CANE'S JUSTICE

by Tamara Lyon

Tamara Lyon

The Sequel to the Award-Winning Novel
"The Ugly Tree"

Final in series, The Road to Justice, available on Amazon!

Comfort PUBLISHING

CANE'S JUSTICE

For information, address Comfort Publishing, 296 Church St. N., Concord, NC 28025. The views expressed in this book are not necessarily those of the publisher.

First printing

Book cover design
by Reed Karriker

ISBN: 978-1-938388-30-9
Published by Comfort Publishing, LLC
www.comfortpublishing.com

Printed in the United States of America

ACKNOWLEDGEMENTS

Thank you to:

Dr. P, who loves me despite my obsessive-compulsive ways.

My talented champion son, who has more drive and ambition than anyone I know.

My mom, who reads, rereads, and supports me all the way.

My dad, who brags about me everywhere he goes.

Nanny, who honestly believes I'm the most talented author on earth.

My twin brothers. One of them has read my books. Let's hope the other one follows suit someday.

Missy, who always wants a sneak preview.

My besties. Munch, EAB, SC, and MH, thanks for always listening.

My family, friends, and fans. A big shout-out to my fellow KHS alums-you'll never know how much your support means to me.

My faithful and sweet Macy, who keeps my feet warm while I write.

Most importantly, to God above, who hardwired me to be a writer. Things finally started to work when I let Him lead me.

For Dr. P.
Always, forever, and no matter what.

PROLOGUE

August 25th, 1998

I pound on the console, threatening and cajoling the car. "Don't you dare quit on me! I know you can do it! We're almost there!"

The check engine light defiantly flickers in my face one last time, and then the engine perishes. I rock all one hundred and five pounds of me forward and backward like a madwoman, hoping the momentum will keep the car moving; but this object in motion doesn't care about Newton's Law, because it's not going to stay in motion. Maneuvering the vehicle onto the shoulder, I stomp on the brake and throw it in PARK.

Now what?

I don't have a cell phone. I'm stranded two miles from the church, and the ceremony has already started. The cherry on top of my day? A wicked thunderstorm is brewing. Impressive stacks of robust clouds stretch across the sky like a defensive line. Poised and ready to tackle, they're throwing off bolts of lightning as a warning.

About the only thing I have going for me is that the car has conveniently managed to break down next to a horse farm. Galloping through the doors of Grace Lutheran Church on a white steed would make quite a statement. However, my equestrian experience is limited, and I'm fairly certain the owners would frown on me jumping their fence and thieving one of their mighty stallions.

All I know is that I have to get there in time to take the pastor up on his invitation to *speak now,* because there's no way that I can f*orever hold my peace.* Not in this instance. I don't have it in me.

CHAPTER ONE

Three Months Earlier – June, 1998

The apple-green walls of my apartment bedroom are riddled with holes that remain from push pins and nails. All my treasured photographs, framed movie posters, and semester schedules have been boxed up or tossed recklessly in the recycle bin. The map of my college life has been tightly creased, folded up, and packed away.

Now that the pomp and circumstance are history and the tassel has been hung on Justice's rearview mirror, the culmination of my four years at Northern Illinois University in the middle of Farmland USA seems irrelevant. Have I accomplished anything at all?

I can't say for sure. I easily recall many titles of books that I've read and studied: *The Canterbury Tales, Beloved, Pride and Prejudice, Iliad, Beowulf, The Invisible Man, The Bluest Eye, Dante's Inferno.* Yet, it's superficial recollection. I only see the image of a cover and an author's name. The stories themselves have gone missing. Afflicted with post-traumatic graduation amnesia, I'm panicked that I haven't learned a thing and won't be able to prove to myself or anyone else that I have educated worth. Tragically, the stories I do remember are the brain-candy romances filled with smut that I would never admit to liking let alone reading. Four years of tuition and I couldn't pass a quiz about Shakespeare. But give me one about any of Danielle Steel's or Kathleen E. Woodiwiss's books, and I would ace it.

Yesterday, Frank gave me a silver compass that had belonged to his mother as a graduation gift. Featured in a glass display case in his office, I'd admired it for years.

I told him the gift was too much, that I couldn't take it, but he said, "I insist. You love it, and you should have it. It belongs to you now. It will come in handy someday."

He'd spoken as if I would need it in the future, but I need it now. I pull it out of my front pocket and flip it open, hoping that it will give me a sense of direction.

The magnetic needle rotates right, pulling north hard and fast, and points directly at the fist-shaped hole in my wall that's barely visible thanks to a patch job. I shuffle over to the spot and push my fist against it, hoping against hope that it won't line up, but it's a perfect match.

The bruises and swelling along the bony ridge of knuckles had long ago faded as had the pink scars from the stitches. The wall, my hand, and my relationship with Justice — they had all been repaired lickety-split.

See, it's as good as new, my roommate, Caprice, had said after helping me mud, sand, and paint the spot seven months earlier. The truth is that nothing is ever as good as new. The damage is merely disguised underneath a thin layer, out of sight but never out of mind.

"Sugar Cane, where have you gone to?" Grandma Betty shouts from the living room.

"Bedroom," I answer. I slip the compass into my pocket and spin myself south. She doesn't know about the wall or what had happened between Justice and me to prompt such an act of rage.

"Are you sure you have everything?" She pops her head in the room.

"I'm sure," I respond wearily and plop down on the floor, sitting cross-legged.

Dubious, she furrows her brow.

"I'm positive," I say more forcefully, but I still haven't convinced her.

"We'll see about that." Nervous as a sparrow, my grandmother darts from room to room checking for anything I might have forgotten and critically eyeing the floors to make sure everything's spick-and-span the way she likes it.

At last she lands in my bedroom and runs a hand down the north wall, right near the patch, causing my diaphragm to seize up. I don't want her to notice it, because her inquisitions are insufferable. With the wiliness of an attorney cross-examining a defendant, Grandma Betty always gets the whole truth and nothing but the truth.

Thankfully, she doesn't notice. Her thumbnail works on a spot of tape I had missed. When she finishes with that, she bends over and pinches a stray piece of lint from the carpet. "Maybe I should have Frank bring the vacuum up from the car. We should give it a once-over."

"I've already gotten my portion of the security deposit back. We're good to go."

Flicking the piece of lint into her purse, she folds her arms and inspects the ceiling, looking for a stray spiderweb. "Still, how you leave a place says something about you, and I want to make sure everything is spotless."

"And what does this place say about me?" I ask Grandma Betty, batting my eyelashes. "Does it say that I'm a fabulously beautiful woman with a college degree?"

Focused solely on making sure I leave the apartment in better condition than when I rented it three years ago, her smile is tolerant at best. "If the walls could talk — it just might say that."

"Doubtful," I mumble under my breath as she scurries out of the room once again. I'm afraid of what these walls would say about me. They'd seen the good, but they'd also seen the bad and the ugly.

She returns to my bedroom and folds her arms. "Did you empty all the closets? The shower? How about the kitchen cupboards?"

We've triple-checked; I know for a fact there isn't anything left. The last of the boxes had been thrown in the trunk of Frank's beefy Lincoln thirty minutes ago.

Let's get the show on the road, he'd said three times before realizing that Grandma Betty and I weren't ready to take the show anywhere just yet. He'd left us alone and went out to the car to reload his Nikon camera and make sure my new video camera, another of my graduation gifts, had full power.

"It's all taken care of." I give her a sunrise kind of smile even though my patience expired long ago. "And when it comes time to unpack, I'll know exactly what's in each box thanks to your label gun. You would be proud of how organized everything is."

"I love that gadget! It has so many options compared to the old one you gave me so long ago. And since Frank and I have been packing like crazy, I've had to replace the cartridge four times."

Grandma Betty and my step-grandfather, Frank, sold their house in Savage, a rural farm town in the middle of nowhere northern Illinois, and are flying south to St. Petersburg, Florida, with no plans to migrate back. Frank says he wants his golden years to be somewhere golden, where he only has to worry about the salt in the water and not the buckets of salt he has to dump on his long driveway in the harsh northern winters.

I don't want them to leave. Although I'll miss Frank, I can live without him, but I'm not sure how to survive without Grandma Betty. The only family I've ever known, she's been the anchor in my life. Without her, I fear I'll get lost at sea.

"Are you ready for the big move?" I ask her.

"As ready as I'll ever be, but honestly, it's going to be so hard leaving. Have you changed your mind? A few months of relaxing might do you some good."

She wants me to stay in their new beachfront condo for the summer, but I've declined the invitation. "My internship starts a week from Monday. I can't."

"Oh, Sugar Cane, please think about it. Ocean, sand, and sun! Frank could take us out in the new boat every day. I heard they have the best snorkeling only a little ways from our place. You could run along the beach-wouldn't that be divine! You wouldn't even have to wear shoes. Samson won't mind if you don't start right away. You know he'll hold the job until you get back!"

"I know." Samson Schaeffer, a longtime family friend who will become genuine family once I marry his nephew Justice Price, owns the prestigious Schaeffer Dairy, a company worth millions. Given my long-standing history with the Schaeffers and the fact that I've worked on the farm from the time I was eleven, Samson has generously carved out a position for me in the marketing department, where I'll be in charge of ad campaigns, press releases, and developing and implementing other marketing strategies. A well-paid and auspicious offer, over which my fellow English majors salivated, I want to start immediately.

"Tell me you'll at least think about it. You don't have to make up your mind today."

"I have thought about it, but I just can't. I want to get started with my life," I say stridently. I have to keep focus. It feels like the rug is being pulled out from under me, and I'm on my hands and knees holding on to the fringed edges of that rug for dear life. If I go to Florida and loaf around, I'll lose what little grip I have.

Adjusting one of her clip-on earrings, Grandma Betty shakes her head and smiles wistfully as she looks at me. "How did we get to this place? You're all grown-up, a lovely young woman who has her whole life ahead of her. And me? I'm a wrinkly old retiree who will spend her days knitting, crocheting, collecting seashells, and going to Friday night bingo with Frank."

I click my tongue. "Come on now. You're going to be a rich beach bum. You look the part." She does look like the quintessential Florida senior resident. Her snow-white hair, perfectly curled and sprayed into place, makes her cornflower blue eyes pop. She prefers to dress her petite top-heavy body in pantsuits. Her shoes, handbag, and even her lipstick and eye shadow must coordinate with whatever she's wearing. By coordinate, I mean match. She dunks herself in a vat of the same color. Today she's wearing a silky lavender getup and has rounded out the look with lavender pumps, lavender eye shadow, and plum lipstick. Even her blush has a purple hue. I call it her purple people eater look, which she doesn't appreciate.

She's aghast at my suggesting that she looks the part. "Have you seen how old some of those people are? I don't look a thing like them!"

"You look better than them! You'll have the most amazing life down there. Martinis on the beach. Beautiful sunrises. Fresh seafood. I'm going to visit all the time." Part of me wants to move with her, but just as she had let me go, I have to let her go. She can't be a mother forever; she deserves her freedom as I deserve mine.

Teary-eyed, she tightens her mouth until her chin dimples from the effort. After sobbing at my graduation ceremony, and *disgracing herself and me,* her words not mine, she's vowed not to shed one more tear. "You better," she says resolutely.

"I will. I promise. For the record — you aren't wrinkly."

Chuckling, she pats my hand. "Don't lie. I am a tad wrinkly and worse for the wear. I ran into Samson the other day at the drugstore. We talked about how fast the time has gone — how it seems like only yesterday you were sixteen years old. He said something that stuck with me. He said that whatever age you are is how fast you move through life. I'm going a whopping seventy miles an hour! Before I know it, I'll be a toothless, doddering old woman, and you'll be married to Justice with children of your own. I'll be a great-grandmother." Her eyes scan the undressed walls and take in the empty closet. "I'm not ready, but I know you are. You've always moved through life at full speed ahead. I admire that in you."

Too much of a good thing usually backfires, and because I always travel at full throttle, I sometimes can't avoid running into brick walls at a hundred miles an hour.

"What about your cap and gown? Are you sure you have those? I don't want to leave those behind! We can put the cap next to your diploma in a shadow box. Wouldn't that be lovely! You could hang it on the wall in your new place."

"Justice packed them. They're in his truck."

"Oh good. If we have time, we should stop at that hobby store on the way out of town and see if they have any display cases. Wouldn't it be nice if we could find some artwork for your walls? And I still want to give you that couch, you know, the plaid one in Frank's den, it will be darling in the living room of your new place. I'll crochet some blankets to match and then —"

I half-listen as Grandma Betty makes plans for my new apartment. This coming Monday, I'm signing a lease on a two-bedroom unit in my hometown of Savage, Illinois. What Grandma Betty doesn't know is that Justice recently ditched his apartment and is planning on moving in with me; a Christian traditionalist, she won't think that's darling at all.

The place I'll be renting is in the same building where my newlywed parents had lived. It seems dangerously circular. Am I tempting fate by repeating history? By following closely in their footsteps, will tragedy find me as it had found them?

"How does that sound to you?" she asks.

"Fabulous," I respond, not knowing what I've agreed to.

Easing myself off the ground, I walk over to the open window and place my fingertips against the screen. I survey the back lot of the apartment building. It's a mass exodus. Half the students in the building, including me, just graduated. Everyone is in such a hurry to leave, and all of them seem relaxed and confident in the direction they're heading. I can't say the same for myself.

Frank must have tired of waiting for us. I hear the front door of the apartment open and then close. The shift in pressure pulls in air from outside, bringing the sweet perfume of late-blooming lilacs. The smell reminds me of childhood springs, when Mikayla, my best friend since infancy, and I would sit beneath Grandma Betty's blooming lilac bushes and play with our Barbie dolls, creating fantasy families. Mikayla, who grew up with a pilot father who not only flew across the country but from one woman to the next and a mother who cared more about appearances than relationships, needed the fantasy lives more than I ever did.

Grandma Betty inhales deeply. "Would you smell that? Isn't it divine? Lilacs smell of heaven itself. I do hope they grow in Florida. I can't imagine living without that scent in the spring."

Frank strides into the room. He's a stocky man with short gray hair, watery brown eyes, and a compact mustache that nearly hides his thin lips. His friendly face reminds me of a worn baseball glove; it's creased in all the right places. Unlike Grandma Betty who matches to a fault, Frank, who's a little zany, prefers to spice up his wardrobe with socks that don't match (he says this is a great conversation starter), loud ties, and plaid golf pants. Today he's sporting a bright green tie that's covered in miniature lightning bolts and green and white plaid pants. "How are my two ladies doing?"

"We're just about ready." Grandma Betty hoists her shiny, lavender purse onto her shoulder and looks at me. "What do you think?"

As soon as I turn around from my station near the window, Frank, ever the prepared photographer, snaps a photo of me. In the last two days, he's taken enough pictures of me to fill an album. He lowers the camera and adjusts the lens.

"I'm not happy with how this is focusing," he grumbles. "Everything blurs at the edges."

Grandma Betty laughs. "It's because you aren't wearing your glasses again! They're in your front pocket."

Grinning self-consciously, he pulls them out, gives them a shake, and then slides them into place. "Ah, much better. It's amazing how the world looks with a new set of eyes."

"I need a new set of eyes — things are looking kind of fuzzy right about now."

Grandma Betty slides her arm around my shoulder and kisses my cheek. Frank captures the moment on film.

She peers into my face. "Your eyes do look a little bloodshot. You can't see straight because you're exhausted! Finals. Graduation. The parties with your friends. The moving. Why, I've only been here for a few days, and I'm pooped. You have to be dead on your feet,and last night I heard you tossing and turning in your bed at the hotel!" she exclaims. "You can give your eyes a rest and nap on the way home."

Lack of sleep has nothing to do with my poor eyesight. My life's moving so fast that nothing is coming into focus. Maybe I need to blindfold myself — maybe then it would be easier.

"Yes, a snooze will do you good. You've run yourself ragged these past few days, and so has Justice," says Frank. "Speaking of which, I hope he's made it back safely."

Justice left a few hours ago, his pickup truck filled to the gills with miscellaneous furniture and boxes. I tried to talk him into putting some of the boxes in Frank's car so that I could ride with him, but he adamantly insisted I ride back with Grandma Betty and Frank.

"Bless that young man's heart," Grandma Betty says, taking my hand in hers and squeezing. "I have a feeling someone will be getting a ring soon."

I smile. My happily-ever-after with Justice. That's all I've wanted from the moment I first saw him six years ago when I was fifteen and he was twenty-one. Only hours after that initial meeting, a tornado devastated my town, my house, and my life. Grandma Betty, critically injured during the storm, was taken by helicopter to a hospital and nearly died. She was in a coma for more than two months. Justice stayed by my side through it all, driving me to the hospital daily, talking with me for hours, and spending time with me when I'm sure he had better things to do. I fell in love with him, a man who not only looked like a superhero with his dark hair, aquamarine eyes, dimples, and muscular physique, but acted like one as well.

Our love story officially began when I turned eighteen. I've always known that I would get my fairy-tale ending. Yet now that I'm so close to having it, I'm spooked. They don't have any articles in *Seventeen* magazine, which embarrassingly enough I still faithfully read, that deal with female-based commitment issues. It's always the other way around. But lately, when I hear the word proposal or engagement, I have the urge to put on my running shoes and head for the hills. It doesn't make any sense, because *I love him. I adore him.* I'm not sure I can live without him.

Or can I?

"He should be home by now," I remark.

"Speaking of home, we need to get the show on the road." Frank taps the face of his gold Seiko watch. "Justice, Samson, and the whole gang are going to meet us at Sorrento's. We don't want to be late. If we leave now, we'll make it with only a few minutes to spare."

"Do you think I could have a minute alone?" I shrug. "It's hard to leave."

"Of course, Sugar Cane," says Grandma Betty. "We'll wait for you in the car."

"Take your time," Frank insists and then adds, "but hurry up!"

I proffer a wry smile. "Very funny. I won't be long."

When they've gone, I explore each room, lightly dragging my hands along the textured walls, because I don't want to just remember the things that happened here, I want to feel them. The matters of the heart are tied to all the senses — even touch.

And as I run my palms across the vertical and horizontal planes of the apartment, so much comes rushing back: Trouncing my friends in late-night Trivial Pursuit games. Fitness competitions with my best friend and roommate, Caprice, which included everything from push-ups and sit-ups to sprints around the collegiate track and even arm-wrestling contests. Celebrating the end of track and field season by running the infamous naked mile on a chilly spring night where I had a distinct advantage over Caprice and my other big-breasted friends. Having midnight dance parties in the dead of winter with all the windows open. Picking up the phone and having Justice tell me that his estranged father had died in the very same way that my parents had been killed — he was struck by a drunk driver. Sitting on the bathroom countertop with my legs drawn up to my chest with a pregnancy stick balanced on the crest of my knees. Offering Jocelyn Ryanne Schaeffer, Samson Schaeffer's daughter, a month of reprieve last summer from her overbearing mother and seven siblings. Splitting a six-pack of beer with Mikayla when she came to see me last fall and lying through my teeth when the subject of her mother's affair came up. Thinking suicidal and homicidal thoughts when Justice told me he wanted me to have my senior year free and clear because he wanted me to *experience life without him.*

I'm leaving behind much more than I've wrapped and placed in a labeled box. My wild, sweet mess of youth is inside these rooms and around campus. This is where I rode the roller coaster of late adolescence into my early twenties, sometimes strapped in and other times barely hanging on. The memories will come with me, but much more will remain here.

I turn off all the lights, place the keys on the counter, and walk out the door of my personal time capsule.

"About time. I think the summer semester is almost over," Frank jokes as I climb into the backseat of the car.

"Don't give her a hard time," admonishes Grandma Betty.

"Here." Frank hands me my new video camera. I flip the power switch and point it at the back of Grandma Betty's head.

She swivels around and frowns when she sees the camera pointed at her face. "You aren't recording again, are you? You're getting to be as bad as Frank with all those gadgets."

"I am recording. You'll be on film for all of time. No pressure, though. Just be yourself."

"Oh schlop!" she exclaims, this being her rather demure version of the word *shit*. "Turn it off."

Frank's brown eyes find mine in the rearview mirror, and he gives me a thumbs-up. "Get a close-up of her."

"Working on it," I tell him as I push the zoom button.

Grandma Betty huffs in protest. "No! I don't want a close-up."

"It's not that close."

"Well, how close is it? I don't have my lipstick on." She self-consciously covers her mouth.

"You don't need any. You're as lovely as ever."

"I'm your grandmother — you have to say that."

"She's right, though, you are as lovely as ever," Frank chimes in.

"Stop," she orders. She turns back around and buckles her seat belt.

"Come on. Be a sport. I want to record this moment," I tell her.

Frank starts the car and eases away from the curb.

"Why would you want to do that?" she asks impatiently.

"Because now that I've graduated college, I want to know what you wish for me and my future."

Looking over her shoulder, she gives me her *don't you already know the answer to that* smile. "All I've ever wanted for you is to be happy, and I know that you are."

I flip off the power button and tuck the camera against my chest. Staring out the window, I watch the squat profile of my apartment building shrink and then disappear. I feel many things, but not one thing that comes close to happy.

*****

Five miles from Sorrento's, I wake and stretch, curling my spine forward into the shape of a C.

Grandma Betty leans on the armrest. "You've had a wonderful nap. Feel better?"

"I feel worse than roadkill."

"Fresh air will cure that." She rolls down the front window. Her permed curls, held in place by a sticky layer of Aqua Net, barely vibrate in the breeze. "This weather is divine. The May sunshine brings out the loveliest smells."

"You're kidding, right?" I grab the small handle attached to the ceiling and pull myself upright. "All I smell is cow shit."

Frank's laugh sounds like a bubble popping. "Me, too!"

"Come on, you two." Smiling serenely, Grandma Betty inhales. "There's more than that. Can't you smell the warm asphalt and the blooming ninebark bushes over there?" She points to someone's front yard. "And I also smell a hint of Scotts fertilizer, speaking of which" — she turns to Frank — "we should donate all our extra bags to the church. We can't be bothered to pack those."

"Sure, we can do that."

A smile of pure pleasure erupts on her face. "Freshly cut grass. There's nothing like it in the world."

Whereas I'm more in tune with my sense of touch, Grandma Betty has canine-like ability when it comes to her sense of smell. If she ever goes blind, she'll be able to navigate the world with her heightened olfactory sense. I roll down my window and stick my head into the fragrant wind. The force of the air snarls my long auburn tresses. Slinking back into the car, I pat Grandma Betty on the shoulder. "Nope, can't smell anything but manure."

"You're only paying attention to the obvious. You have to learn to appreciate the subtleties. Take your time with it."

"Says the Zen-sniffing master," I quip.

"Almost there!" Frank announces grandly.

Sorrento's, all stucco and arches, looms in the distance. An Italian mecca of fine dining, it's oddly located off a rural highway with cornfields as its only neighbors. Despite the bizarre setting, it's the most popular restaurant in Savage and Clinton, the larger neighboring town. The parking lot is crammed full of cars. I recognize Justice's truck and the Schaeffers' family van.

As Frank pulls into the entrance that's punctuated with a fountain, I spot Mikayla's conspicuous yellow Corvette.

"Is that Mikayla's car?"

"That it is," Frank says with a grin.

Mikayla has been living in Chicago, working as a catalogue and runway model. According the Chicago modeling agent who snatched her up right after senior year while she'd been dining at Navy Pier with one of her boyfriends, she's the perfect combination of Kate Moss and Niki Taylor. I'd always known that someday she'd be profiting off her long legs, translucent blue eyes, high cheekbones, and perfectly symmetrical face. I'd talked to her earlier in the week and she'd said her schedule was impossible and that she wouldn't be able to make it.

"She wanted to surprise you," says Grandma Betty.

I smile. "That's her style."

Mikayla doesn't plan; she lives life in a pulling-a-rabbit-out-of-a-hat mode. She loves surprising me most of all. She never calls; she simply shows up at my door. And she's always bringing me gifts. She's given me: designer clothing, a Tiffany necklace, shoes with brand names I can't even pronounce, stacks of *Seventeen* magazines and *Vogue* (her favorite), cosmetics (she always wanted me to try a new look), smutty romance books, mittens that were ten sizes too big but I wore anyway since she'd knitted them herself, a case of microwave popcorn (I'm addicted to the stuff), and sometimes, upon returning from a particularly lucrative photo shoot, hundred-dollar bills.

Her hectic schedule and jet-setting lifestyle usually mean thousands of miles separate us. But when I truly need her, she takes planes, buses, and cars to be with me. When I thought I was pregnant two years ago and scared out of my mind, I'd called her hotel in France, where she was working the runway for a fashion show, and told her that I was three weeks late.

"Have you told Justice?" she asked.

"Not yet. Before I say anything to him, I want to be sure."

Twenty-four hours later, she was at my door, jet-lagged beyond all recognition, her sleek blond hair a frizzy mess.

Stunned, I couldn't believe she'd flown across the world to be with me. "What are you doing here?"

She shrugged off her coat and kicked the door shut. "You needed me."

"I didn't say that."

"I could hear it in your voice."

"But your job!"

"Blood or not, you're family. Family comes first. I told them it was an emergency and here I am." She handed me a paper bag. Inside, was a gallon of triple chocolate ice cream and fifteen home pregnancy tests.

Before I'd recovered from the shock of her being there, she dragged me into the bathroom and opened the first test. She took my hand and pressed the plastic stick into my palm. "Pee on it and get it over with," she commanded.

I pulled down my pants and sat on the toilet. My bladder didn't cooperate. I couldn't go through with it. "I know that you came all the way here, but I want to wait for Justice. I want him to be here when I do this."

She nodded. "Fair enough. But we don't have to wait for him to eat ice cream, do we?"

Together, we polished off the gallon of triple chocolate and fell into a sugar coma sleep, which is where Justice found us when he showed up later that night.

"How exciting is this? I can hardly wait." Grandma Betty pulls her pick out of her purse and gives her curls a fluff. Lowering the vanity mirror, she swipes on more plum-colored lipstick and then carefully blots her lips with a tissue.

Scooting over, I appraise myself in the rearview mirror. As usual, I'm so far from pulled together, I look undone. After spending too much time outdoors running, my freckles have come out in full force against my milky white skin, and although I keep trying, no amount of makeup can subdue them. These freckles, along with my petite Tinker Bell face, make me look much younger than my twenty-one years. My best feature is my almond-shaped hazel eyes. They're glorified mood rings and change colors several times a day, depending on my state of mind. Presently they are a matte, boring gray. I work my hands through my long hair and at the same time slip my feet into high-heeled sandals. When I pull my skirt into place, I sigh in frustration; my knobby knees, ankles, and lower legs, despite a careful shave this morning, glisten with patches of fine blond hairs that I can never see when in the shower.

Frank parks the car. "Why don't we bring in your new camera? I think it would be nice to video the evening, don't you?"

"A brilliant idea." I pick it up off the seat.

"You have too much in your hands. Why don't I carry it for you?" Frank asks solicitously.

His offer is polite but unnecessary; I hold nothing but my purse in one hand and the camera in the other.

"Yes, Sugar Cane. Give it to Frank." Grandma Betty rolls her lips together as she tries to squelch a sly smile.

Something fishy is going on. There are quite a few cars here. Maybe it isn't just the Schaeffers, Justice, and Mikayla. A surprise party, perhaps? I can play along.

"Okay." I place the camera in Frank's hands.

"I want to get the door for my ladies." Frank hurries ahead and opens the door for us.

We step into the dimly lit restaurant that's strung with thousands of tiny white lights. The air is so heavily infused with the aroma of marinara sauce, garlic, and freshly baked bread that I can already taste it on my tongue. Instrumental Italian music whispers from the wall-mounted speakers. The atmosphere is drowsy and relaxed.

Resting her hands on my shoulders, Grandma Betty steers me toward the hostess table manned by a rough-looking Italian man with meatballs for cheeks.

"Good evening! How can I help you?"

"Kallevik party," Frank announces.

"Ah, yes! So, here at last, eh? And did you have a pleasant trip?" Meatball Cheeks gives me a curious smile.

Grandma Betty is about to say something, but I beat her to it. "Yes. We smelled the most lovely cow manure on the way here!"

His curious smile is replaced with a jovial laugh that shakes his entire body. Frank, who appreciates my humor, laughs as well, but Grandma Betty isn't as easy to win over.

She gives me an *only you would say that* sigh.

"Right this way!"

He leads us to a back room and nods in the direction of the closed double doors and then backs away. Frank and Grandma Betty hang behind me. I hear the beep of the camera as Frank pushes the record button.

Now, I'm sure that something is up. I'll play along. Placing my hands on the door pulls, I form my mouth into a mystified smile — the perfect expression to wear when everyone jumps up and shouts, *Surprise!*

I open the doors. The room is empty except for him. He's wearing a tuxedo. I have that pins-and-needles feeling all over. My heart beats faster and faster. A wicked trembling starts in my toes and works its way up until my hairy knees knock against each other.

He smiles, making those two dimples that I love so much appear.

"You're finally here," he says nervously.

I walk toward him only somewhat aware of Frank moving closer with the video camera.

He takes my hands in his and then gets down on one knee. He slips the diamond ring on my finger — my mother's ring.

"The timing wasn't right when we met, was it? And even though some things have gone wrong these past six years, so much more has gone right. You make me crazy. You make me sane. You make me laugh harder than anyone can. You make me want to be the best person that I can be. You are the love of my life, Cane. I don't know how to live without you. I want you by my side for all of time. Will you marry me?"

The fairy-tale proposal. The one that I've always wanted from him. *It's finally happened,* I think, and then my next thought is, *Not yet.*

In the fraction of a second before I answer, I have a flashback.

I'm a feisty sixteen-year-old girl kneeling in the damp grass on a summer night, and Justice, twenty-one at the time, kneels in front of me. We're separated by a span of years that requires separation and patience.

"I love you," I say, knowing that it isn't enough — not yet.

I splay my hand and press it over his heart. Through his crisp white dress shirt, I feel the rapid push of his heart against my palm. He moves his hand up to mine and gently takes hold of my wrist. Words aren't exchanged. No promises are made or sealed with a kiss, but I swear we are both thinking, until death do us part.

Until death do us part. He's offering me that very thing and waiting for an answer.

Before I know it, before I'm aware my mouth has opened and my lips are moving, I answer with a zealous, "Yes!"

When Justice sweeps me off my feet and spins me around, all my friends and family, who have snuck up behind Grandma Betty and Frank and have been standing in the doorway watching and waiting, spill into the room with whoops and hollers. My stomach does a rapid series of somersaults.

By the time he sets me on my feet and seals the deal with a leisurely, less-than-PG kiss — we're talking French all the way — and Frank zooms in for the close-up and then pans the crowd, capturing raw reactions, I know that I've managed to hit another brick wall.

I should have given him a different answer.

CHAPTER TWO

"Love you," he whispers in my ear.

My euphoria is sullied with trepidation, but I don't want Justice to know that I'm anything but sure. I love him too much to hurt him, and I won't ruin this for either of us. Haven't we been working up to this point for years? I give him a glowing smile. "You look dashing."

He grins. "For effect. I had to go all-out. It's not like you get the chance to propose more than once."

"How long have you been planning this?"

"For months. And you like the ring?" he asks.

"How could I not? It's my mother's."

"When I told Grandma Betty what I was planning on doing, she gave it to me. She said you should have it."

I hold it aloft, admiring the sparkling square diamond set in gold. I smile up at him. "If only I would have known you were going to propose, I might have done a better job at shaving my legs."

He runs a hand down my waist and presses himself close. "I love you — hairy legs and all."

"Good, I'll stop shaving immediately. I'm going native."

"Oh! Isn't this thrilling!" Grandma Betty kisses Justice and then me on the cheek. "She's getting married!" she trills, loud enough so that the hundred guests in the room, who include all ten of the Schaeffers, employees from Schaeffer Dairy, Justice's friends, and many of my friends as well, can hear her.

"Where's your mom?" I ask him, scanning the room.

"She didn't make it back from her trip in time," he explains.

Sara, his mother and Samson's sister, had taken a year off from her career as a nurse and for the past six months had been backpacking across Europe.

"When will she be home?"

He grins and raises his brows. "She said she'll be sure to make it in time for the wedding."

I'm about to ask him if he's already set a date for our wedding when his buddies steal him from my side and drag him over to the bar to celebrate. He's razzed for wearing a tuxedo, slapped on the back, punched in the shoulder, and handed a shot glass. He downs the glass of amber liquid. When he finishes, he looks across the room.

Our eyes meet. His expression, the way he smiles with only half his mouth, says, *This is the way it was supposed to turn out.*

Waiters bring in champagne, wine, and appetizers. Dozens of conversations start at once. I stealthily drink one, two, three flutes in a row, hoping to slow things down, but it has the opposite effect.

The phrase "speed of light" comes to mind as I'm bombarded by a series of well-wishers, including Jocelyn Ryanne, Samson's seventeen-year-old daughter, a blue-eyed brunette with puffy, heart-shaped lips and round cheeks who tries to hide her acne by styling her long hair so that it falls all over her face. She throws her arms around me with gusto, causing me to lose my balance. Teetering on my heels, I nearly fall backward, but she grabs my hands and saves me. We laugh at the near mishap.

"I've missed you so much! Now that you're finished with college we can spend so much time together. I'm just so happy you're finally home and here to stay." She lowers her voice and leans in to whisper in my ear. "Mom has been driving me crazy, and ever since I stayed with you last summer, she's been on my case about how I shouldn't put you on a pedestal. She's been making nasty remarks about you and about how you're a bad influence." Jocelyn sneaks a look at her mother, Jenny Ryanne, who stands across the room with her arms crossed and a scowl lurking under the surface of her ribbon-like smile that could come untied at the slightest provocation.

Sighing, Jocelyn's eyes skate back to me. "Seriously, I'm ready to move out for the summer. My mother is a neurotic head case. Worse than usual lately."

I nod sympathetically. Jenny Ryanne, whom I had long ago nicknamed Jelly Roll because of her round figure and fondness for wearing glittery clothing, isn't my biggest fan. She never has been. An unhappy, hostile woman with a squishy, marshmallow face and body to match, she isn't satisfied with herself or anyone else. She has a talent for driving people up walls and keeping them there by honking her horn. "You can spend the night at my apartment as often as you like," I offer.

"Do you mean it?"

"It's a two bedroom, and I plan on having you as a guest all the time."

Her face lights up. "I'm going to be in the wedding, right?" she asks.

"Of course you are."

"Because I'll have lost the rest of the weight by then, I promise."

"You're beautiful just as you are."

"Yeah. Well, maybe." Jocelyn nibbles on her thumbnail. "It's just that I want to be super-duper skinny like you."

She's always struggled with her weight, and two years ago, because of my influence and encouragement, she revamped her diet and started running and lifting weights. To date, she's lost almost eighty pounds. Instead of celebrating this, she's prone to criticizing herself. "Don't try to be me. Be you. Be healthy, not skinny."

"Yeah, okay," she says without making eye contact and then wanders off to find something to drink.

I glance over and finally spot Mikayla. She's standing by the bar with her arms wrapped loosely around Jeremy Schaffer, the eldest of the Schaeffer siblings. He'd been in our high school graduating class. From her animated expression and dynamic hand movements, I know she's telling a story. Mikayla, gorgeous and charming, was born an enchantress, and all the men in the group, including Justice, have fallen under her spell. If I didn't love her so much and trust her implicitly, I would be threatened by her dangerous talent. She looks up and winks at me, and then she continues making the men eat out of the palm of her hand.

Samson Schaeffer, a man as large as Paul Bunyan with a jawline reminiscent of Arnold Schwarzenegger and cheeks that remind me of

Theodore the Chipmunk, comes over and gives me a hug. "All grown up, graduated, and now you're going to marry my nephew, the best guy I know."

"I'm one lucky girl."

"And he's one lucky guy," he replies.

Grandma Betty and Frank, who are nearby, turn at the sound of Samson's voice and come over to join in our conversation. After hugs and handshakes, Samson suggests having the wedding at the farm.

"Wouldn't Jenny Ryanne love that!" I exclaim.

Though Samson knows his wife and I don't get along and has even had to break up fights between us over the years, he misses the slap of sarcasm in my statement. Possibly it has something to do with the sixteen-ounce beer he holds in his hand. Grandma Betty, however, never misses a thing; she gives me the stink eye.

Frank agrees that the farm would be a prudent choice but that a destination wedding might be the way to go. "After all, we'll be living in Florida. We could have the ceremony and the reception right on the beach. Nothing beats the Atlantic as a backdrop. Now that would be classy."

"I like both ideas! Either one would be spectacular," gushes Grandma Betty. "If we have it on the farm we could do it this summer, but if it's in Florida, it would have to be in the fall — it will have cooled off by then. What do you think, Sugar Cane? Which option sounds better to you?"

A rolling, bubbly kind of laugh comes out of my mouth. I don't know what to say because I'm still trying to come to terms with the fact that my enthusiastic *yes* may have been a bit premature.

Thankfully, Mikayla chooses that moment to crash our small group. She throws her arms around me.

When she releases me, she flaunts her million-dollar smile, or in her case, her three-thousand-dollar smile, since that's her average earning for a photo shoot.

"Just like that you're getting married," she says. "We've all been waiting for this day."

"I bet you knew it was coming, didn't you?"

"Since I have frequent lunch dates with your fiancé, yes, I knew it was coming."

Justice oversees the financial growth and management division of the Schaeffer Dairy business, and although his office is at the company headquarters in Clinton, he frequents Chicago to meet with investors and financial strategists. He occasionally meets up with Mikayla to have lunch. "You couldn't have told me?"

"And spoil the fun? I wouldn't do that to you."

Something about the way she says this makes my scalp tingle. With a deft hand, she snatches two glasses of wine from a waiter's tray and hands me one.

"I'm trying not to have anything to drink."

She guffaws. "Please. Don't bother playing the role of Saint Cane. You can't get anything past me." She raises her brow and narrows her eyes knowingly. "You've fallen off the sobriety train already. I saw you slam three flutes of champagne."

"Think anyone else did?"

"Obviously not Grandma Betty or you would have heard about it."

"I just don't want to have too much to drink tonight."

"You might want to rethink that. It's going to be a long night." Her eyes wander over to the bar, and she smiles at Justice before looking back to me. She takes a long draught of wine, pulls me close, and murmurs in my ear, "Wait until you see what's going to happen next."

"What do you mean *happen next?* What else could there possibly be?"

As soon as the question's out of my mouth, Frank points the video camera at Mikayla and me.

"Just wait and see," she says before turning her face toward the camera and giving away one of her three-thousand-dollar smiles for free.

*****

While at my college apartment this afternoon I had pondered the idea of a blindfold. With my eyes covered, I figured I wouldn't have to watch life whizzing by me.

As luck would have it, I don't have to blindfold myself. Justice has done it for me. Before we left the restaurant, he tied a black bandana around my eyes and set me in his truck, and now we're driving to an undisclosed location.

"You should have left your tux on. It was getting me hot and bothered." As the party was winding down, he'd changed into jeans, a flannel shirt, and work boots.

"Now you tell me?" He laughs. "A tux isn't that practical for where we're headed."

"Can you be more specific?"

He laughs. "You're not getting a thing out of me. It's a surprise."

"I've had enough surprises tonight. Speaking of which, I was surprised not to see Caprice at the party."

"I sent her an invitation but never heard back."

"Huh. That's weird. Did you try calling her?"

"No, I guess I should have, but I've had a lot on my mind lately."

Join the club.

The blindfold thing is starting to freak me out. Having no vision is terrifying. All motion and no orientation. I have the disconcerting sense of rocketing violently through the night. "Can I take this thing off?"

"You're so impatient. We're almost there. Promise."

"That's what you said ten minutes ago. I've got the spins, and this thing isn't helping." I tug at the outer edges of the bandana. "I swear I'm going to blow chunks all over the dashboard."

"Make sure to stick your head out the window."

"I would if I knew where the window was."

"It's to your right, and you aren't that drunk and disoriented."

"Did you see me try to walk to the car? It wasn't so much in a line as in a zigzag." For effect, I moan loudly. "Seriously. I'm going to puke."

"Don't be such a drama queen." He laughs. "Two minutes, and we'll be there."

"Why am I blindfolded?"

"Because it's suspenseful and fun." I hear him push a button. The cassette tape ejects.

"No more Bon Jovi. I'm so over that album," I tell him.

"Radio, then?" He turns to a pop rock station out of Chicago, and Gwen Stefani sings, "I really feel I'm losing my best friend, I can't believe this could be the end."

In a dreadful falsetto, Justice sings along, and I join in, more so to drown out the sound of his voice than to entertain myself.

When it finishes, I turn in his direction and give him an evil smile. "Are you sure you're not going to join the church choir with Samson?"

"You know," he muses. "I like you blindfolded."

"Seeing as how half my face is covered, I'm not sure I should take that as a compliment. Are you implying that I have a gross face and you like it better when it's hidden?"

"I love your gross face."

"Now that I think about it" — I swing my head in his direction — "you look a whole lot better with this thing on."

The truck comes to a stop. I hear the *click* of his seat belt being released, and then he shuts off the ignition. He reaches across me and unbuckles my seat belt.

He slides his hand up my leg and between my thighs, working his way up farther. The lack of vision heightens every sensation.

"I would like to do so many things to you right now." His whisper has the rumble of gravel and the sensation of a feather.

I shiver. "You have my permission to do every one of those things. And the blindfold? I changed my mind. I like it — leave it on."

"Has to be later, because we have an audience."

"An audience? Why?" I reach up to rip off the black bandana that he tied around my head twenty minutes ago, but he grabs my hands and pins them to my sides.

"Hey! Come on! I want to see what's going on. What audience are you talking about? What do you have planned?"

"Stay put." The door groans and squeaks as he opens it. He jumps out of the vehicle, slams his door shut, causing me to startle, and comes around to the passenger side.

When he opens the door, I reach out and feel the hard line of his shoulders. "Are you backward?" I ask.

"Climb on my back."

"A piggyback ride?"

"Hop on."

I climb onto his back. He walks forward, and then I feel the angle shift as he begins ascending a hill. I start to slide, and he tightens his hold under my butt.

I cling to him. "This is kind of fun, but I feel like a preschooler."

"The best part of this situation? Easy access. I like the fact that you're wearing a skirt right now." He pinches one of my butt cheeks.

I squeal and squirm, and he laughs, tightening his grip on me.

"Put me down!" I yelp.

"I would, but you said you couldn't walk in a straight line."

"She can't! Her blood alcohol level is way past the legal limit."

Mikayla's here? I turn my head toward the sound of her voice. "Like your level is below the limit?" I shout in her direction.

Her drunken laughter rings through the night. I hear her running over to us. "I never said it was. In fact, I'm pretty sure I could short out a breathalyzer machine right now."

"You told me that Jeremy was giving you a ride back to the hotel."

"He did. We stopped there so I could change clothes," she responds. "Isn't that that right, Jeremy?"

There's something cozy about the way she says Jeremy's name. I wonder what else they did at the hotel. Could Jeremy Schaeffer be her next potential victim? Mikayla shoots cupid arrows for fun, toys with her impaled victims, and when she has them right where she wants them, she yanks out the arrow along with their heart.

Justice walks ten more feet.

"You'll tell me what's going on, won't you?" I direct my question at Mikayla.

"Even if I told you, you wouldn't believe it. Hell, I don't believe it. You've got to see this for yourself."

Although I can't see anything through the fabric, not even a faint shadow or outline, I sense a crowd around me and beyond me.

There's an eruption of tittering, punctuated by howls of laughter. Next to me, the metallic pop of a can being opened and the telltale fizz of carbonation. In the distance, the smell of smoke and the sound of a crackling fire set against the backdrop of hushed conversations.

Justice carries me farther. By the cautious way he maneuvers I know that he's making his way through a maze of trees. A low-hanging branch sweeps across my face. Finally, he sets me down.

"Ready for this?" His voice vibrates with excitement.

He unties the bandana. It rolls down the front of my chest and falls to the ground. My vision adjusts gradually.

Justice takes my hand in his. "What do you think?"

I see Frank and Grandma Betty first. Frank stands directly in front of me and has the video camera pointed at my face; Grandma Betty stands at his side, cheeks puffed up and wearing a gigantic smile. The entire crowd from Sorrento's and at least twenty more additional friends and acquaintances stand around the wooded area watching me and waiting for a reaction.

Flustered by the attention and unsure of exactly what I'm supposed to react to, I paste a fake smile on my face and turn toward Justice. "An engagement party?"

"Take a closer look," encourages Frank from behind the lens. The camera swivels away from me. I follow the movement.

My gaze lands on a large, rectangular concrete hole and a flat concrete slab on the side. I'm not slow on the uptake; I'm at a dead stop. *Is this a gift or something?*

Seeing my perplexed expression, Justice explains. "Remember when we were in Chicago last summer, near the lake? We were driving through this neighborhood, and you made me stop because you saw that two-story Craftsman house with the wide front porch. You stood on the sidewalk in front of it, and I took your picture. You told me that you wanted to build that exact house someday. I'm building it for you, for us. This is our house."

Stupefied, I shake my head. My hands find their way to my mouth. Reeling from shock, I take a giant step backward. *Fall back, fall back,* my mind screams. *Retreat! Run for the hills!* "Our house?" I ask.

"No walls yet, only the foundation. But with Samson's help it will be finished by late summer, early fall."

I spot the black bandana lying on the trodden grass; it's within reach. I want to pluck it from the ground and tie it back into place. Instead, I lunge for Justice's arms. A loud and bizarre, garbled sound escapes my lips. I'm not sure if it has the ring of horror or delight, but it lights the crowd's fuse and causes them to explode with excitement. They whistle and cheer as they had done earlier in the evening.

My suction cup embrace is more about necessity than affection. Maybe I succeeded in pulling the wool over the crowd's eyes, but I can't fool Justice. His radar, finely tuned to my moods and actions, detects trouble.

"What's wrong? You don't love it?" he whispers the questions in my ear.

My sinus cavities thicken with snot, and my eyes burn. Tears are at the ready. I relax my hold on him. "I don't even know what to say."

"Cane, what's —"

Before he can complete his sentence, Mikayla ambushes us. She snakes her arms around my waist and rips me away from Justice. She jumps up and down in excitement. "Ha! Can you believe it!"

"Speech! Speech! Speech!" someone starts to chant. Others join in.

Grandma Betty smiles ferociously and sidles up to me. I know by the way she's rapidly blinking and puckering her lips that she's seconds away from blubbering. I could say the same for myself.

"Oh honey, what do you think? Isn't this something?" she marvels.

Craving my reaction, the crowd gradually falls silent.

Justice is craving a reaction as well. His eyes find mine, and in that brief look I can't hide what I've been feeling all night. I'm not ready. Maybe it isn't too soon, it has been six years after all, but it's too much. My visible panic prompts him to push his lips together in a smile that hints at disappointment.

I hear the electronic whirring of the camera as it zooms in for a close-up.

"Say something already," Mikayla murmurs insistently in my ear and then shoves me.

I lurch forward, stumble, and then steady myself. I'm on display in front of everyone I know and many others I don't. A fire starts on the top of my chest and works its way up, leaving a blazing trail. I'm mortified not by what's happening at this moment in time, but rather by my reaction to it all. Where, oh where are my gratefulness and my dignity? Where, oh where could they have gone?

Clearing my throat, I run one hand down the side of my long hair, resisting the urge to braid, a nervous gesture that would give me away to all those who loved me. I smile, but my mouth quivers like barely set gelatin. I hate making spontaneous speeches, especially under duress.

In my peripheral vision, I see Justice take a promising step toward me. Will he swoop in and rescue me from this awkward situation? Unfortunately, he doesn't have a chance to intervene, because Jelly Roll, who stands not ten feet behind the video camera, crosses her arms and tips her generous body forward. "Come on now, what do you have to say for yourself?"

Her tone may be jovial, but her body language is overtly confrontational. I'm not going to let her rattle me.

"I'm the luckiest girl in the world. Thank you all so much for coming tonight."

A round of applause ensues, and just like that I'm off the hook. Now that I've finally spoken, everyone feels free to indulge their hedonistic party desires. The crowd splits apart, and things get exponentially louder. Someone cranks up the music. Conversational volume rises. Sharp laughter punctures the night.

"That about sums it up, ladies and gentlemen!" Satisfied with his handy-dandy camera work, Frank smiles and snaps the lens cap back into place.

He hands the camera back to me. "Why don't you hold on to this, Cane. I'm going to go find Samson so I can talk to him about the house! Wish I could be around for this project from start to finish."

Grandma Betty rushes over and hugs me.

"Did you know about this?" I ask her.

"Not at all! I kind of wondered why Justice would be having a party out in the middle of the woods. Samson filled us in when we got here. This is simply over the top, isn't it? Honey, it does my heart a world of good to know that I'm leaving you in such good hands. Justice will take such good care of you — he has already been doing that for years."

After planting a kiss on my cheek, she leaves me to go find Frank and Samson.

With no idea as to where Justice has gone to, I look around, feeling disastrously confused about everything. Mikayla comes over and snatches the camera away from me. "I'm your official videographer for the night. I'm going to document this whole evening for you so that in sixty years you can show everyone at the nursing home the video of your engagement party."

Tucking the camera under one arm, she sets her empty beer can on the ground and promptly squashes it with her foot, kicking it to the side. Squinting thoughtfully at me, she asks, "What's with you?"

"Nothing is with me."

"You're freaked out. Your mouth is practically hanging open, and your eyes are all glazed over."

"It's a lot to take in. That's all."

"You can't tell me you didn't know this was coming. This is what you've always wanted and now you have it. Well, aside from the house thing, which is a little insane. And this party? Did you see how many people are here? There are so many kids from our graduating class it's like a flipping high school reunion." She pries off the lens cap, hits the record button, and sashays away, already garnering the attention of every male within a thirty-foot radius.

Justice magically reappears; I wrap my arms around his waist and lean my head against his chest. I breathe in his spicy cologne and the familiar smell of his skin, recently burned by the sun. So deep is my exhaustion that if I close my eyes, I would be asleep in an instant.

I snuggle closer to him. "I'm not sure how I can thank you for what you've done for me tonight. The engagement, the party, the house."

"I can think of some ways," he says flirtatiously.

I glance up at him. "No way do I deserve this kind of treatment."

"You deserve the world, and I want to give it to you."

I frown and give a quick, nervous shake of my head. I don't deserve this. I don't deserve him.

"What's going on with you tonight?" he whispers in my ear. "You aren't yourself."

"Who am I then?"

"Come on. Tell me what's wrong so I can fix it."

For once, I'm going to think things through instead of giving him a knee-jerk reaction that would leave both of us down for the count. As an almost twenty-two-year-old woman, I need to start checking myself, because I have a proven track record of wrecking myself.

For instance, freshman year of college I told off the arrogant and pedantic classic American literature professor, Dr. Heath, after he bullied a shy classmate of mine, reducing her to tears when she'd answered one his questions incorrectly.

Placing my hand on the poor girl's shoulder, I'd stood up, stared down Heath, and with as much eloquence as I could muster said, "You're a dickless, chauvinistic Neanderthal who berates others to hide your own idiocy."

The lecture hall applauded me; Dr. Heath ejected me. Turns out verbally abusing a professor, no matter how warranted, is frowned upon. After a stern talking-to from the English department, I received an incomplete in the class. Dr. Heath received tenure the next semester. Life is never logical and rarely fair.

Though I'm not very logical either. One November Saturday night, sophomore year of college, I couldn't sleep and decided that going for a run at one thirty in the morning around DeKalb was a brilliant idea. I narrowly avoided being mugged by a thug who'd been lurking in the shadows. He'd chased me two blocks and then vanished when I ducked into a gas station and called Caprice from the pay phone. She was furious, but not as furious as Justice would have been had I told him.

I also wreck myself when it comes to wagers. I'm a sucker for any phrase that begins with *I bet you can't.* As soon as someone tells me I can't, I'm not resting until I prove that I can. When Mikayla mentioned that it was physically impossible to stay awake for forty-eight hours straight, I made it my mission to do just that. Cut to thirty-six hours in, when I ended up in the emergency room because my heart became a rocket ship after ingesting too many caffeine pills.

Four months after my caffeine overdose, my heart nearly stopped again when, without thinking, I signed up for the Polar Bear Plunge fundraiser for the American Cancer Society. Eighteen degrees outside, and I thought it would be a great idea to cannonball into Lake Michigan. Twice. Not such a great idea, according to the EMT who had to cut off my swimsuit and wrap me in a warming blanket so that I didn't die from hypothermia.

The list goes on.

I speak before I think and act before I'm sure that's what I want to do or am able to do. More than once, I've relied on level-headed, capable Justice to fix things, like the time he had to play lifeguard and pull me into the boat after I nearly drowned while attempting to swim across Lake Geneva in Wisconsin on a day when the water was so choppy it felt like I was getting punched in the face every time I tried to move forward.

Tonight, I'm going to turn over a new leaf and think things through. Instead of spilling my guts, which would only prompt Justice to get out the cleaning supplies, I calmly and sweetly ask him to show me our house.

He walks me around the foundation, circling to the rear where the walkout basement will exit. We walk inside the structure. He gestures enthusiastically, showing me the location of the living room, kitchen, office, and bedrooms. He explains how the second floor will be supported and where the staircases will be located. He also wants a few hidden passageways — or doors disguised as bookcases — to make things interesting.

Frank, Samson, Jelly Roll, and Grandma Betty soon join us. Frank and Samson discuss the best local electricians and plumbers to hire and where to get decent flooring and fixtures for a bargain price. Grandma Betty, who adores decorating and selecting wall colors, is ready to run home and get her Sherwin-Williams fan deck of paint colors.

Everyone in the group is enthusiastic and positive, with the exception of Jelly Roll, who loves to cast a pall over everything.

"You have some pretty high-end finishes planned. Cedar shakes as siding! Do you know what the upkeep on something like that will be? Constant sealing every year, and if you pay someone else to do it, you better believe you'll be paying top dollar. Not to mention it will be a losing battle. The sap from these trees will ruin it all. And that slate you have planned for the walkway and porch? What an expensive waste. Totally unnecessary investment. Trust me, that will be chipping and flaking off so fast you'll be left with nothing after a few years."

Samson tries to minimize his wife's negativity. "It will all work out fine in the end. Justice knows what he's doing, and we can help with some of the upkeep."

Yanking the hem of her sparkly, bedazzled shirt down over her gut, she screws up her nose. "We have enough going on at the farm and business; we can't be running over here helping out. They'll have to learn how to handle it on their own. Constant headaches are guaranteed, and they are so young, especially you, Cane. You'll be in way over your head." She sneaks a look at me and covers up her stinging insult with a ringing laugh.

Jelly Roll cheers for herself to succeed and all others to fail, but she cheers the loudest for my failure. I'm about to make a witty retort, something to the effect that the only thing giving me a headache is her, when Grandma Betty says, "I have faith in them. They'll handle it effortlessly! These are two of the smartest kids I know."

She looks at Justice. "You can bet we'll be coming up to visit all the time! Especially during the summer months when Florida is too hot to handle."

Frank laughs and gives Justice a jolly slap on the back in a consoling way. "Hope there's a mother-in-law suite in those plans?"

"Finished walk-out basement, complete with a bedroom and attached bath. You're welcome to visit whenever you like."

"Be careful what you say, young man." Frank grins. "You might come to regret that invite."

"He won't regret it one bit!" Grandma Betty places her hand over her heart. "I promise to keep my visits short and sweet, though they might be frequent."

Shortly after the tour, Grandma Betty and Frank say their good-byes. After they've gone, Justice and I stand alone by the foundation. He talks in detail about the finishes: carpet versus hardwood floors, tile versus laminate, gold fixtures versus antique bronze fixtures. When he inquires about what I want, I throw my two cents in but don't offer anything more than that. Talk about role reversal. Usually I'm the one who can't shut up.

I gaze down in the vast, smooth square that will soon be sectioned off with wood and drywall.

"It's huge," I remark. I feel a squeezing tightness in my chest, a swell of anxiety that leaves me shaky. I ease myself onto the ground and dangle my legs over the ledge of concrete.

"Oh, come on, it's not that big."

"If four thousand square feet isn't huge, then I guess we have different definitions of big. It could house a family of elephants."

"How about we keep it simple and get a dog, maybe a chocolate lab or golden retriever."

"Yes, but an elephant is infinitely more interesting, a total conversation starter."

He sits down next to me. "We'll never have to move. That's the point. No starter home."

There's a doughy lump in my throat that's expanding. I try to swallow it. "I know, but *five bedrooms?*"

"For our three kids and one extra for guests."

A diamond ring, a house, a lab, and now kids? Sure, we've talked about all of this before: the house, dog, kids, and even the guest bedroom. We've had six years to hash out the details of what we want our life to be like and have discussed hot button issues like religion, politics, finances, and even sex. Given that we're both fairly right-wing Christians with a similar upbringing who believe a penny saved is a penny earned and view family, love, and loyalty as the bedrock of a fulfilling existence, we've never had a major disagreement. And any minor disagreements were swept away by communication and hot sex.

That's not to say we're two peas in a pod. Our personalities and proclivities are on opposite ends of the spectrum.

Tranquil Justice, whose feathers are never ruffled, appreciates simplicity from the food he eats (plain vanilla ice cream and no condiments ever), to the way he dresses (he owns five pairs of the same

Levi's and twelve different colors of the same Gap T-shirt), to the way he interacts with others. He shies away from confrontation at all costs, keeps his opinions to himself unless goaded and provoked, usually by me, and errs on the side of practicality. An athlete at heart, he loves to run, jump, and play ball. Even when he's not exercising he has a baseball or basketball in his hands or nearby. However, he also has the patience to sit perfectly still for long periods of time, like when he fishes with Jeremy for eight hours straight.

I, on the other hand, am more like a hurricane in both temperament and in the way I approach life. The mere thought of idleness, or being trapped on a boat staring into a calm lake for hours with a pole in my hand, makes my skin crawl. My feathers are usually sticking straight up in the air, stuck on backward, or sometimes falling out. I don't own one thing from the Gap. I frequent secondhand and vintage stores and go for a bohemian look, buying fun and colorful clothing that may or may not match. My favorite outfit, a flowing, cotton, sequined skirt and tight navy polka-dot shirt, was purchased out of a trunk in Venice Beach, California. I prefer messy food (never plain vanilla, the more flavors and condiments the better), throw a welcome mat down when it comes to confrontation, and relish my gigantic soap box.

Our relationship is a delightful balance of harmony and passion. We're alike in the ways that matter and different enough to create a spark and keep us both on our toes. Obviously, we want the same things out of our relationship and life. But Justice is sprinting toward our future, and I'm not sure I'm ready to start the race.

Those feathers of mine are falling out right now. "Three kids, as in *right now?*"

"Mrs. Justice Price, I want to have our family young so we can enjoy it. My goal is to get you barefoot and pregnant as soon as possible."

I blanch at his statement. *Mrs. Justice Price?* That sounds like a fifty-year-old woman. I'm twenty-one! And what if I want to keep my name?

"Are you serious?" I ask breathlessly. "Because I know we've talked about it but-"

"Not right this second. Maybe a year or so after the wedding."

Again, we've talked about this timeline, and I remember thinking it would be a fantastic idea. We both agreed the earlier the better, but the earlier is almost here. Now I'm thinking the later the better might make more sense. In less than two years I could be pregnant? A mother? The notion that I will have to be responsible for someone else, *an infant,* strikes me as ludicrous. I can't take care of a baby! I can barely take care of myself.

"Um, what about the lease I'm supposed to sign?"

"We'll sign a six-month lease instead of a year. We'll still need somewhere to stay while this place is being built."

"Yeah, okay." I don't want a new apartment or a fancy dream house. What I want right now is to return to my college apartment bedroom with the apple-green walls that are riddled with holes, patches, and memories. I long for another month, another semester, another year. Maybe I can get my graduate degree, maybe I can put my nose in a book and leave it there for a while and worry about research papers, studying, and exams as opposed to wedding reception venues, cabinet and tile selections for the house, and bouncing babies that are going to spring from my womb. The piece of dough in my windpipe must have a load of yeast in it, because it's narrowing my airway. I push my hand against my throat trying to offset the pressure.

"This is . . ." I can't finish the sentence.

He turns and looks at me. "It's what?"

I let all the air out of my lungs and tentatively try on a smile. "Unbelievable," I respond, masking my horror with amazement. I can't say much more without opening a can of worms, and for tonight, even though they are squiggling like mad trying to get out, I'm going to hold the lid down tightly.

"Cane."

The way he says my name is an invitation to speak. I look over at him. He knows something is up. I can dump my load of insecurities and uncertainties later, but I'm not about to bury either of us tonight.

Get a grip, Cane.

Scrambling to my feet, I dust off the back of my skirt. "We're being rude. We've been ignoring our friends for the last hour."

He gives me a quizzical look as I hold out my hand to him and help him up.

We both look down at the expanse of the foundation one last time and then at each other. Hand in hand, we walk toward the bonfire. As we make our way closer to the circle of our friends, Jocelyn approaches holding my video camera aloft.

"Hey guys! Hope you don't mind, Cane, but Mikayla gave the camera to me. She said she was having a hard time dual tasking."

I glance over at Mikayla. She's doing a silly kind of lap dance for Jeremy Schaeffer, who's sitting on a lawn chair looking immensely pleased by her attention. I turn back toward Jocelyn. "Meaning she couldn't hold her beer, dance for your brother, and also wield a camera at the same time."

"Bingo," she says laughing. "I'm going to keep recording unless you want it back."

"Go ahead and have fun with it. You can't be catching anything that interesting."

She waggles her brows and looks around. Many of our friends have coupled up. New romances are blossoming all over the place.

"You would be surprised," she says.

"I'm going to go get a beer," announces Justice. "Want anything?" he asks me.

"I'm good."

He meanders off toward his friends and the row of coolers. I mill about for the next hour or so, trying to talk to everyone. When I tire of mingling, I sit down on a large blanket near the fire. Mikayla, who spies me by myself, abandons her position near Jeremy and saunters over.

Taking a swig of beer, she belches loudly. Only Mikayla can make bodily functions sexy. A few of the guys look over and give her a thumbs-up. Holding one hand out to the side, she bows and then sits down across from me.

"You and Jeremy should get a room."

"Haven't decided yet, but he's hot."

I shiver. "Yuck. I've known him so long — I see him as a brother."

"I don't."

"Clearly. It was a lovely lap dance. Where did you learn those moves?"

"I've been to a few strip clubs in Chicago, a few in Vegas. Even one in Paris. I've picked up some skills." She takes another drink of beer. "What's Justice's problem?"

"He doesn't have a problem."

"It looks like he swallowed a screwdriver." She glances at him over her shoulder. "You guys sat by yourself for an awfully long time. What were you talking about?"

There's a frantic edge to her question that doesn't jive with her drunkenness. "Countertops, paint colors, tile versus hardwood floors, and then of course the three or four babies I will birth. Apparently he wants to place a domestic goddess crown on my head and host a coronation."

She looks furtively in his direction and leans closer. Her eyes, glassy from her inebriated state, have a hard time focusing on me. "And that's it, right?"

What is she getting at? Her skittish tone sets off a warning bell inside my head. *Is there something else coming?* What more could he possibly give me? A new car? A trip around the world? "We also talked about retirement funds and where our kids are going to go to college. In case you're wondering, they'll all be getting into Harvard on full scholarship."

She howls with laughter. "Retirement funds? Knowing your fanaticism with saving money that doesn't surprise me."

"I thought the Harvard thing was funnier."

"No, the retirement thing is, because knowing you, you probably did discuss this. I know what a tight wad you are. I bet you and Justice have already hired a financial planner."

No financial planner yet, but I do have a strong IRA and retirement account started. I love getting the statements and watching the numbers multiply. Money doesn't grow on trees, but it does on paper. Still, I'm not going to give her the satisfaction of admitting that I'm already preparing for my golden years.

My time alone with Mikayla is short-lived, because she's hotter than the fire. Like moths to a flame, the men fly closer. Jeremy ambles over and sits next to her, and others hang around the periphery of the blanket, trying to act slick and cool and interesting all at once. All the machismo makes me want to gag.

I inch over to make room for three guys who take up residence next to her. When I look up, I happen to catch Justice's eye. He's standing on the opposite side of the fire chatting it up with one of his college buddies, and I nod slightly with my head toward Mikayla and her ever-growing harem of men as if to say, *would you get a load of this?*

I'm about to let Mikayla have the group all to herself and go over to Justice when she yelps with delight. She jumps up and launches herself at Mike Branzel, throwing her arms and legs around him.

My heart shoots up into my throat, and I nearly choke on it. The last time I saw the jerk was at the end of my sophomore year when he graduated and left for Kentucky to attend college. He knows the secret I've been keeping from Mikayla for years. And I know this because of what he said to me six years ago when he confronted me in the hallway right after Mikayla's mom, Annette, gave birth to her baby boy. "I appreciate a girl who knows how to keep her mouth shut. Let's make sure it stays that way," he said.

What is he doing here?

Mikayla puckers up and kisses every part of Mike's face. Clearly reveling in this kind of greeting, he's smiling.

"How's my cover girl doin'?" he asks.

Apparently, a degree isn't the only thing he picked up in Kentucky. What an annoying drawl.

"Mikey — what in the hell are you doing here? It's been ages and ages! I haven't seen you since your graduation party!" she says.

"I'm finally back, honey. Figured six years was way too long to be away. Had to come back to Savage, Ill-I-No-Is to see how ya'll was doin'!"

He grins as she unwinds herself from his body and slides back to the ground. "And it looks like you're doin' mighty fine, sweetheart. Heard through the grapevine that this party was going on and figured

I'd drop on by if that's okay with you, Cane."

I give him a snappy smile. For obvious reasons, I do mind. "The jury's still out."

"Heard you're getting married."

I hold up my hand and showed him the ring. "This is my engagement party."

"You knocked up or something?"

I point to my concave stomach. "Observant, aren't you? Eight months along."

"You always were a sassy thing."

"Funny, but I don't remember you talking to me at all in high school. So, um, I'm trying to figure out why you're here exactly?"

He feigns a wounded look. "I'm not welcome?"

"Actually, it would be great if you —"

"It's so nice of you to drop by," Mikayla interrupts. She shoots me a how-can-you-be-so-rude look and loops her arm through Mike's.

Apparently, she's decided that Jeremy is out and instead she'll be shooting arrows at Mikey tonight.

"Why don't we go get something cold to drink," suggests Mikayla.

"I am mighty thirsty," Mike responds.

"Then why don't you go get yourself a *mighty* beer, Mikey."

Mike and Mikayla ignore my comment and waltz off like long-lost lovers. In the meantime, Justice meanders over.

"Who was that?"

"*Mike Branzel.* You need to ask him to leave."

"Why?"

"You don't remember who he is and what he said to me?"

"No clue," he remarks.

Incredulous, I scowl. "You honestly don't remember that name?"

"No bells are going off."

I grab on to his arm and whisper frantically into his ear. "He's two years older than me — a senior when we were sophomores, and he happened to be one of Nate's closest friends. Remember? He cornered me after Annette had the baby and told me to keep my mouth shut. *He knows about Nate and Annette.*"

"So what if he does?"

I look at him like's he lost his mind. How could he be so dense! "What if Mikayla brings Nate's name up? What if she asks Mike about him? *What then?*"

He shrugs. "You're making this out to be much worse than it is. She's not going to ask about Nate. That was high school stuff. Don't worry. It will be fine."

"Maybe," I concede, though I'm not entirely convinced.

He sits and lounges on the blanket. "Come sit next to me."

I sit and someone hands me a beer. It tastes bitter and tangy, and my stomach doesn't want any more fizz than it already has. I'm too keyed up about Mike being here. I offer it to Justice.

"Come on, ask the guy to leave. Pretty, pretty please?" I wheedle.

Justice furrows his brow. "Why?"

"For obvious reasons, and because he wasn't invited and because I don't want him here," I say petulantly, slipping into *I'm a baby mode.* "I would do it, but Mikayla would be pissed."

"I can't just tell the guy to get lost."

"Oh yes, you can. I have this feeling he's going to cause trouble." Frankly, it isn't really Mike that's the problem — it's his association with Nate, Mikayla's former high school boyfriend, that makes him a dangerous addition to this party.

Nate had been the most popular boy in school, the handsome, rich, Mustang-driving quarterback with reptilian green eyes. He had done so many evil and twisted things back when we were in high school that there was enough material for at least a week's worth of Jerry Springer episodes. Unfortunately, Mikayla had worshiped Nate. They had dated for a year or more, but what she hadn't known, and would never know if I could help it, was that he had been having sex with her mother. I was the one who had found out about the sordid affair and confronted Annette, but the damage had already been done. A little less than nine months later, she had given birth to a baby boy with reptilian green eyes.

Rumor was that an out-of-town construction worker that frequented Savage Suds, the local bar and grill, had knocked her up. Annette, knowing in this case the truth was more dangerous than fiction, corroborated this gossip, divorced her husband, and hightailed it to California shortly after the baby was born and before anyone had a chance to wonder why her baby boy had the same eyes as the high school's star quarterback.

Also in self-preservation mode, Nate kept his mouth shut about the ordeal. He told only one person, his football teammate and best friend, Mike Branzel.

I've been carrying this grenade of a secret around for years and by some miracle have managed to keep the safety pin securely in place even though the subject has come up on more than one occasion, including this past fall when she'd visited.

"Please, ask him to leave, pretty please," I implore in a sugarcoated, suggestive voice that implies he'll get a cherry on top and more.

Just as I make my request, Mikayla and Mike reappear. And, Justice, being the consummate, non-confrontational gentleman that he is, rises and introduces himself. Then, to top it off, he says, "Why don't you have a seat."

An introduction and an invite when I want him to boot Mikey's ass out of the party? I shoot him an I'm-going-to-strangle-you look, and he smiles innocently at me, dimples popping and goodwill radiating. Sometimes, I wish he were a little meaner, a little rougher around the edges, a little more willing to see the bad in people and not always the good. He shrugs his shoulders.

Come on, he doesn't seem like that bad of a guy, his face says.

Only, Mike is that bad of a guy. He was best friends with Nate, which says more than enough about his character.

Mike, who stands behind Mikayla, accepts Justice's invitation. "Don't mind if I do."

Mike then bear-hugs Mikayla, picking her up clear off the ground; and then as a unit, they sit down on the blanket.

I roll my eyes. Obviously, Mike's here to stay. Spectacular. And to top things off, Justice, who thinks this is no big deal, has wandered off with Jeremy to get a beer. With the way their heads are pressed together, I know they're talking dairy business per usual.

Mikayla, who isn't thrilled with being confined to Mike's lap, wiggles her way free. When he reaches out with his meaty football player hand to grab her butt, she reacts with catlike swiftness, swatting him away.

"Play nice, Mikey," she warns flirtatiously, looking over her shoulder.

She crawls over next to me, so that we now we're both facing the enemy.

"I play, ma'am, but I'm rarely nice." He makes a biting motion, his teeth clinking together.

Unimpressed, Mikayla coolly regards her manicured nails for a moment before finally saying, "I seem to remember that. You and Nate had a lot in common."

Oh no, this is not a safe direction. *Dangerous, slippery slopes ahead.*

Mike guffaws shrilly. "Not too much in common. Don't go puttin' me in the same category as him."

Jocelyn, who stands on the opposite side of the fire, shouts, "Hey, Cane, I'm getting some great footage!"

Distracted, I smile and wave. "Awesome," I yell back, missing some comment that Mike made about Nate, something about him being the biggest playboy there ever was.

"Come on now, Nate wasn't that bad," simpers Mikayla. "From what I remember about the hallway behind the boy's locker room and the illicit activities that went on there after the football games" — she gives him a level stare — "I would dare say that you were worse."

Mike looks at Mikayla with his eyelids a fraction too low and says, "I have excellent recall of those illicit activities, and if memory serves, weren't you involved in one of them?"

"Who the hell wants to talk about high school?" I ask, trying to derail them. "It was ages ago."

"Wasn't that long ago, honey pie. Only been six years since I graduated."

Tilting my head, I give him a way to go smile. "You're so great at subtraction!" I commend mockingly. "Math major?"

"Guess nothin's changed. You still have that sarcastic mouth."

I need to steer them away from the subject of Nate so I keep flapping my sarcastic jaw. "But so much has changed. Your accent, for instance. It's a little much. I feel like I should fetch you some sweet tea, a rockin' chair, and a piece of straw to put in your mouth. Maybe a corncob pipe as a backup accessory."

Mikayla snorts. "A corncob pipe? Not sure if he could pull off that look."

Mikey, who is well on his way to being plastered, takes affront to my jeers. "I know it's your party and all," he says, "but you aren't being nice."

Lowering my chin, I give him an impressively innocent smile. "Don't you know? I'm not a nice person." I throw his mock term of endearment back in his face and add, "*Honey pie.*"

Annoyed with me, he sniffs angrily and finishes off his beer. "I've gathered."

Mikayla, who still sits beside me, leans back on her elbows, and Mike, who seems magnetically drawn to her, compensates for the distance by leaning toward her.

She pegs Mikey with a curious stare. "I lost touch with Nate after high school, what with his family moving away and him going to FSU. You keep in touch with him, right? What's he been doing with himself?"

Mike chortles. "Seriously? I thought for sure after what happened you would have written him off. You honestly want to know what he's been up to?"

Slippery apprehension squirms around in my stomach. That grenade safety pin is in jeopardy. "*No, she doesn't want to know.*" I grab Mikayla's hand, intending to get her the hell away from there. "Come on, I want to show you my house!"

"Not now, Cane." She wrenches her hand free and gives Mike a level stare. "Yes, I want to know! Why wouldn't I?"

"Come on, Mikayla, come with me!"

Mike regards me with annoyance, and Mikayla gives me a *you're being so annoying* look.

"Because," he half-snorts, half-laughs, "I would have thought the whole fiasco of Nate messing around with your mom would have left a bad taste in your mouth. I'm not sure how anyone could ever get over that. I mean, if my mom screwed around with one of my friends and got knocked up, I think I would kill the bastard."

"Wait —" Mikayla flips her hair over her shoulder and sits upright. "What did you just say?"

Ka-boom. The grenade just discharged, and I didn't even have time to duck and cover. Shrapnel and carnage all over the place. "He said nothing!"

Unfortunately, my comment goes unnoticed, because at the same time I speak, so does Mike. "You're not telling me that you don't know . . . I mean, by now, darlin' I was sure that you would. Hell, thought it would be kind of obvious."

"You're kidding me with this!" she bellows. "Cane, come on? This asshole is making this up, right?"

Good old Mikey has backed me into a corner. I can barely look at Mikayla.

"Right?" she screeches again and scrambles to her feet.

Mikey, who has been following her every move like they're in a synchronized dance of sorts, stands as well.

This is one dance I don't want to be a part of, but what choice do I have? I stand.

While Mikayla's waiting for my tongue to come loose, Mike says, "Whoa, whoa, whoa. First off, I thought for sure that by now you would know about it. I mean, man, Nate showed me a picture of the kid about six months after he was born. It was kind of obvious."

"Asshole!" she shouts piercingly.

Her voice, a crack of thunder, carries through the night. Immediately, the party goes deathly silent. A storm is brewing, and we're at the center. Justice snaps to attention. Our eyes meet, and even before I open my mouth to tell him to please help, he's on his way.

"Listen, Mickey D," Mike says, using Mikayla's underground nickname from high school that was a playful twist on her name and reference to her breast size. "You were always a little cock tease, shaking that ass and those tits, but your follow-through wasn't so hot. Maybe your mom was an easier target."

"Is there a problem here?" Justice asks forcefully, inserting himself into the quarrel.

His interference, though welcome, is a fraction of a second too late, at least for Mike.

Mikayla's fist comes out of nowhere and thwacks Mike across the cheek. The impressive right hook knocks him off balance. He recovers from his shock faster than I think possible, perhaps because he's used to getting hit by women. The punch washes all that glossy southern boy charm away, leaving behind his true, shadowy character. Scowling, he shifts his jaw first one way and then the other.

"Get the hell out of my party, you loser!" I shout.

"Listen, you little bitch, I've had enough of your mouth," he says, snarling and stepping toward me in a menacing way.

Adrenaline courses through me. Fight-or-flight kicks in, and if he comes at me, he's not even going to live to regret it, because he's going to be dead.

Before he can lay a hand on me or I can lay a hand on him, Justice and Jeremy rush in, grabbing his arms and pulling him backward.

"Don't you dare touch her," Justice growls menacingly.

"The truth hurts!" Mike shouts at Mikayla. "Sorry to break the news, honey pie, but hey, don't shoot the messenger."

"Leave it be!" yells Justice. "You've done enough."

"*Let go of me!*" Mike tries in vain to shake them off, but more of Justice's friends step in to help restrain him and haul him back to his vehicle.

The dramatic scene prompts dozens of wildfire dialogues around us, and word of what has happened and of what was revealed burns through the crowd in mere seconds.

In the distance, I hear a skirmish, cursing, shouting, and finally the roar of an engine.

Mikayla, who's holding her fist against her stomach and looking like she either wants to pass out or start another fight, visibly trembles.

Wanting her to know that I'm on her side, I reach out to place my hand on her shoulder. She jerks away from me.

By this time, Jeremy and Justice have run back to where we're standing.

"We should call it a night," suggests Justice.

"I can take you back to the hotel, Mikayla," Jeremy offers gallantly. "Or to wherever you want to go."

She scoffs. "No way. I'm. Not. Going. Anywhere." She glares at me, her eyes flinty and unforgiving, her body rigid with fury. "It's true then, *isn't it?* I can see it in your face that you knew. You knew, and you didn't tell me! And we just talked about it this last fall! What the *hell?*"

I have a flashback to last October. I'd been plowing my way through a rather dull classic novel, highlighting passages, scribbling notes in the margin, and trying not to drown in a puddle of my own drool, when Mikayla, whom I hadn't seen in six months, showed up at the door with a six-pack tucked under her arm.

She plucked the highlighter from where it was perched on my ear.

"You take this school thing much too seriously," she said as I threw my arms around her neck from sheer joy.

We were each two beers in when she told me that her youngest brother, Seth, had been asking questions about his father.

"Seth has a right to know. I thought by now my mom would have come clean about who she had an affair with. Everyone thought it was that guy from Savage Suds, that construction worker, but I don't buy it. She's never mentioned him, never tried to go after him for child support or anything. It can't be him, but the question is: who was it and why is she keeping it from Seth and everybody else? You're home more often than I am. Have you heard any rumors over the years? Do have any idea who she was having an affair with?" she asked.

Without hesitating, I lied. "I have no idea. I haven't heard a thing."

"*How long have you known?*" Mikayla screams now.

Justice tentatively proposes a solution. "Why don't you and Cane get a good night's rest and then you can sit down and talk things out in the morning."

Mikayla, furious and determined, stares him down. "I'm getting to the bottom of this, *now.*"

Justice gives me an *uh-oh* look, and it's obvious that he's finally acknowledging those slippery slopes. Only now, there's an avalanche, and I'm about to be buried alive.

He claps his hands once and makes a loud announcement. "Party's over. Thanks for coming out, but I think everyone should call it a night."

There's murmuring, feet shuffling, and palpable unease, but no one makes a move. It's a train wreck. The crowd had witnessed the impact and now they want to gawk at the bloodbath.

Get a clue, people! Go home! I would shout this, but my tongue, which feels like it's coated with superglue, is stuck to the roof of my mouth.

Jeremy, Justice's right-hand man, walks over and shuts off the music, hoping to make the message louder and clearer, but it backfires. Without the buffer of noise, the crowd's attention to our escalating drama is more conspicuous.

Mikayla's glower cracks at the edges, leaving room for her vulnerability and hurt to poke through.

I throw a *help me* look at Justice, but he can't save me from this. No one can. I dug my own grave years ago when I kept quiet, and now I'm about to be rolled into it. I only hope Mikayla won't pick up the shovel and start burying me alive.

"*Say something, damn it!*" she yells. "I want to know how long you've known. I want to know why you've never said anything to me!"

My stomach turns into a hardened pit, and bile rises in the back of my throat. "I caught them in high school at the forest preserve, the summer of the tornado. I wanted to protect you."

Her eyes bug out, and she covers her mouth with her hands.

"I'm so sorry. It wasn't a secret that I wanted to keep, but honestly, I didn't know how to tell you. I mean, I just couldn't do it, not with all the junk you had to go through." Mikayla's life had been so turbulent at that time. She'd suffered through screaming matches between her parents and their rancorous divorce. While she was trying to adjust to her family's demise and shouldering the embarrassment of her mother's affair, her mother took off for California with the baby without explanation, deserting Mikayla and her younger brother. I hadn't wanted to add to her misery.

"Cane's intentions were pure. She wanted to protect you from this," Justice says.

Mikayla's expression reminds me of Mike's after she'd cold-cocked him. Just as he had recovered quickly, she does as well.

Her eyes harden at the edges. "I can't believe you did this to me! That has to be the worst thing —"

"*I* didn't do anything to you!" I interrupt. "Your *mother* did, and let's not forget about Nate. Put the blame on them," I say pleadingly, "not me."

She throws her head back and laughs mirthlessly before looking me in the eye again. "A true friend would have said something to me. We've been friends from the day we were born, Cane. You never should have kept this from me. You lied to me."

"Only to protect you." Mikayla and alcohol aren't a great combination; the more she imbibes, the uglier and more volatile she becomes. "Why don't we talk about this tomorrow, in private?"

She throws her hands up in the air. "Since everything's coming out in the open now, *why the hell not.* Friends tell friends everything, right? No more secrets, no more hiding things and pretending they didn't happen, no more protecting anyone from anything. Why not —"

"Mikayla, don't," warns Justice.

I notice Justice's strained face and the way his fingers curl into his palms.

His nostrils flare. "*Don't* do this, Mikayla. *Don't.*"

Wanting an explanation, I look at him, but he's too busy staring down Mikalya. They seem to be a having an argument without saying a word. The hairs on the back of my neck rise, and a shiver skates its way down my spine, paralyzing me as it goes.

What is going on?

"Oh Justice," Mikayla remarks in a maliciously, teasing tone. "It's already been done."

Justice finally looks away from her to me. "Cane, let's get out of here."

I want to flee with him and run away from all of this. But I don't have the chance.

Mikayla smiles with a malevolence I've only seen her use on enemies. "Your knight in shining armor, your forever love, your soon-to-be husband and father of your future children, why don't you ask him what happened three weeks ago after we had lunch together?"

Her smile, sharp and curved, is reminiscent of a sickle. She takes a step closer. "Why don't you ask him why he so willingly made out with me?"

CHAPTER THREE

I don't understand what's happening at first. It starts as a tickle in my throat. I cough, or at least I try to, but what comes out instead is a mangled giggle. To my amazement and everyone else's, most notably Justice's and Mikayla's, I start laughing.

It isn't, *woe is me, I can't believe I just found out the love of my life cheated on me with my best friend and I'm in shock laughing.* It's a true, robust, howling kind of laughter that makes me fearful I'll lose control of my bladder and piss my pants in front of everyone. It has happened before, actually this past fall on the night when Mikayla had come to visit. We'd watched Dumb and Dumber at two in the morning, and the bathroom scene, where the laxatives that Jeff Daniels's character unknowingly ingests finally kick in, had made me lose control. Drunk and overtired, I'd found the scene torturously funny. I'd wet my pants, and when Mikayla realized what was happening, she spewed beer out of her mouth all over to the wall and laughed until she almost did the same thing.

Justice and Mikalya look at me, wondering what screws have suddenly come loose in my brain and what they should do about it. Their bemused expressions make me cackle harder. Tears roll down my cheeks. I bend over, clutching my stomach and trying to get control.

The news is so bad and ridiculously awful that for some reason it seems hilarious. It's like my funny bone has been overstimulated, and my body, not knowing what to do, convulses with laughter.

"I'm not making this up!" Mikayla shouts. "There's *nothing* funny about this. This *seriously* happened."

I pause, mid-laugh, look at her in all her indignant sincerity, and that's the end of my chortling. The bad news finally sinks into the core of my cerebral cortex, and the well of laughter dries up. I have nothing left in me.

I emit a heavy, rumbling kind of sigh that has the makings of a groan. Justice and Jeremy had tried in vain to shoo everyone away, but it turns out ridiculous and inappropriate laughing does the trick. Our friends and acquaintances shuffle and slink away, wearing embarrassed, smiling grimaces, and clearly at a loss of what to say. *Congratulations* no longer makes sense. *Good luck with this mess* seems more apropos.

Justice, looking like he may vomit, stares at the ground and shakes his head. Mikayla looks from Justice to me and back again, trying to figure out what to make of this scene.

Someone calls, "See you later, Cane."

I give a halfhearted wave.

Jocelyn sneaks up behind me and quietly clears her throat. "Um, I like, so I just …" Pausing, she hands me the camera. "Here."

Leaning in, so only I can hear, she whispers, "I forgot to stop recording."

"*Everything* is on here?" I ask.

Jocelyn, looking teary and nervous, sucks on her bottom lip and gives a barely perceptible nod before scooting away to stand next to her brother.

I briefly glance at the camera in my hands trying to come to terms with what has happened and with the fact that it's all on film. Forever recorded in time, it's better than a scrapbook or a diary entry. I can watch my tragedy unfolding second by second. It's the ultimate documentary. Maybe if I sent it in to *America's Funniest Home Videos,* Grandma Betty's second favorite TV show only to *Wheel of Fortune,* I could win the $100,000 prize.

Out of nowhere, my emotions do a back handspring, and when I stick the landing, I'm furious. My wrath, with the heft and strength of a boa constrictor, slithers its way up my body and squeezes. The pressure builds until I'm sure my head will blow apart in a million bloody pieces.

"*This really happened?*" I direct the question at Mikayla.

Justice, eager to explain, jumps in before she can say a word. "It's not what you think at all, Cane. She's blowing it out of proportion. Let's go somewhere and talk about this." He runs his hand down my upper arm and leaves it there.

I look at him like he's crazy for thinking it's okay to touch me, and he drops his hand.

His show of affection and his eagerness to reconcile prompts Mikayla to emit a hissing noise. "Not what you think? That's classic guy bullshit." She gives me a sharp look. "It happened, just like my mother slept with Nate, I made out with Justice. No more secrets."

"It was only a kiss. You initiated it, and I stopped it as quickly as it began," Justice adamantly specifies. "We both know that."

She gives me an enigmatic smile, and then turns to him. "Do we?" she asks coyly.

I know Mikayla well enough to know that she's playing this for all it's worth, but still, she kissed Justice. This rocks me to the core.

"Come on!" he yells. "This is *ridiculous.* And for you to bring it up *tonight?*" He looks stricken as he meets my eyes. "Sugar Cane, I swear to you — nothing happened."

She rolls her eyes. "Keep telling yourself that, buddy."

"You've always had a flair for the theatrical. Cooler heads will prevail in the morning after you sober up, maybe you'll remember it —"

Before Justice can say another word, I put an end to this nonsense. "I'm finished."

Mikayla rolls her eyes and throws her beer can into the fire. The flames eat up the alcohol. The aluminum blackens and shrinks. "*You're finished?* That's all you've got to say? Well, I have something more to say, this friendship is over. I don't care how long we've been friends, or how many years we've invested. As I see it, it means *nothing,* not after the secret you've kept from me."

"For the hundredth time, I was doing it to protect you. And you're so *innocent,* Mikayla? You kissed the man I love! You probably threw yourself at him! All you care about is having every male in the universe wrapped around your finger, or should I say *body.* You're desperate to have everyone worship you."

"This isn't about worship, or making out, or anything superficial. This is about love. Here's another newsflash for you, Cane, another secret I've been keeping. *I love Justice,*" she announces piercingly.

And with that, she strides off, calling for Jeremy to give her a ride back to the hotel. Like a well-trained puppy, he follows her, with Jocelyn trailing them both.

She loves him?

Justice runs his hands down his face. "Please, honey, let's go home and talk about this."

"Go home?" Standing on my tiptoes, trying to lift my five-foot-three frame up high enough to see over Justice's six-foot build, I spot the concrete foundation in the distance. "Aren't we already home?"

"Good point, but it's not comfortable, no furniture yet or anything," he says, trying to infuse lightness.

"I'm *leaving,*" I proclaim with finality. I'd made up my mind as soon as my laughing spell had passed. I knew what I was going to do and had it all plotted out in my head. Mikayla's announcement had been the straw that broke the camel's back, and I'm not sticking around until its bones are mended.

He flips over his hands, an entreaty of sorts, and rushes to explain. "What happened with Mikayla, listen, it was harmless. We met for lunch, and she proceeds to have three glasses of wine and doesn't eat but two pieces of lettuce. She was completely drunk. Then she started unloading about all her bad relationships and how thankful she was to have a friend like me, that I had always been there for her and had been such a gentleman and always listened. The next thing I knew I was walking her to her car and she was telling me that she loved me, that she couldn't live without me. I told her it wasn't going to happen, that I loved you, and the next thing I know, she jumped me. Started shoving her tongue down my throat. I was shocked — I swear I stopped it as soon as it started."

"And yet you didn't tell me?"

"I wanted to protect you," he says.

Clobbered by a boomerang. He'd thrown the same excuse I'd used with Mikayla back at me.

"You're her best friend, and I didn't want you to think less of her. You know how she is. Nothing changed because of what happened. It was just Mikayla being Mikayla. She doesn't love me. She'll be onto the next guy in no time at all."

Because he hadn't told me I think less of him, not her. I narrow my eyes. "Protecting me like I had protected her from an ugly truth? Don't kid yourself, this ugly truth is a little different."

"Come on, Cane. It's not a big deal."

"Let's play devil's advocate and flip this coin around, shall we? Let's say for instance, your cousin, Jeremy, or one of your best friends professed his love for me and started making out with me, and I didn't tell you. How would *that* feel?"

He places his hands on either side of my face and murmurs, "It would feel awful. Sugar Cane, I'm so sorry." The heated electrical pulse of desire that I had first felt when I met him when I was fifteen and he was twenty-one, the one that had grown more potent over the last few years, has lost its charge. It's gone stone-cold just like that.

I love him, but I can't deny that something has changed. It's happened so suddenly that my heart can't quite keep up with my brain, and vice versa. A bolus of tears pushes behind my eyelids, and the surface of my eyeballs burns. "I need some time to think about things."

His eyes bore into mine. "To think about things?" he asks slowly.

He knows something is up, but I can't tell him out here in the middle of the woods, standing next to our future home.

On the way to Frank and Grandma Betty's, Justice doesn't stop talking, which is unnerving in and of itself, because I usually do enough talking for both of us. He tells me how sorry he is that the night had been ruined, how he hoped that we could forget about this and move on, how Mikayla is so flaky that she'll get over it and that we can all find a way to move past this. He says he should have kicked Mike Branzel's ass, but who is he kidding? Justice is a lover, not a fighter. He wouldn't pummel someone unless absolutely necessary. I, on the other hand, a hothead to the core, have been in more than one fistfight, even with inanimate objects like walls. I have the scars to prove it.

When he finally pauses for a moment, I say, "You know everyone in town knows about this by now, including Jelly Roll, who is going to have a field day with this new development since she doesn't want me anywhere near your family tree."

He gives me a conciliatory smile. "That's not true."

I seek clarification. "The part about the town not knowing or the part about Jelly Roll not wanting me securing a branch on your family tree?"

"Neither is true."

"Sure, uh-huh." *Right.* He's trying to make me feel better; both are true. Although Savage, Illinois, has gone through a population boom in the last four years, it is still a small farming town at heart, filled with big mouths and Dumbo ears, and by now everyone has heard a version of the story. The next morning the local paper will probably run a headline that says something to the effect of *Sugar Cane and Justice, Longtime Sweethearts Gone Sour.* And when Jelly Roll finds out what happened, I'm sure she'll call Mikayla and thank her for sabotaging my relationship with her nephew.

Hesitantly, he broaches the subject of our wedding. "Where do you think we should get married? Do you think it should be this summer?"

I give him a glassy-eyed stare. "I don't know," I mumble.

He rambles on, changing subjects faster than a speeding bullet, which makes me wonder. What really happened between him and Mikayla? They've had quite a few lunches together over the past couple of years and had even gone out at night together in the city.

Is he hiding something other than a post-lunch parking lot smooch session? I look over at his Superman profile. Is this man who always fights for truth, justice, and the American way capable of lying to me?

When we pull into Frank's driveway, Justice suddenly runs out of words. He rests his hands at the top of the steering wheel and looks at me.

I have to tell him what I'm going to do. If I wait, have a good night's rest, and think things through, my backbone might soften. I might forgive and forget a little too easily.

I wrap my hands around my knobby knees and steel my resolve.

I look straight ahead, because looking him in the eye is out of the question. "I'm leaving town for the summer," I announce. "I won't be back until the end of August. I want some space and time to think about everything." I chance a look to the left and observe Justice taking this in.

He turns off the engine and rests his arm on the windowsill. "You're overreacting to all of this."

Justice constantly accuses me of overreacting, but he underreacts. Whose responses are right and whose are wrong? Are we supposed to meet in the middle? Am I supposed to put some starch in my upper lip to stiffen it up, and is he supposed to tenderize his so that he can feel a little bit more? "I *hate it* when you say things like that. Maybe instead of laughing, I should have decked Mikayla and then you and then thrown the ring back in your face! Maybe I have no interest in marrying you and moving into our dream house and having three or four babies and walking our chocolate lab!"

Rubbing his hand over his mouth, he gives a tolerant sigh, the one I know all too well, the one that translates, *here she goes again.* "You don't mean that."

I mean it, and I don't. My emotions, contradictory and unreliable, are swinging like a pendulum, and I'm not sure where they're going to land next. "I mean everything I say. I want out."

Justice's voice ratchets up a notch. "Want out of *what,* Cane? Want out of this relationship? Want out of the truck? What do you want out of? Don't say things you can't take back."

"I have every right to be pissed, you know!"

"For once, why don't we stick to the conversation at hand?"

"Fine. I want a break from us. I want to leave for the summer. I need to think things through."

"You are *unbelievable!*"

"No, you are!" I throw back, realizing how juvenile I sound, how the tone and cadence sound like the saying *I'm rubber you're glue, whatever bounces off me sticks to you.* Trying to save face, I calmly say, "You made out with my best friend and didn't tell me. I'm not unbelievable. You are."

To punctuate my statement, I hop out of the truck and resist the urge to slam the door.

Normally Justice would say something like *I'll let you calm down and we can talk tomorrow and I love you,* and I would begrudgingly say *I love you, too,* and that would be the end of it. But, tonight, he jumps out of his truck and slams the door.

It's so unexpected and so unlike him that I actually jump off the ground. He comes around to where I'm standing and fixes his hands against his hip bones.

"This was supposed to be the best night of our lives, and I'm sorry about the Mikayla thing. It sucks, and yes, I should have told you, but I don't understand how you can let it ruin everything and leave for the summer to think things through. What exactly do you need to think about?"

His anger, like a virus, infects me. "You want to know what *I* need to think about? I need to think about *us* and whether I want all of *this!* I want to see what life is like without you and on my *own* for once! I want some *separation!*" These toxic words pop out of my mouth before I can stop them.

Justice's face looks like Mike's had after Mikayla punched him. "I can't believe you."

I've never seen him so wounded. He raises his palms to his forehead and shakes his head.

To hell with my plan. To hell with leaving. To hell with it all. Clearly I'm not thinking straight. I'm about to take everything back, when he recycles the words I'd said earlier. "*I'm finished.*"

Something about the way he says this causes the pit of my stomach to fall out and land between my feet. *Finished?* Finished with me, finished with the relationship, finished with talking?

"What specifically are you finished with?" I ask in my most reasonable tone.

"Last fall when I said that you should take a few months to make sure this is what you wanted, to make sure that you could spend the rest of your life with me, you flipped out on me and said you didn't need any time because you knew it was right! Do you remember?"

How could I forget?

Justice had driven up and surprised me on a Saturday night, the last weekend in September. After a romantic dinner at an French bistro, we went back to my apartment and capped off the night with intimate, passionate sex.

Then, while we lay in bed, he stroked my bare thigh and said, "Cane, you know I love you more than life itself, but I want to give you a shot at figuring out what you really want. I've had other relationships, you haven't. I want you to take three months, or more time if you need it, to see what it's like without me. Date other people if you want. Live it up with your friends, but I think if we took a break — just for a short time — it would make me feel better about the direction this is headed. I won't see other people at all, I promise. This is for you. You're so young, and I don't want you to end up regretting anything."

"I don't need to do that." I pulled the sheet up under my chin and put on my most obstinate face. "I'm not doing that."

"It's not up for discussion. I think we should break things off for a while."

Overheated with rage and fear, the blood rushed to my head and pushed against my skull, threatening to split the bone down the middle. In a shaking, teary rage, I kicked him out of my apartment, told him I never wanted to see him again, and then when he was gone, I put my fist through my drywall. Caprice came home to find me stewing on the couch with my bloodied hand swaddled in a towel. The doctor at the emergency clinic stitched up my mutilated knuckles, and Caprice and I mended the wall.

"Vividly," I snarl. "I still have the scars from the stitches!" I hold up my fist in front of his face for a visual aid. "By the way, your timing sucked! Maybe if you had waited to have that discussion until we were at least dressed!"

"Timing? You want to talk about timing? On the night I propose and throw you a surprise party and show you our dream house, you're questioning *everything*. And I know you well enough to know that you were freaking out even before you found out about Mikayla.

"All those months ago, I gave you your shot at freedom. I told you to take it, and you didn't! So, if you want freedom, fine, but I'm making up some rules. We're not talking. At all. I don't want you calling me in a few days telling me you're sorry and this was all a mistake and that you want to come home." He moves closer to me and drops his voice an octave. "That's *not* how it's going to work. The rest of June, July, and all of August — there will be no contact between us. Got it? And, we are both free to see other people. As of now — it's all up in the air."

It's so unlike him to actively participate in an argument and to make threats and demands that at first I'm not sure whether to duel with him or lay down my weapons. But then, I recover my wits. Of course I duel. I live and die by the sword. "Fine by me, and for the record you're the one who's going to be begging to have me back!"

"You want this, then? We're doing this?" he asks in a low, hostile voice.

Is this a test of sorts? I literally dig my heels into the ground. "I'm leaving, so yes, I guess we're doing this."

Disgusted, he throws his arms up in the air, gets in his truck, and slams the door again. I don't want him slamming doors! I'm the one who slams doors!

"*Don't you want to know where I'm going?*" I scream the question as I walk backward and brace myself for what's about to happen.

He starts up the engine, backs over the pit of my stomach, and before he pulls away he says, "I'm sure I'll know by tomorrow morning. It's a small town, word spreads fast."

His truck roars down the gravel road away from Frank's house. When his taillights are no longer visible, regret ravages me, shattering my heart to pieces.

A highlight reel of our relationship flashes before my eyes:

After delivering my valedictorian speech at high school graduation, he presents me with a gorgeous bouquet of two dozen red and orange poppies. And finally, after two long years and two months of having to be just friends with him, he asks me out on a date.

A freshman in college and missing him so much I can barely navigate the day, he surprises me on a snowy November night outside my dorm. With a boom box held above his head and the speakers blasting Peter

Gabriel's "In Your Eyes," he reenacts the scene from my favorite romantic eighties movie, Say Anything.

On a hot August night, we drive to the gravel pit near the forest preserve; stripping off our clothes, we dive into the deep body of water, our bodies humming with cold and desire.

We sign up for a marathon and spend countless hours during the spring and summer religiously training. Come October, we run the twenty-six-point-two miles side by side and finish in less than four hours despite the freezing drizzle that pelts us the entire way.

He wraps me up in his arms on a cool spring night after making love for the first time, runs his fingers along the cross-shaped birthmark on my forehead, and vows to love me forever.

After his father dies, I drive home and hold him in my arms all that night, knowing that he was both angry at his absent father for all he had done and had not done, and also tragically indifferent.

He stands in front of me in the bathroom and together we stare at the pregnancy test that rests on the crest of my knees, praying for a negative sign. "No matter what it says, or what you decide, I will always be by your side," he promises.

Our lives have become so intertwined and codependent that I no longer know where I begin and he ends. Without him, do I even have an identity?

"You want this, then?" he'd asked only moments ago, but now I realize that what he'd really been asking is *you're throwing all of this away?*

He's already put so much distance between us that I can barely hear the powerful yet mournful sound of his truck.

What have I done?

That stupid No Doubt song "Don't Speak" pops into my head, and the lyrics worm their way through my brain.

Have I lost my best friend? Could this be the end?

CHAPTER FOUR

"You're shitting kidding me with this, right? You're actually here!" Caprice slaps me hard on the arm and then crushes me in a hug, lifting me clear off the ground.

With the body of a goddess and the mannerisms and mouth of a rough-and-tumble boy, Caprice is an anomaly. She's not conventionally beautiful, more like striking and intimidating; her broad brow and sharp cheekbones are tempered somewhat by her jade eyes and long, thick dark hair. Men love and fear her in equal measure, and women admire her bravado but are sometimes put off by her aggressive in-your-face demeanor.

"Holy. Shitty. Balls. What the eff are you doing here?"

Before I can formulate a response, she grabs me by the hand and jerks me into her uncle's vacation home that's located on the outskirts of Briar, Colorado, a quaint resort town minutes from Boulder. Caprice, a business major with an economics minor who graduated six months before me, has spent the past few summers living out here running a successful cleaning business called *Maid Right in Time.* Upon graduating this December, she relocated here permanently and turned her part-time cleaning business into a full-time, profitable venture.

I appraise the enormous two-story great room, with the hardwood floors, cedar ceiling, soaring fireplace, and wall of windows that frames a perfect view of the Rocky Mountains. It looks like the cover of a real estate brochure for million-dollar Colorado homes. "Don't tell me this is where you get to live for free? Not even fair."

"I know, I'm lucky. The uncle's loaded. But not free. Now that I'm here permanently, he's putting me in charge of paying taxes, upkeep, and maintenance." She waves her hand, indicating that she's done with the subject. "Speaking of living arrangements, I thought you were signing the lease on your apartment yesterday and starting your job at Schaeffer Dairy. What the hell happened to all of that?"

I scan her nearly six-foot Playboy body up and down, suddenly aware of her outfit. "You're wearing a hot pink bikini?" I unzip my sweatshirt and tie it around my waist. "In case you didn't get the memo, it's not quite sixty-two degrees outside. Cover yourself, you look like a beached tramp," I joke.

She grins. "Don't give me any crap, or I'll kick your ass. I just got done with work. This is my uniform." Twirling around, she gives me a view of her perfect butt. In black, script letters it reads *Maid Hot.*

I cock an eyebrow. "You're kidding me? That is your *uniform?*"

"Yes." She grins slyly and proudly. "I'm still running *Maid Right in Time,* my conservative cleaning business. But I've also launched *Maid Hot,* a raunchier, edgier alternative to a boring maid service. If the clients want, and the male demographic, old and young, always does, we clean in bikinis. Business is booming. Honestly, I can't keep up with the demand. We're the Hooters of the cleaning world. At this rate, I'll be able to open franchises in resort towns across the west and hang up my cleaning gloves and manage a million-dollar business."

"Why bother with the cleaning business? You could be a model and join Mikayla in conquering all the men of the world, including Justice."

I wearily sink down onto the leather sectional, lean forward, and hang my head between my legs. I start braiding my hair in an upside-down position, starting from the nape of my neck and working my way up to the top of my scalp.

"Oh. Shit." Caprice knows that braiding is never a good sign. "What *happened?*"

I finish off some braiding and flip my head back up. "Short version? Surprise proposal." I hold up my hand, why I'm still sporting my mother's ring, I'm not sure. "Surprise engagement party, followed by another surprise party in the woods where Justice showed me our future house dream house that he's building, followed by a dramatic scene where some ass that knew Mikayla's high school boyfriend, Nate, shows up and tells Mikayla that her mother screwed around with Nate and had his love child, finally outing the secret I've been hiding from her for years. The icing on the cake? Mikayla breaks the news that she loves Justice and kissed him on one of their lunch dates this spring. Follow that up with a fight between me and Justice where he wants" — I make air quotes with my fingers — "no communication for three months and we're allowed to see other people."

Caprice blows a stream of air out of her mouth, waits a full minute, and then says. "Holy. Shitty. Balls." She walks purposefully to the fridge and yanks out a beer. "That shithead didn't even invite me to the engagement party!"

"He said he sent you an invitation."

"Heads-up!" She tosses it to me. "Slam that. He probably sent it to my home address in Chicago, and since my dad is pissed as hell that I'm making my own life and not slaving away for that godforsaken family restaurant slash catering business of his, he only forwards my mail when he feels like it." She points at the beer in my hands. "Come on now, drink!"

I dutifully twist off the top. "I don't feel like it." Despite this, I lift it to my mouth and drain half of it anyway. I burp for a full three seconds and then lay my head against the back of the couch.

Caprice paces the room like a boxer. "I want to kick Mikayla's ass! Had I been there, you can bet there would have been fists flying in her direction."

"I don't doubt it."

"I've never told you this, because I know that she's your best friend since birth, you have the same birthday, blah, blah, blah, but I've never been crazy about her. She strikes me as a person who only cares about herself."

"She can be selfish, but deep down, she's a good person. I owe her my life," I say quietly.

"That doesn't mean she has a get-out-of-jail-free card. I can't believe she did this to you! I'm seriously itching for a fight with that girl."

Caprice is furious, but I can't say the same, not anymore. On the eighteen-hour drive out west, the wrath had been replaced with a numbing fatigue, the kind of tired that makes my bones feel brittle and my brain fuzzy. "I don't even care anymore."

"*That's a load of balls!* You know you care! You didn't see it happen? You didn't see her kissing Justice or anything?" Caprice inquires.

At first I'm confused by her questions, but then I know what she's referring to. "You know it doesn't work like that. It would be convenient if it did, but it doesn't. Only works in a crisis."

Mikayla and I have an unusual psychic connection; we are mediums for each other's trials and tribulations. It began when we were young. I woke in the middle of the night and instinctively knew that Mikayla couldn't breathe; she'd been having an anaphylactic reaction from medication and would have died had I not insisted Grandma Betty call her parents. This pattern continued during our childhood and into adolescence. I'd been sitting in a Sunday morning church service when I knew that her beloved golden retriever had been hit by a car. In high school, I'd been competing at a track meet when I had a vision of her getting into a car crash. In turn, Mikayla had known when I'd fallen out of tree and broken a bone and when I'd contracted the chicken pox. Most importantly, the summer I turned sixteen and an inferno ravaged what was left of my tornado-damaged home, she'd known I was trapped in my bedroom. It would have been my premature cremation had she not dragged an extension ladder over to my house, placed it next to the second-story window, and played fireman and rescued me.

I've never been able to figure out why we have this connection. Does it have something to do with sharing the same birthday? Are our souls that tightly bound together? I'd lost a twin brother at birth, and Mikayla, in many ways, has been his replacement, a constant by my side, and, more often than not, a thorn in my side.

Scoffing, Caprice says, "As if her kissing him wasn't a crisis."

"Good point."

She plunks down next to me on the couch. "This Justice thing, this pseudo breakup or temporary separation or whatever you want to call it, you must be freaked out about it," she surmises.

"I don't know how I feel about the Justice thing right now. It's all the things leading up to the breakup. I'm freaked out about settling down. It felt like two thousand pounds were strapped to my chest when he was giving me a tour of our future home. I was suffocating. Right now, I feel like I can breathe again."

She puts her feet up on the coffee table and studies my profile. "If all that would have happened to me? I would have had a panic attack. They would have had to call an ambulance and the paramedics would have had to run a Valium drip."

"He kept calling me Mrs. Cane Price," I tell her. "I've waited what seems like my whole life to hear that, but now … I don't know. I just don't."

Clapping her hands together in an impromptu round of applause, she grins like a maniac.

I regard her curiously. "What's with the clapping?"

"Ms. Cane Kallevik, you've finally come to your senses. Take time for yourself. Take time to grow up. You have your whole life to be tied to a man. This last fall when Justice offered to give you a break, I was pissed as hell that you didn't take it."

"Why didn't you say anything?"

"Not my place, and besides, I found you sniveling and bleeding on the couch. I couldn't tell you that I thought the temporary break was a good idea."

I bury my face in my hands. "What the hell am I going to do? I can't go back. I can't go to Florida, I can't —"

"You can live here for the summer, or indefinitely if you want. But I have to warn you, my two cousins, who are working for me, live here. They're a handful. Lizzie, honest to God, she's a box of rocks. Not kidding, when you take her shoulders and shake them, you can hear rattling in her head. She just joined the company. Can't clean for shit, but I only give her to the clients who strictly want eye candy, so it's fine. Then there's … Nikeo." She purses her lips. "He's a hothead, and now he's even more of a pain in the ass thanks to a girl who took an ice pick to his heart. Anyway, he's a business genius, so he's on the marketing end of things."

"I can't stay here."

"Like hell you can't! You are staying here." Caprice gives me a what-I-say-goes look, picks up my beer, and guzzles the rest of it.

"Are any places hiring? I need a job."

"Honey, you have a job." She springs up from the couch, stands with her back to me, and points at her butt. "Welcome to *Maid Hot.*"

"Do you not see me? Obviously you're wearing beer goggles." I stand and hop up onto her coffee table and spin slowly for her. "Exhibit A. I'm pale with a zillion freckles. I'm not much bigger than a stick figure. I'm still waiting for puberty to arrive." I glance down at my boobs. "Training bras are my reality."

"Get down from there." She rolls her eyes. "We'll talk logistics later."

I step off the coffee table. "Under no circumstances am I wearing a bikini," I proclaim.

She smiles. "So you're staying?"

"I haven't officially said yes yet, have I?"

"You're going to need a bedroom. Follow me," she says and walks out of the room down a wide hallway.

I follow her into a bedroom. "You can stay here. My room's right across the hall."

"Caprice, I'm serious. I'm not cleaning houses wearing a bikini."

"I didn't say that you had to." With a flourish, she throws open the curtains, exposing a grand view of the mountains.

The landscape is such a change from the cornfields of Illinois and the flat, endless plains of Nebraska that I had driven through it feels like I've crash-landed on a different planet.

"Here's what I figure. You can have three of my *Maid Right* clients, because I'm getting too busy to clean for them anyway with all the *Maid Hot* clients we're picking up. I'll give you the family cut — meaning you can take home seventy-five percent of what the client pays. And, Ms. English major, you can co-chair the marketing department with Nikeo and help grow this business. You'll get a bonus for every new client you bring in. How's that? Clean one or two days a week and the rest of the days you'll do marketing."

"Rent?" I ask.

She shrugs. "Minimal, about three hundred a month, plus you'll have to chip in for food."

"How much income are we talking?"

"I figure with the cleaning gigs and marketing, you'll be pulling in around six hundred a week if not more depending on how fast the business grows."

"You're saving my butt here. It was either this, or spending the summer in St. Petersburg with Grandma Betty and Frank."

She chuckles. "Don't get me wrong, I love those two. But I can't see you hanging out with the bingo, blue-hair crowd, getting your picture taken by Frank every two seconds, and going to the paint store with Grandma and picking out colors for the new condo. I'm so glad you showed up at my doorstep."

She gives me a juicy kiss on the cheek and then a stinging slap on the butt. "Make yourself at home. *Mi casa es su casa.* I've got to inventory our supplies, wash all the rags from today, return some calls, and do some accounting. But top priority is getting out of these clothes and into something more comfortable."

Even as she says this she's already untying her bikini top, freeing her perfect C-cup boobs. She isn't into exhibitionism for shock value; she's simply neutral about nakedness and doesn't understand the need for privacy.

However, I'm a bit of a prude. Though, in this case, prudishness has little to do with it. I'm envious of Caprice's centerfold curves, and when they're on display it only makes me more aware of my twelve-year-old boy body. "I can't deal with nudists. Put on some clothes."

As soon as I say this, she gets the weirdest look on her face.

"What?"

She squelches a laugh. Her jade-colored eyes sparkle with mischief.

"*What?*" I demand again.

She hums *I know something you don't know* and breezes out of my room.

After I drag my suitcases in and scarf down a bag of fat-free, salt-free, taste-free microwave popcorn, dousing it in ketchup to give it some flavor, I call Grandma Betty.

"Tell me you're safe and sound."

"Alive and well."

She takes a deep breath. I hear Frank in the background asking if I've made it okay and how long it took. I know she's shushing him with her hand. "What are your plans?"

"I'm staying."

She doesn't respond. I know she's waiting for me to offer more details, but I'm not in the mood. I'm still angry that she's not supportive of my decision.

Two days before as I was studying the map on the dining room table just after sunrise, figuring out what highways and interstates would get me to Briar, Colorado, the fastest, she'd waged a campaign against me leaving. According to her, I was making the *biggest mistake of my life.*

She breaks the silence and fishes for details. "What are you going to do out there?"

"Work for Caprice. Clean houses."

I can hear her careful breathing as she struggles to hold back a disapproving sigh. "He's not going to wait around forever."

"I think you told me that before I left."

"But I want you to understand it. Actions have consequences."

"I'm doing what I have to do," I insist.

"But Cane —"

"But *nothing,* Grandma. Please understand. Please be behind me."

"I'm always behind you. But he gave you your mother's ring. He's building your dream house. He loves you and only you, more than life itself. Don't you want a future with him? A family of your own?"

There's a mournful sound in her voice, and then I know why she's opposed to what I'm doing. This has everything to do with the past. Her son, my father, and my mother died right as their life was getting started and right as I was preparing to enter this world. She wants a do-over, and I'm her shot at that.

I twist my mother's ring off my finger and set it on the dresser. Should I have taken it off before coming out here? Should I have left it with Grandma Betty? With Justice? "I need to figure some things out first."

Another heavy silence passes between us.

"What does the air smell like out there?" she asks in a subdued tone.

Opening the window, I inhale deeply. My nostrils filter the many layers of the mountainous air. "It smells like aspen and pine trees, melting snow, fresh water, and the purest oxygen you can imagine. It smells solid, old, and brand-new."

She's silent as she absorbs this description.

"It's absolutely breathtaking," she declares, as if she were standing right next to me.

CHAPTER FIVE

The heavy front door slams.

"Caprice, I swear to God, if you don't fire Lizzie, I'm quitting! She neglected to tell me about three messages from potential clients. It's getting out of hand," declares a gruff male voice. "I can't run my business like this!"

"First off — it's *my* business, not yours. Secondly, she's family. We're keeping her!" Caprice fires back.

He responds to her statement with a string of expletives. When he's finished, he asks, "Hey, what did you make for dinner?"

"This isn't your mother's house, Nikeo. No one's going to serve your ass. You know where the refrigerator is and the stove."

The front door opens and closes again. "Hey, guys, like whose car is in the driveway? It's totally blocking me."

Imitating an announcer, Nikeo bellows, "And here she is now, ladies and gentleman, the employee of the year!"

"Nikeo, get off it already! Like, I told you, I was sorry, okay?"

"It's called *taking a message.* Pen, paper, writing it down, handing it to me."

"*Whatever.* You are so annoying," she complains.

"You're an airhead," he retorts.

I know I have to go out there and introduce myself, but my brain has flattened and dulled at the edges. Less than twelve ounces of beer and I'm well over the legal limit and ready for sixteen hours of sleep. I glance at my mother's ring on the dresser. To wear or not to wear, that is the question. Not to wear seems to be the right choice for now. Forcing myself out of the room, I amble down the hall and into the kitchen.

Caprice sees me and smiles. "Lizzie, Nikeo, this is my roommate from college and best friend, Cane Kallevik."

Lizzie swivels around to face me. She's Caprice's blond counterpart. They look more like identical twins than cousins. Although she has more sparkle than Caprice. She's wearing obscenely large diamond earrings, a diamond necklace, a stack of glittery bracelets on each arm, a silver tennis bracelet, and has smeared glitter all of her chest and abdomen. She's bedazzled every inch of herself and her clothes. The edges of her Maid Hot bikini are studded with rhinestones.

"Like, we've heard so much about you! Nice to meet you," she says.

"You, too."

Lizzie bunches up her generous lips as she regards me. "Like, what's up with your hair?" she asks.

The tightly woven braid, still in place, makes my auburn hair puff out at odd angles and sprout at the top. I probably look like a ripe carrot ready to be yanked from the ground. I give a self-deprecating laugh and rifle my fingers through my updo, undoing my handiwork. "A braid gone bad."

"Oh." Her mouth curves into an ingratiating smile. "Hey, by chance do you have any pot?"

"Are you *kidding* me with that?" Caprice snaps and gives her cousin a sharp look. "*No drugs*, and besides, my girl here" — she points to me — "isn't into that. I have a little announcement; Cane's staying for the summer and joining the company. She's going to take over a few of my *Maid Right* clients, and she's going to help you with the marketing end of things," she declares, directing this last statement at Nikeo.

Nikeo, who's bent over with his head buried in the refrigerator and hasn't yet bothered to say hello, now seems to be paying attention. He stands up and kicks the door shut with his heel.

As a way of introducing himself, he says, "The infamous roommate that I've heard *too much* about. Huh."

I'm not impressed with him or his attitude. "Huh yourself."

Wearing a cockeyed, arrogant smile, he appraises me in a cool, leisurely way, and turns toward Caprice. "I work alone. You know that.

This is not up for discussion."

"You either work with her," Caprice states in an unyielding voice, "or you're fired."

He looks at me again. He laughs mirthlessly and cruelly, making me self-conscious and irate at once. What is his problem?

I told you he was a pain in the ass, Caprice tells me with her eyes. "Be nice, Nikeo," she warns.

He gives me another cocky smile. "I'll try my hardest."

He removes a pot from a cabinet, fills it with water, and sets it on the stove. "I'm making pasta. Lizzie, cut up some peppers and onions," he orders and then moves around the kitchen, gathering all the ingredients.

"I can't cut up onions. They make my eyes water." Rolling her eyes, she sits down on a stool at the breakfast bar. "Besides, I'm not interested in food, I want to get high."

He pauses and raises his eyes to her. "If you don't watch yourself, you're going to end up with tracks up your arms and a stint in rehab."

"Lay off, Nikeo. I smoke pot now and then. I haven't partied in two months, okay? All I want is one joint, so stop being an anti-drug freak. It's been a long day," she whines and then extracts a wad of bills out of her bikini and sets it on the counter.

"What's with that?" demands Caprice.

Nikeo explodes with laughter. "We aren't running an escort service, Lizzie. It's a cleaning service."

"It's just a tip. Don't get all up in my face."

Caprice gives her a dubious stare.

Lizzie slams her palms on the counter. "*What?* I'm telling you, it's a tip. A roll of ones, okay?"

"No more strip teases. I mean it, or I *will* fire you," threatens Caprice.

"I only do it for Herman. He's like eighty-five, and I feel sorry for the guy, okay? He's super lonely, and all I have to do is flash him my boobs, jump up and down a little, and he gives me sixty ones. Doesn't touch me or anything. The guy is so sweet and harmless. Why not give him a thrill?"

Disgusted, Nikeo shakes his head and dumps the pasta into the now boiling water. "Stripping for the geriatric clientele. Way to keep it classy."

Exasperated, Caprice frowns at Lizzie. "No more Herman. I'm taking over."

Pouting, Lizzie slinks off the stool. "You're a total buzzkill. I knew I should have stayed in Chicago and worked for your dad's restaurant."

Later that night after Lizzie has gone to a friend's house in search of a joint, Caprice, Nikeo, and I camp out in front of the fireplace and discuss business.

Caprice wants me to start working on marketing strategies and promotion literature right away, but Nikeo isn't having it.

"She needs to clean for a week to get an idea of what this business is all about," he insists. "You have to know it to market it. If she can hack it, we'll go from there."

Offended, I glower. "I started working on a dairy farm when I was eleven. I worked from sunup to sundown sweating my butt off doing manual labor. I think I can hack cleaning houses."

"Shoveling cow shit, pulling on teats, and riding on a tractor with a piece of straw hanging out of your mouth doesn't make you qualified to clean houses or handle marketing."

"You don't have any idea what I did or didn't do on the farm,and, by the way, I love that visual of me on a tractor with a piece of straw hanging out of my mouth," I retort, my words dripping with sarcasm. "I'm sure in your fantasy I'm wearing bib overalls as well."

"Bib overalls, nice visual touch," he says as he leers at me.

A panther personified, everything about Nikeo is dark and strong. His hair. His skin. His voice. Even his body language and the way he moves are stealthy and predatory. His eyes, a light green with a translucent quality, are otherworldly. He doesn't look at me as much as he looks through me.

He intimidates me, and no one intimidates me. I won't allow it. "I'm sure I can outperform you in every way," I state smugly.

"I'm sure you can, sweetheart," he mutters condescendingly.

"What's your problem?"

"I don't have a problem."

"Clearly, you do."

He leans back against the couch, crossing his feet at the ankles. "Clearly, you're misinterpreting. You amuse me."

Now I'm not intimidated, just pissed. "I *amuse* you?"

Caprice reprimands her cousin. "Leave her alone. For once in your life, be pleasant."

He eases himself off the ground, seizes the guitar from the stand near the fireplace, and places the strap over his head and onto his shoulder. With deft expertise, he plays the first verse and chorus of "I Shot the Sheriff" by Eric Clapton.

He strums the guitar with such fervor it's like he's accusing me of something.

When he finishes the impromptu performance, he looks down at me. "I give you a week of scrubbing toilets, and then you'll be packing up your bags and heading back home to the cornfields with your overalls and piece of straw stashed in your suitcase."

I smirk at him. "Did something crawl up your butt and die or do you just have a sunny personality?"

He regards me coolly. With his guitar still strung around his neck, he walks out of the room and down the hall. His bedroom door closes, and minutes later I hear the muffled but familiar chords of "Layla."

"He won't stop playing Clapton. It's wearing on my nerves," grouses Caprice.

"What's his problem with me?"

"It's not you. Don't take it personally. He's combative, and, in general, not the easiest to get along with or figure out, which is why you can see that I need help with the marketing side of things. He's great at ideas, but sometimes when it comes to his people skills, things fall apart."

"Why did you hire him then?"

"He quit school, got dumped by his girlfriend, was fired from the family restaurant and catering business because he and my father butted heads, and he desperately needed a job and wanted to get out of the Chicago area. He's family. I couldn't say no. He does have an incredible business mind."

Can I put up with him for the summer?

Caprice and I may not have a psychic connection like Mikayla and I do, but she's pretty adept at reading my thoughts.

"If you don't want to work with him or clean houses for that matter you don't have to. It's up to you," she says.

That's the problem. It is all up to me, only I don't have any idea what my next move should be. I've got no one to blame for putting me in this awful position but myself, because I skipped the hills and ran straight for the mountains. Now that I'm here, I have this twitchy, nervous feeling that's making me indecisive and has stripped me of the ability to make prudent decisions.

"I don't know what I want anymore," I admit.

CHAPTER SIX

A few days later, I'm officially an employee of *Maid Right in Time,* thankfully sans the hot pink bikini. Caprice outfits me with a bag of rags, a bucket overflowing with cleaning supplies, several mops, a vacuum, and a brown bag lunch that she sweetly packed for me.

She sends me off with a sloppy wet kiss on the cheek. "It's a fresh slate today. Things are going to get better."

These words are exactly what I need to hear after the maddening phone conversation I'd had with Mikayla last night, a conversation that prompted me to run a speedy thirteen miles, thus inducing a spell of wicked altitude sickness that left me praying to the porcelain god and crawling on my hands and knees because of dizziness. Lack of oxygen certainly hadn't done me any favors physically, but it had also emotionally crippled me. Because I was so ill and my defenses were down, the *Woe Is Me* army snuck in for a surprise attack. I'd cried for two hours straight.

My sinuses are achy and swollen this morning from last night's blubber fest. I slow the car and glance at the clipboard Caprice has given me. I double-check the address and pull up in front of a magnificent log home nestled between two mountains. Before I left, Caprice told me that it would take about four hours to clean the house from top to bottom but said I might move faster than usual today. When I asked her why, she flashed an inscrutable smile.

I pop open the trunk, haul all the gear to the front door, and ring the doorbell.

A lady with a head of dazzling silver hair that falls to her shoulders peeks through the window and smiles brightly. She throws open the door. "I'm Arlene! You must be Cane! What a thrill to have you, dear. Come in! Come in!"

As soon as I step into her house and realize what I'm seeing, my mandible hits the floor so hard it nearly cracks off. Obviously, my eyes aren't deceiving me, but my brain is having a hard time coming to terms with it.

She is completely naked. Not a stitch of clothing on her. Her seventy-year-old breasts look like tube socks that are only half-filled with sand and hang to her belly button. Her nipples point downward to her generous, gray bush.

I'm so startled and so focused on not gagging that my bucket drops from my hands, and a bottle of Windex slides across her hardwood floor and right between the legs of a naked man. My eyes can't help themselves. They land right there, smack-dab on a seventy-year-old penis that's cushioned by a pair of wrinkly, saggy balls.

Gravity. Is. Evil.

"Whoops! Sometimes I drop things, too," says the naked man with a jovial voice.

He turns around, bends over, giving me a prime view of his pasty, wrinkly old butt, and retrieves my Windex.

I'm barely able to stop my eyes from rolling into the back of my head. My retinas, burning with the image of their nakedness, are permanently scarred. When I close my eyes, I'll see flopping genitals and drooping, mushy breasts. *Welcome to fifty years from now,* I think.

My head and neck flush a deep crimson, even the roots of my hair are embarrassed. While I'm thrown for a loop, this naked couple is completely at ease, and from the looks of it, accustomed to reactions like mine.

Arlene, with her hands on her hips, proudly introduces her mate. "This is my husband, Skeeter."

Immediately, I think of the well-known song that the boys used to endlessly sing in middle school. *There's a skeeter on my peter, whack it off.*

If I wasn't such an impulsive, reckless idiot, I would be sitting in an air-conditioned office right now coming up with innovative slogans for dairy products. I'd already had success in the advertising arena. A few months back Justice casually mentioned that Schaeffer Dairy wanted to revamp their ad campaign for Cow Pie, one of their bestselling ice creams, and were looking for ideas. I had a brainstorm later that night while studying for an exam. It was an unorthodox idea, but I thought it might be worth mentioning. The next morning I called Samson and suggested having a picture of a farmer wielding a giant shovel and standing next to a giant tub of Cow Pie ice cream. Next to the tub of ice cream would be an even larger bowl filled with several scoops. The caption would read, "Shovel up as many piles of Cow Pie as you want!" I'd been half-kidding, but Samson thought the idea was genius and rolled out the ad, plastering it on ten billboards around the Chicago land area. Sales of Cow Pie doubled, and that was when he offered me the job at Schaeffer Dairy.

Skeeter wedges my Windex back in the bucket. "You're the new cleaning gal, huh? Caprice said the business is growing like gangbusters!"

Arlene closes the front door. "I was hoping you were going to wear that darling new bikini that she showed me. I love the new direction of her company! That gal has vision, doesn't she, Skeeter?"

"Absolutely." He looks at me. "No bikini under there?" he asks, laughing.

Flustered and mortified, I squeak out two words. "No bikini."

"That's okay, dear! You know, if you're open to it, you could clean naked. We embrace nudity," Arlene declares earnestly.

Skeeter crosses his arms and nods his agreement. "It's so comfortable! No restrictions."

"Should I start upstairs?" I ask, wanting to get away.

"Sure, I'll take you around the house before you get started."

With that, Arlene ascends the stairs, and I follow, my eyes unfortunately level with her curdy butt. I suddenly remember Caprice's enigmatic smile earlier this week when I'd said I couldn't deal with nudists. I'm going to strangle her.

For the next twenty minutes, Arlene gives the grand, naked tour and tells me her expectations about what she wants cleaned. She also tries to persuade me to join a young nudist group called *Bare and There* that meets twice a month.

"They're always looking for new members," she says.

"I don't think so."

"You just moved here, right?"

"Only for the summer," I qualify.

"Ha! That's what I said fifty years ago when I came out West and decided to stay! Met a boy and that was that."

"I have a boy back home." At least I think I do.

She laughs. "So did I, but things change. Anyway, you should think about dropping in on that group. It's a great way to meet new people. You could bring Caprice with you. I'll leave a brochure next to your check. Be sure to grab it before you leave." Arlene rushes off to find the brochure and some informational literature.

I begin the tedious process of dusting, vacuuming, and mopping, systematically moving from room to room. When I'm in the second-story loft that overlooks the backyard, I catch a glimpse of the married nudists through the window, sitting on their back deck. They're sipping their morning coffee and reading the paper. Aren't they freezing? The morning air still has a crisp bite. At least one of them is freezing; it's one-inch cold. But, apparently, Skeeter doesn't notice or care.

Gross.

I try to focus on the tasks at hand, such as scouring the shower and wiping up after Skeeter's peter; I quickly glean his aim isn't that great as evidenced by the yellow-streaked walls. However, cleaning only occupies the tiniest fraction of my mind, and I can't help but think back to when I'd called Mikayla's cell phone yesterday evening.

Our conversation had lasted barely two minutes.

"I want to know how you could have done this to me. How could you have fallen in love with Justice? How could you've even given yourself permission to do that? And, then, throwing yourself at him?"

"Whoa, let's back up here for a minute. I didn't throw myself at him. We've spent a lot of time together over the last few years, and you were the one to encourage that."

She waited for me to deny it, but how could I? She was right.

Despite how well Mikayla treated me, Justice had always been slightly annoyed by her behavior and had once called her a "princess with a questionable conscience." Because she was my best friend and a fixture in my life, I'd pushed him to spend time with her and get to know her.

"That doesn't give you the right to fall in love with him," I countered.

"I didn't say I had the right."

"Find someone else, Mikayla."

She snorted in response, and I knew she wouldn't back down. When she wanted something or someone, she couldn't be stopped.

"Heard you're hiding out in Colorado with Caprice," she said. "Thought you might be interested in what I'm doing."

"Not really."

"I'm taking a hiatus from modeling. I need time to process what I found out about my mother and Nate. Jenny Ryanne personally invited me for the summer," she said, sticking her betrayal knife deeper. "I'm staying at the Schaeffer Farm. And, seeing as how you didn't rent that apartment, Justice had nowhere to go with his lease up so he decided to stay at the farm until the house is finished. I'm two doors down from his room."

With that bomb dropped right on target, she'd hung up the phone.

I scrub Arlene's sink until it shines, wad up the dirty rag, and shove it into the canvas bag. Hand-to-hand combat against dirt is an excellent conduit for anger.

Not wanting to chance another interaction with Arlene or Skeeter and his peter, I work without even stopping to breathe and finish cleaning the three-thousand-square-foot house a full hour shy of Caprice's estimate.

The next client is a sweet old woman named Harriet who's recovering from hip replacement surgery and thankfully believes in covering up her skin rather than exposing it. Her ranch house takes me only an hour to clean, but I end up staying for another hour talking to her and fixing her a peanut butter and jelly sandwich for an afternoon snack.

"Please, you make yourself one, too, and we'll have a picnic together right here in the living room!"

Because she's lonely and reminds me of an older version of Grandma Betty, I oblige. When I bring our food out to the living room, she gives me the biggest smile.

"Would you look at that! You cut it in triangles!" Her delight is genuine. "You're the sweetest young woman I've met in a long time."

"Thank you."

"Are you going to be working for me every week?"

"Yes, but only for the summer. I'm heading back home to Illinois in September." Even though I sound definite, I'm anything but.

"I wish you would stay! It would be so nice to have a young person like you for a friend. Everyone my age is dropping dead. The ones my age that are left-they spend hours talking about their aches, pains, surgeries, medications. You name it — they gripe about it. When they're not complaining, they're busy talking about when they're going to die or how they're going to die. It's not much fun to listen to, and it's rather exhausting and depressing. I don't like being around people my age that much." She munches thoughtfully on her sandwich and wipes the corner of her mouth with a napkin.

"My grandma says the same thing. She has many younger friends, simply because she can't stand people who focus on the negative. She always tells me that if you get so busy looking down you'll miss seeing what's right in front of you and all the great things up ahead."

Harriet laughs gleefully. "She's absolutely right! That's my philosophy."

I clean up our plates, settle a blanket on Harriet's lap, and make sure the television is tuned in to Nickelodeon, her favorite channel.

"I can't wait to see you next week," she says and pats my hand. "Only here for the summer, huh?"

"I'm afraid so."

"What's waiting for you back home, dear?"

If someone would have asked me a question like this last week, I would have told them that I was going to go home, ditch my *Seventeen* magazines for *Bride* magazines, marry Justice, and live happily ever after. Now it feels like I've taken a gigantic eraser to the storyline that

I've been writing for the past six years and doing a hasty, hodge-podge revision with one of the main characters missing. Instead of giving Harriet the down-and-dirty drama that my life has become and looking down, I choose to look at all the great things ahead.

With all the conviction I can muster, I say, "Justice Price is waiting. He's the love of my life. He just proposed."

I can see the question she wants to ask — it flickers across her face. *Well then what are you doing all the way out here in Colorado?* Good question.

She smiles knowingly. "Don't keep him waiting too long!"

When I arrive back at the house, I throw the grubby rags in the washing machine. Knowing Caprice is a stickler for details and could give Grandma Betty a run for her money when it comes to cleaning, laundry, and all things pertaining to organization, I make sure to add the appropriate amount of bleach and detergent per Caprice's instructions, which are laminated and taped next to the washer. Slamming the lid shut, I lean against the wall, close my eyes, and take a private moment to wallow in misery.

I know it hasn't been that long since I've been separated from Justice, but I miss him. I miss the way he twirls a basketball on his fingertips when we watch movies or television. I miss the way he runs into walls first thing in the morning and how at the end of the day when he comes home from work he can't wait to get out of his starched shirts and confining ties so he starts undressing the moment he walks through the door. I've discovered his clothing in every place imaginable: on top of the refrigerator, in the dishwasher, covering the television, and under the pillow in the bedroom. I miss the way he plows through a pack of Double Mint gum in minutes, chewing for a maximum of sixty seconds, long enough to enjoy the flavor burst. Once the sugar has dissolved, he spits it out and moves on to the next piece. I miss the way he kisses the back of my neck in a circle, insists on howling at a full moon, and every so often shakes me awake me up in the middle of the night to ask me a random question.

"Would you consider skydiving?" he once asked at two in the morning.

A daredevil and adrenaline junkie, I told him that I wouldn't consider it; I would do it in a second.

He had no recollection of this query or any of the other questions he's asked over the years. He doesn't sleep walk, he sleep interviews, a trait I find adorable.

I miss how when we're lying in bed and I'm reading or studying, he takes a pen and meticulously connects the freckles on my leg to make up words, phrases, and even art. The most memorable phrase he's ever written: *forever, for always, no matter what.* A true romantic, Justice said he'd seen this phrase on a plaque in a restaurant hallway, and it had made him think of me. The most impressive drawing: us as a bride and groom.

Leaving was impulsive and a tad reckless, a total Cane Kallevik knee-jerk reaction to an overload of stress. I'm a fool. Should I put on a bib and eat a big crow dinner? But, at this point, would Justice even accept an apology?

"Trying to erase the image of saggy boobs and genitals out of your head, aren't you?" Nikeo asks, startling me.

I jump away from the wall and give him a sour look.

"No use trying. I'm afraid it's going to be stuck there forever," he adds. "Caprice took me with her once because I didn't believe her. I wish I hadn't gone." He taps the side of his head. "That's a Kodak moment that doesn't require a picture to remember. It's burned into my mind."

"It was no big deal," I say, only because I don't want to agree with him about anything.

He snickers. "I can tell from your face it was no big deal."

"I have no problem with nudity," I proclaim. I exit the room, hoping he'll leave me alone, but he tails me into my bedroom.

"What do you want?" I ask irritably.

His eyes scan my room and settle on my mother's diamond on my dresser. He appraises it, and then his eyes find mine. "I bet you said yes."

I hate his feline grin, the catlike slant of his eyes, and his arrogant, albeit insightful assumptions. "Why is it any of your business what I said or didn't say? How do you even know there was a proposal?"

"You're out here, so I'm assuming trouble came to paradise," he surmises. He removes the ring from the dresser and inspects it. "Where did he buy it?"

"He didn't. It was my mother's ring."

"A man with family values who respects tradition."

"You don't know anything about me or about Justice."

"His name is *Justice?* Of course it is."

"What's wrong with his name?"

"More like what *isn't* wrong with it? And I know more than you think I know. I'm an excellent judge of character."

"You're incorrigible. Get out of my room."

"You're coming with me." He sets the ring down. "We're going out for dinner at The Elephant Ear, this awesome restaurant downtown with killer live music."

"Why would I want to go anywhere with you?"

"This isn't about *wanting* to go. This is about business and brainstorming on how to build this cleaning company into a mega empire," he says as he walks out of my room. "Meet you outside in five."

"You're cracked. I'm not going anywhere!" I yell after him.

"I'll be waiting in the car."

He's infuriating. Using my T-shirt, I buff my mother's ring like I'm trying to erase boy cooties.

The back door slams and seconds later, Caprice, wearing her teeny-tiny cleaning bikini, pops her head in my bedroom and smiles wickedly. "Survive your first day?"

"I could kill you," I say, glancing up at her. "A warning would have been nice."

She chortles. "I thought about it, but the element of surprise works wonders. Bet it took your mind off everything."

I give in and laugh along with her. "His name is Skeeter!" I cry disbelievingly.

"Kind of perfect, right? And Arlene's boobs?"

I shake my head. "Our tragic future." I glance at my small chest and then at Caprice's. "Or maybe just yours."

She smiles self-assuredly. "Yes, but that's what plastic surgery is for."

"Nikeo wants me to go out to dinner with him to talk business."

"I know. He told me this morning. He wanted me to go with to strategize as well, but I'm swamped. We've got three new girls starting this week, and I've got to meet with them tonight, go over schedules and expectations, and I'm also going over to a couple houses to give quotes."

"I can't tolerate him. I'm not going."

"You have to go. As your boss I say so. His bark is worse than his bite."

"My bite is worse than my bark," I counter.

A grin slithers onto her face. "You two are a perfect match. Have dinner with him. He'll grow on you."

*****

"I can't believe you smoke," I say with disdain.

Nikeo cups his hand around the end of a cigarette and lights it. He makes a show of taking a big drag and then blows it toward me. With his free hand, he picks up his gin and tonic. "Only when I'm having a drink."

I press a napkin against my nose to block out the smoke and lean as far back in my chair as possible. "That makes it okay?"

"You're honestly as straight as an arrow, aren't you? Never deviate from the path of perfection?"

Unwilling to engage, I narrow my eyes. "This dinner is supposed to be about business." I take a gigantic, un-ladylike bite of my Southwest salad and slide my gaze away from him.

Amused, he studies me for a moment before turning his attention to the stage where a band called Unarmed Scandal, who sounds like a hybrid of the Dave Matthews Band and Counting Crows, croons about love gone wrong.

When they finish the song, he flags the waitress over and orders another gin and tonic.

"Are you an alcoholic?"

He carelessly shrugs. "Business partners need to know each other very well-maybe tonight I am an alcoholic."

"Yeah, well." I toss my napkin aside and push my plate back. "I already know all I need to know about you, and I'm not interested in learning a thing more."

"I could write a thesis paper on what I know about you."

"Let's get one thing straight." I look him in the eye. "You don't know anything about me."

He settles comfortably into his chair and pulls out another cigarette.

"You must really like those cancer sticks. Addicted to carcinogens or something? Or do you just like tarring your lungs?" I ask.

He gives me a smooth smile. "Here's what I know. You're Midwest born and bred, raised in a Norman Rockwell house by a mother and father who loved and adored you and thought you could do no wrong. You probably have one sibling, maybe two, and he/she is your best friend in the world. You went to church every Sunday to praise Jesus. You fell in love when you were young, and like a good girl you guarded your virginity until you were eighteen, maybe nineteen? I bet you've only slept with one man. You value health and wellness supremely and can't stand people who don't take care of themselves. You're anxious, nervous, and very annoying. You run every day, sometimes twice a day, because you can't ever keep still." He looks down at my foot as he says this.

I immediately stop bouncing it. "Finished yet?" I ask, giving him a level *I hate you* stare.

"Honey, I'm just getting started. You're impatient" — he smiles at me; I'd just proven that I was —"judgmental, critical, shrewd, and intelligent. Yet you're always saying and doing things you don't mean. You're a reactor. You get yourself into trouble. You're too loyal and trust too deeply, although" — pausing, he regards me for a moment — "you don't seem to trust yourself enough. You have commitment issues when it comes to trusting your instincts. How am I doing?" he inquires innocently.

He's taken some kind of psychoanalytic machete, eviscerated me, and put all of my insides on display. Enraged and stunned by his precise, cutting assessment of my psyche, I flush deeply.

"I can't tell you the *exact* reason you came out to Colorado, I'm not a mind reader after all, but I know it has something to do with the engagement. Because when I asked you about that earlier, you looked like you wanted to cry." He raises his brow expectantly and waves his hand my way. "Your turn," he says with airy politeness, as if we're playing some kind of mundane board game.

My fingers twitch; I've never wanted to wring someone's neck so badly. All the blood has fled my organs and tissues and has collected right under my skin.

If I lose my temper and go with my instinct and hurl insults at him and then my dinner plate, which I'm considering, it only proves he's right about everything. To prove that I'm nothing like he thinks I am, I reach across the table and snatch the cigarette from his hand. I put it up to my mouth, sealing my lips around the end. I take my first ever drag. The powerful inhale smolders my lungs. The urge to sputter and cough and vomit comes, but I hold it in, my eyes watering from the effort. I then pick up his gin and tonic and effortlessly drain it. Then I plunk the lit cigarette into the ice.

He observes this with nonchalant amusement, grins playfully, and then says, "I forgot to mention one thing-no matter what the cost, you love proving everyone wrong."

Screw my bark. I want to bite. "Are you about *finished?*"

"For now."

"Here are my ideas on business. First, we need to set up a state-of-the-art website. Everything is headed for cyberspace, and we need to be there before any other company in the area arrives. We contact all the Realtors, mortgage lenders, bankers, and small business owners in town. For those who are game, we set up one-on-one meetings, tell them about our business, ask if they'll recommend us to their clients, and, in turn, we promote them. Stick their logos on our cars, put their names on our literature, and place their ads — for free at first — on our website."

Satisfied with my tidy delivery of ideas, I fold up my napkin and toss it onto my plate.

"Bravo." He leans back in his chair. Catching the server's eye, he signals for two more drinks.

"I don't want one," I insist.

"You could use one. You're so intense that if someone stuck a piece of coal up your ass, it would be a diamond in a matter of minutes."

I sputter in disbelief. "Give me a —"

"Save yourself the embarrassment and don't deny it."

The server delivers our drinks.

"Given your treatment of me tonight, you're footing the bill."

He frowns and pulls out another cigarette and lights it. "Aren't you a split-the-bill-down-the-middle kind of girl?"

"You don't have me figured out as well as you think you do."

He pushes the drink he ordered for me my way, and I push it back.

Using his cigarette, he points at the gin and tonic sitting between us. "I *know* you want it."

I don't want to admit it to myself, and most certainly not to him, but he's right. Like one of Pavlov's dogs, my mouth waters. I loved the taste of his and the way the alcohol had worked itself into my bloodstream, loosening my muscles and calming my agitated state. I grab the drink, avert my eyes, and drink half of it. I chew on a piece of ice.

"Better, right?" He laughs. "I knew it."

"Can we leave now?" My question has a sharp, impatient edge.

He exhales in a leisurely, indulgent way. The smoke creates a wreath around his head, a devil's halo. "Why are you always in a hurry?"

"Why are you always busy analyzing me? And FYI, I have no interest in emphysema or lung cancer. Put that thing out."

Unarmed Scandal starts playing a Dave Matthews's cover, "Crash into Me."

He stabs his cigarette in the ashtray and raises his intensely green eyes to mine. "You're going to dance with me."

Irritated with the way he never asks anything but instead demands or decrees, I shake my head. "No, I'm not going to dance with you."

He smiles, and it's so silky that it seems almost liquid.

And just like that, it happens.

I am undeniably attracted to this man. I'm attracted not only to his dark and dangerous appearance, but also to his antagonistic and audacious behaviors. He's Justice's polar opposite. Justice is the tried-and-true superhero who bravely swoops in for the save, and Nikeo is the mischievous villain who goes in for the kill.

He stands and moves gracefully around the table, and before I know it, I'm standing in front of the stage with Nikeo's arms wrapped around me. He moves seductively and easily, almost as if he's operating on instinct and not thought. Uncomfortable with what I'm feeling and with how my body buzzes with desire, I redden and feel the prickle of sweat under my arms and on my lower back where his hands are tightly pressed.

I put my hands on the front of his shoulders as if to push him away. "I don't want to be here." I breathe the words as opposed to speaking them.

"Why bother saying things you don't mean." Reaching up, he takes hold of one of my hands and repositions it behind his neck, and then does the same thing with my other hand.

I'm much too close, close enough to smell the gin, lime, and smoke on his breath. Close enough to inhale his scent — he smells like the air in a sauna, all heat and cedar. If I stay around him long enough, I'll melt.

Redirecting my thoughts, I focus on the reason we came here tonight. "We should be talking about business."

He pushes a strand of my hair off my face, leans down, and places his lips right next to my ear. "Don't ruin the moment," he cautions.

His voice tickles the inside of my ear, and his subtle touch sends a rippling shiver down my spine. My breathing stills. My heart races. My lips part slightly. Detecting my weakness and knowing he has power over me, he pulls me in closer.

The night has gone from all business to all pleasure. The low lighting, the purified mountain air, the sexual lyrics of the song, the way he moves seductively, taking me along for the ride, it feels like we're doing something illicit. Something wrong. I want it to go on forever. I want it to end.

It has to end. I tear myself away from him. "I've had enough."

His disappointment translates into a disgusted frown. "And just when you were starting to let yourself go and unwind."

"I'll walk home," I announce with pluck and spin around to leave.

Before I know what's happening, he's two steps in front of me. He throws cash on the table and declares, "You're not walking. I'm driving."

Because it's a long walk home, I reluctantly follow him out to the parking lot.

I hate being in the car with him. I'm trapped inside with everything I don't want to be feeling, and my heady desire swirls around us both. I fairly squirm in my seat and hug the passenger door.

He looks over and gives me that silky, liquid smile again, and I know that he knows precisely what I'm feeling and thinking.

When we pull into the driveway, I can't get out of the car fast enough. I slam the door and plan a sprint getaway when he tells me to wait a minute.

"Where do you get off barking orders?"

"I'm disappointed," he says as he saunters over to me. "You said, and I quote, 'I already know all I need to know about you,' and yet you didn't tell me one thing. You never took your turn."

At the mention of this, I'm reminded of his brutal appraisal of my character. The anger that I'd thought hadn't survived the attraction stampede rises up and rears its ugly head. Now I remember why I don't like him.

I give him a sardonic smile. "Fine. You want my analysis? I'll give it to you. You grew up with a mother and father who didn't pay much attention to you, because you have seven, maybe eight siblings? To get attention, you learned how to use your smart mouth and bully people and generally act like an ass. I don't know when you lost your virginity or how many people you slept with, and honestly I don't care. You're always on that ridiculous road bike of yours, wearing those ridiculous cycling shorts. You go hundreds of miles each week and yet you always end up in the same place you started. You're arrogant, selfish, and only care about looking out for your best interest. *The tattoo on your arm, the barbed wire?* Please. It's cliché. You're lost, desperate, and sad; to make yourself feel better you pretend to be an authority and expert on everything and everyone when in reality you're ignorant and insecure. People like you, who pretend to know the most, know the least."

He takes a step closer to me and then another, and all of a sudden that anger of mine goes docile on me, rolling on its back and playing dead like some sort of crafty opossum.

"You forgot one thing," he whispers.

Wake up, anger! Wake up! Glaring I cross my arms and lean my upper body away from him. "I don't care to know what that one thing is."

He compensates for the distance I've put between us by moving even closer. Before my alcohol-addled brain can process what's happening, he pushes a strand of my hair behind my ear, and my body absolutely betrays me. Every inch of my skin tingles from the delicate touch, and places I don't even want to think about at the moment hum and ache with anticipation.

He traces one of his fingers across my bottom lip, and my mouth automatically parts. "I'm an excellent kisser."

Against my judgment, if I even have any left, I find myself moving closer to him, like he's pulling me into his orbit. Our eyes are locked, neither of us willing to back down or go an inch further. I can't look a second longer, or I might do something I'll regret. My eyes travel down his face. I study his feline-like lips that rise at the edges, instinctively knowing that if I allow him to kiss me, I'll never want to stop.

"Maybe if you're into licking ashtrays," I remark caustically.

"I don't taste like an ashtray, but why don't you see for yourself."

His touch, his challenging invitation, the ridiculous, inexplicable chemistry between us along with my suppressed inhibitions — it's too much to resist. I'm about to close my eyes and go for it when the front door opens behind us, breaking the ridiculous enchantment.

Instantly flushing, I take a large step away from Nikeo and assume a defensive pose.

"You guys are back later than I expected. Did you come up with any good ideas tonight?" Caprice asks as she flips open the mailbox and pulls out a stack of envelopes.

Nikeo leers. "Some very interesting ideas."

I stride toward the house, eliciting a curious stare from Caprice.

"I'm not sure how much longer I'll be staying." The words fly out as I walk past her. I've surprised even myself with this declaration.

Stunned, her eyes widen. "What happened?"

I shake my head tersely, a clear indication that I don't want to talk about it, and enter the house.

"What the hell did you do to her?" Caprice shouts.

Lizzie, who sits in the kitchen noshing on a tray of fresh vegetables, waves at me. "Seriously! I heard you cleaned for the nudists today." She giggles. "I've never seen them, but Caprice said Arlene's boobs scrape the ground."

"They come close."

"Someone called for you today," she announces as she chomps on a carrot. "Simson Schmidt or something like that. Whatever. I can't remember his name."

"Samson Schaeffer?"

She snaps her fingers and smiles. "Yeah, yeah, that's it. I'm bad with names."

"What did he say?"

She shrugs. "Can't remember, something like he's just checking in. I wrote it down somewhere" — she rifles through the papers that litter the counter — "but I lost it."

"Did he want me to call back?"

"Um, yes. No … wait." She shakes her head and taps a piece of celery against her bottom lip. "I'm not sure."

I glance at the clock. It's ten at night here, eleven back home. I'll call him tomorrow morning.

I hole up in my room for the rest of the night, trying to figure out what I should do to make things right. Even though nothing overtly physical happened between Nikeo and me, I've crossed an emotional line and betrayed Justice in every imaginable way. I'm terrified that my attraction to Nikeo will lead me to places I don't want to go and that I may never find my way back to what is safe, true, and real.

Is avoidance the answer? Should I leave? I can't keep making messes and then bailing.

Before I fall asleep, I hold my silver compass in my hand, wishing that my moral compass worked as well as this one and would lead me in the right direction.

CHAPTER SEVEN

Before I left this morning, Caprice told me that Misty Moreland, a client who was rich but difficult, paid exceptionally well so I was instructed to put up with her.

"I mean it, Cane," Caprice cautioned in her I'm-the-boss-and-what-I-say-goes voice. "Watch your mouth today. We're talking two hundred twenty-five a week. That's a lot of cash flow right there."

Unfortunately, I've yet to master the art of watching my mouth so this should be interesting. I ring the doorbell and wait, dreading what is to come. Misty opens the door, and I step into the foyer with all my cleaning supplies and set them on the floor.

"Hi, I'm Cane," I say politely and extend my hand to Misty Moreland, a husky woman in her mid-forties with alarmingly stiff hair that resembles Nikeo's bike helmet in shape and density.

Refusing my handshake, Misty points at my shoes. "Not allowed."

I lower my hand. "No shoes?"

"No shoes," she reiterates.

I do a double take, because one of her brown eyes stares straight at me while her other eye strays slightly to the right. I don't know which eye to focus on. "I only wear these shoes for cleaning, and I need the support on my feet. Would you mind?"

"Absolutely, I mind! Which is why I mentioned it in the first place!" Misty pulls the door shut and turns the lock, dead bolt, and punches in a security code.

Two locks and an alarm system? Is she trying to keep someone out or keep me in?

"I'm very, very serious about the no shoe policy! Sometimes a pebble gets caught in the tread of a shoe and scratches up my hardwood floors. I have three thousand square feet of hardwood on this floor, and let me tell you, not one scratch. Not to mention that shoes are the dirtiest thing in the world."

Smiling my *you're crazy but you're the customer* smile, I untie my shoes and place them in the special hidden shoe rack she has by the front door.

"Here put these on," Misty says as she thrusts a pair of blue hospital booties in my direction.

I take them in my hand. "But I'm wearing socks. New white socks. They aren't dirty at all."

"Socks aren't enough of a barrier! Your skin has oil, and oil transfers, stains, and ruins hardwood. I'm not having that. Everything in here is spotless, and I'm keeping it that way."

I don the booties and do a quick scan of the expansive house. Every surface looks like it's been buffed for hours. It's scarily clean.

"Why did you bring that in?" she points to my array of cleaning supplies.

I glance down at the vacuum, cleaning bucket, and rags that I'd brought inside with me. Then I remember Caprice saying that Misty has her own arsenal of supplies. "I'm sorry, I'd forgotten that you have your own."

"Leave all of it here and come with me," she says impatiently.

I follow her down to her basement where she stops in front of three stainless steel shelves that are stocked with cleaning supplies and a table that boasts three vacuums, each vacuum labeled according to what floor it should be used for. Her inventory rivals Walmart's.

Misty gives me directives about what cleaning product should be used for what surface. She then shows me the vacuums, and after using the vacuums I'm supposed to vacuum out the vacuums and rinse out the canisters with bleach and water.

Obsessive-compulsive cleaning disorder in full effect. This lady doesn't need a maid; she needs medication and a shrink.

Misty fills two buckets with supplies, gives me a new pair of cleaning gloves, and ties a surgical mask around my face. With the mask, booties, and gloves, I'm officially a cleaning doctor. If only my fellow English majors could see me now. I can't believe I gave up my cushy office job at Schaeffer Dairy for this.

We ascend the stairs to the second floor and she tells me to start in the bathroom. I hope to be rid of her once I start cleaning, but she stays pasted to my side and criticizes nearly every move I make.

"You have to polish every cabinet handle, doorknob, and hinge in the house. Every week. No exceptions." She hands me a container of brass cleaner.

I methodically clean each handle, moving so slowly it actually pains me. However, I'm learning that the slower I move, the better. Misty takes this as a sign that I'm doing the job correctly.

"I'm going downstairs," she finally announces.

It's about time.

"Be sure to clean all the light switches too, especially in my sons' rooms."

This whack job procreated? "You have kids?" I ask pleasantly, trying to keep the dismay out of my tone.

She frowns. "Two boys. They're five and seven. Why?"

"Just wondering." How can two children live in a place like this!

Misty appraises my work one more time before leaving. "I'll be downstairs. If you have any questions or concerns come get me immediately. And if you see any insects, spiders, or anything at all that's crawling, please let me know. I have the exterminator come out here every other week. We live in the country so it's a constant battle."

"I'll be sure to take insect inventory," I say cheerily. If I were a bug, I would take one look at this crumb-less, spotless place, and fly away as quickly as I could.

I attempt a snail's pace, but I'm not capable. I'm built for speed. Every time I slow down, I automatically start to pick up the pace. I have an internal race mechanism, and I'm always trying to outdo myself and everyone else.

Like a whirling dervish, I scrub, polish, dust, and vacuum. The rags are cleaner after I finish wiping something down than before I started. When I go into one of her son's rooms to start dusting, my heart aches for this young boy.

I look around the room. Not one thing is out of place. All the toys are perfectly aligned on the shelves. The wood blinds on the windows are tilted at the exact same angle. The bedding and dust ruffle are practically starched into place. I think back to my childhood bedroom. Although Grandma Betty regularly harped on me to put away my things, she gave me the freedom to run my own room and permitted a certain amount of disorder.

I push the vacuum across the immaculate floor and stop. Glancing at the dust ruffle, I wonder if there's proof of this child's real identity under his bed. That's where I had always stored and hoarded all my treasures: magazines, books, rock collections, movie ticket stubs, the newspaper article about my parents' accident, ribbons, and friendship bracelets. Curious, I take a peek under the bed. There's nothing, only a pristine pile of carpet that's standing at attention. This strikes me as incredibly tragic. This woman is doing her children more harm than good, going to an extreme that's squelching their creativity, repressing their true persona, and requiring them to be robotically perfect.

As I finish vacuuming, making a perfect fan pattern on the floor as instructed, I vow that I'll let Justice's and my children keep their rooms as they please and require only a semblance of order.

When I finish and am winding the cord up tightly, I realize that every time I envision my future Justice is there. Even now, when everything in our relationship is a mess, he's present and accounted for. I try to imagine what it would be like with someone else in his stead, someone like Nikeo. It's a ridiculous notion. Nikeo isn't the *marry me and live happily ever after* kind of guy, he's the *have hot sex with me but don't expect me to stick around afterward if I don't feel like* it kind.

When I make my way downstairs to the main floor, Misty nearly has a cardiac arrest.

"You can't be done! You can't! It takes at least three hours to clean the upstairs bedrooms and bathrooms."

I look at my watch; it's taken me an hour. "I did everything you said, and, besides, the rooms were already immaculate."

She snorts in disbelief. "No, they were filthy. Absolutely filthy."

She's kidding, right? Does she have sight in her wandering eye? Maybe she's crazy *and* legally blind. I have the urge to tell her this but wisely keep my mouth shut and paste a smile on my face.

"When you're finished with this floor, I want you to go back upstairs and do it again."

I smile as kindly as I can. "Are you serious?"

The wandering eye nails me for a moment, and then it floats away.

"Why wouldn't I be!" she exclaims.

I commence dusting, and am forced to use cotton swabs to get in those hard-to-reach corners in the kitchen that according to Misty are laden with bacteria and mold. With the help of an extension ladder, I wipe off all the light fixtures and bulbs. When dusting is completed to Misty's specifications, I vacuum all the floors with a soft brush attachment and prepare to mop the unbelievable expanse of hardwood. I fill a bucket with warm water and vinegar as instructed and carry it to the living room. I search for a mop in the basement and find one. I carry it back upstairs, dunk it in the water, and start mopping the floor.

When Mindy sees me, she emits a bloodcurdling scream. "Stop! Right now! Stop!"

Slowly lowering the mop, I turn toward her.

Gasping for breath, she asks, "What are you doing?"

"Mopping."

"No. Absolutely not. Hands and knees only, remember? I told you that in the basement! *Hands and knees only.* That's why I put knee pads in the bucket."

Reluctantly, I lower the mop and hold in the world's longest and biggest sigh. Forcing myself to be obedient and compliant, which is no easy feat, I pull on the knee pads. In Cinderella fashion, I wipe down the gleaming hardwood floors. After another hour of pointless cleaning, I return to the upstairs so that I can clean it. Again.

At noon, I'm famished and inhale all the contents of my lunch. Then I have to clean the finished lower level. By four in the afternoon, I'm exhausted. The house has been cleaned, and now it's time to vacuum out the vacuums and rinse them out with bleach and water.

When I'm finished and have returned everything to its place, Misty hands me a check for two hundred twenty-five dollars. "You could use some lessons on how to clean."

I dazzle her with an innocent grin. "And you could use a bottle of Valium and a shrink." Did I just say that out loud? I'm not sure, and then I know I must have, because Misty narrows her eyes and gasps.

"You are unequivocally the rudest person I've ever met!"

Oh well. I've already sunk the ship, might as well slash the life rafts. "Or maybe the most honest," I reply curtly.

Misty's shaking with such fury that she looks like one of those bobble-heads; her helmet of hair vibrates. "*Get out of my house.*"

"Gladly."

When I'm in the car, I repeatedly bang my forehead against the steering wheel. Caprice has a temper, and when she finds out what happened, that I've potentially blown her biggest account because of my big mouth, she's going to blow a gasket.

Annoyed with myself and even more annoyed at Misty, I drive away wondering if Caprice will fire me, beat me up, or both.

When I arrive home, the coast is clear. I slink into my room and close the door. Sitting on my bed is a stack of mail that Caprice must have left for me. There's an envelope from Jocelyn Ryanne. Seeing this triggers a memory from a week and a half ago. I'd forgotten to call Samson back!

I tear open Jocelyn's letter.

Dear Cane,

Hi. How are you? I got your address in Colorado from Grandma Betty. I wish you would call me. Are you mad at me or something?

I'm sorry I recorded all the stuff at the party. I didn't know that was going to happen. I should have erased it or something. I'm so, so sorry.

Things are horrible around here. My dad is upset with Justice, because he says that Justice should have told you about kissing Mikayla right away. Justice seems ticked off all the time. When I bring up your name or ask him questions he says he doesn't want to talk about it. Also, Justice, my brother, and Mikayla are inseparable lately! They're always hanging out! I don't get it at all, especially because of what happened. Did you know that Mikayla is staying at our house? Mom invited her, and Dad isn't happy about it at all.

My mom and dad are fighting a lot, because something horrible happened. Not the Mikayla thing, but something else. But I don't want to talk about it. It's too awful.

I have a favor to ask. Can I stay with you for a few weeks? I need to get out of this house before I go crazy.

I wish you had a cell phone. I tried calling a couple of times and talked to this girl named Lizzie, and she said she would give you the messages. Have you gotten them?

Please call.

Love, Jocelyn

I rush into the kitchen, grab the phone off the counter, and call the Schaeffers.

"I was wondering when I'd hear from you," Samson says kindly and without accusation.

"I'm sorry. I should have called back last week. How's Justice?" I ask. This general question only scratches the surface of what I want to know.

He sighs heavily. "You should ask him that."

Even when asked, Samson never voluntarily delves into someone's personal business. I sit down on the bar stool and stare glumly out the window. "I can't, and besides, he wouldn't talk to me."

"You know that he would."

Samson sounds certain, but I have my doubts. "How are things?"

He clears his throat. "Things around here ... well, they aren't so great right now," he says. "Jocelyn would like to get out of the house if she could. She needs some breathing room."

"I know. I just got her letter today. She can come out to Colorado and stay here as long as she wants. I'll take her to work with me and keep a close eye on her."

"Good to know," he says, laughing sheepishly, "because I've already bought the plane ticket. She'll be there a week from today. Next Friday."

"How long does she want to stay?" I ask.

"I haven't bought her a return ticket yet. I'm thinking two or three weeks of being away from home would do her a world of good. I'm hoping it's enough time to restore some peace around here."

"Jenny Ryanne is okay with this?" I inquire.

"I haven't told her about it." Uncomfortable, he coughs. "We aren't on speaking terms right now."

"Because she's allowing Mikayla to stay at the farm?"

He hesitates and then says, "That's part of the reason."

"How do you think it's going to go over with Jenny when she finds out Jocelyn is flying out to Colorado?"

After a long pause, he says, "About as good as it went over with Justice when you left."

Ouch. That tells me everything I need to know. "He didn't think I would actually go through with it, did he?"

"When you come home, you're going to have to do some damage control," he confides.

After I write down Jocelyn's flight number and arrival time, I hang up the phone and hold my head in my hands.

What if I return and the damage can't be controlled?

Lizzie and Nikeo come through the back door. Keys are thrown on the entry table.

"How many people did you invite?"

"I don't know," Lizzie responds evasively.

"Does Caprice know about this?"

"You're acting like a parent, Nikeo! *Yes,* she gave me permission. Not that I need it! I live here. I pay rent just like you. Anyway, what's the big deal? It's a party. Loosen up."

"Last time you had a party someone trashed two of my guitars. It was like having a bunch of toddlers on the loose."

"Maybe if they trash them you'll finally stop playing Clapton. If I hear 'Layla' one more time, I'm going to puke."

"Get used to puking, because I'm not stopping."

They enter the kitchen.

"You only play it because of your infamous breakup."

Nikeo shoots her a dark look.

"Hi, Cane," Lizzie says and gives me a small wave.

Nikeo says nothing to me, but gives me a smoldering *I want to sex you up* stare that makes the hair on the back of my neck rise. I quickly avert my eyes.

Lizzie opens the fridge and takes out her vegetable containers. Is that all she eats?

"My friends aren't a bunch of toddlers. You're getting on my nerves lately," Lizzie informs Nikeo.

"Ditto," he responds.

She pops a tomato in her mouth. "And as for attendance tonight? Fifteen, twenty, thirty. Who knows. And we're probably going to smoke some joints, so get over yourself."

He rolls his eyes and grabs a Pepsi out of the refrigerator.

"Has anyone been calling for me?" I ask Lizzie.

She adjusts the strap on her bikini and shrugs. "I don't know, why?"

"Because I got a letter in the mail today from a friend, Jocelyn. She said she's talked to you a few times, but you never told me she called."

Nikeo chuckles humorlessly. "Maybe if Lizzie knew how to use a pen and paper and write words down, it wouldn't be an issue."

"Jocelyn sounds familiar. I probably wrote it down, but sometimes I forget."

"Try *not* to forget. It was important."

"Sure, okay," Lizzie says distractedly as she fishes inside the cabinet for a bowl.

Something occurs to me. "Has anyone named Justice tried calling?"

"Um, no. No one by that name. I have to get out of this damn bikini. It's been riding up all day." She dumps a heap of vegetables into the bowl and stalks out of the room.

Nikeo and I are left alone in the kitchen. No escaping him now. I've been trying to fly under his radar, and we haven't had a conversation since last week.

He glances down at my hand. "What I want to know is why you suddenly decided to wear that diamond ring? Were you afraid that someone was going to steal it off the dresser?"

I knew at some point that Nikeo was going call me out on this. I'd seen him eyeing it at breakfast the other day. Last week, after my near indiscretion with him, I pushed the ring on my finger. My motives for wearing the ring, however, are suspect. I can't figure out if I want to let Nikeo and everyone else know that my heart is taken or if I'm wearing it to remind myself. "You can't be trusted," I say, implying that it wouldn't surprise me if he were a thief.

He raises his eyes to mine, and that oily smile slips onto his face. "You're right. I can't be trusted."

The sexual suggestion of his statement causes that weird, intoxicating chemistry that we have to churn. He's at least six feet away, and yet every cell of my body stands at attention. I want him to touch me. To kiss me. To do things to me that only Justice has done. Not wanting to betray my feelings, I maintain a stone-faced expression and fold my right hand over my left so that I can feel the ring dig mercilessly into my palm. I'm taken, I remind myself.

The phone rings shrilly. I push it toward Nikeo, hop down off the bar stool, and escape down the hall.

"Caprice isn't here right now, but I'm Nikeo, marketing director of the company, and I would be happy to help you, Mrs. Moreland," he says in a professional, friendly voice.

Immediately, I stop and lean against the wall.

Busted, I think. I'd been so wrapped up in the letter from Jocelyn and in the conversation with Samson that I'd forgotten about what I'd said to Misty — the wandering eye — Moreland.

"Yes, yes, I understand but —"

I creep closer to the kitchen to eavesdrop.

"Cane Kallevik is a new employee, and I do apologize for her behavior. We would like to keep you as a client. Please tell me what I can do to make this right."

A long pause follows. Then Nikeo says, "I know what she said was very upsetting and rude. I apologize for that. However, I stand behind Cane's work. I know that she does a stellar job when it comes to cleaning. If you are that dissatisfied, we can refund you for today."

More silence. If only I could hear the other end of the conversation.

"I'm sorry you feel that way, but we will not be terminating her for this."

"I understand. I'm sorry we've lost you as a valued client. If you change your mind, we will send you a different employee and provide you with excellent service."

I hear him hang up the phone. "Damn it," he mumbles.

He defended me? Maybe he doesn't have such a rotten core. Maybe he's not the villain I think he is. I walk into the kitchen.

He looks up at me. "Couldn't keep your mouth shut, could you?"

"A moment of weakness."

"She wants a full refund for today, and she no longer wants our company to clean for her."

The back door opens and then closes.

I nod. "I kind of guessed something like this would happen. Caprice can take it out of my paycheck if she wants."

Caprice waltzes into the kitchen and catches the tail end of my statement.

"What about a paycheck?" she asks as she scrutinizes my guilty expression.

She knows me too well. It doesn't take her long to figure out what happened. "*Damn it! Shit!* I *told* you to keep your mouth *shut.*"

"Misty wants a refund for today. But that's not the worst of it," says Nikeo.

"She fired us, didn't she?" Caprice asks.

"Sorry," I mutter.

She curses me out, using every expletive in the book and some that she invented, and then pounds her fists on the countertop. When we were first living together and had only known each other for a year, I used to fight back. But when I understood her better and realized her sudden outbursts of anger were much like a thunderstorm that packed a wallop but then dissipated quickly, leaving blue skies and sunshine behind, I stopped engaging and let her have her verbal tantrums.

Sure enough, after three minutes of thunder, lightning, and very frightening words, she takes a deep breath. "I'll have to take it out of this week's check. From now on, keep your mouth shut."

"I'll try."

"Try harder."

"Out of curiosity, what did you say?" she asks, a grin snaking its way onto her face.

"I told her she needed a bottle of Valium and a shrink."

Caprice and Nikeo burst out laughing.

"Can't fault you for that, because that's exactly what she needs," states Caprice. "She's a nutcase."

When I leave the room, I hear Nikeo say, "Take it out of my paycheck."

I stand at the entrance to my bedroom and listen closely.

Caprice laughs incredulously. "You're kidding, right?"

"We've gotten ten new clients in a week because of her ideas. She should be marketing full-time with me."

"What's gotten into you?"

"Nothing," he responds casually.

"I don't like where this is headed. She's my best friend, Nikeo," Caprice declares emphatically, giving him a *stay away* warning.

Even though I'm not in the room with them and can't see Nikeo's face, I sense his defiant smirk.

He won't heed her warning. He doesn't listen to anyone.

Is it possible that he and I have more in common than I care to admit?

CHAPTER EIGHT

Jell-O shots on trays. A quarter barrel. Loud techno music. A disco ball, provided by one of Lizzie's many boyfriends, strung to the ceiling fan. A counter full of liquor. Miscellaneous junk food strewn about the great room. A circle of people playing a sophomoric game of Spin the Bottle — only in this game from the looks of it the stakes are higher than a kiss. Bodies bumping and grinding.

I wish Caprice were here, but she's gone off on a date leaving me to fend for myself.

"Come on, Cane, smoke a joint with us!" trills Lizzie, who sits on the floor, glassy-eyed and smiling.

"Thanks, but no thanks."

"It makes you feel good," purrs Lizzie.

"I bet it does."

I want to escape to my bedroom and finish reading the smutty romance I bought at Goodwill, but the hallway, clogged with couples groping in the dark, is impassable. Seeking peace and quiet and space to think, I go outside on the patio.

Nikeo sits in a chair with his guitar pasted to his chest. Staring off into the distance, he strums chords absentmindedly, not even noticing at first that I'm there.

I feel like prey that hasn't yet been seen. I could sneak away unscathed, and yet I move forward and clear my throat.

He stops playing and looks over. "Couldn't take the excitement."

"I don't feel like toking up."

"You've never toked up. You've never done drugs in your life." He meets my eyes looking for confirmation.

"Shouldn't I be proud of that?"

He laughs. I sit down across from him.

"I heard you tell Caprice that she should take the money out of your paycheck. I'm the one who lost the account. It's my responsibility."

"It's not that big of a deal. We've already covered our losses with new accounts."

"Thanks for covering my ass."

Shrugging off my gratitude, he starts playing "Cocaine."

When he finishes, I ask, "What's with you and Clapton?"

He sweeps his eyes to me and then away from me. He tilts his head back and stares at the stars that are sprinkled across the mountain-tops. "I was going to spend two months backpacking across Europe with Tonya, this girl I dated for a couple of years. I wake up the morning of our flight, and she's gone. Ditched me in the middle of the night. No note. No explanation. No conversation. Nothing, just gone. We had planned that trip for a year. I went to a bar that night. There was this guy performing there, all Clapton covers. Ever since then?" He gives the subtlest shake of his head. "I can't stop playing him."

He's human after all, and even though I haven't heard Clapton ballads like "You Look Wonderful Tonight," it's evident he's hurting. The inside of my heart goes all gooey and empathetic. "Are you still getting over her?"

He gives a stunted laugh. "No way are we going to sit here and discuss my feelings."

The wind stirs, rattling the delicate leaves on the aspen trees that surround the patio. The air pulses and vibrates thanks to the strong bass from the music inside the house. The thumping sound goes straight to my head, giving me the feeling of heady anticipation. Though stone-cold sober, I feel drunk.

"It's past my expiration date," I remark offhandedly.

"I'm not going to even pretend to know what you're talking about."

"I've been here for much longer than a week, and I haven't packed up my bags and left as you predicted."

"But you've wanted to. You said as much to Caprice last week. In the driveway." He looks over to me. "Why aren't you gone yet?"

His inquiry, acidic and cutting, feels like a verbal shove.

I stick my hands into the front pocket of my funky rainbow hooded sweatshirt that I bought at the art fair Caprice and I went to last weekend in Denver. "Do you want me to leave?"

"Interesting that you care what I want."

"I don't care."

"But you do. You need to know what everyone is thinking and why they are thinking it. Not that you can help yourself. It's your nature."

"And that" — I point at him — "is one of your most maddening qualities. Drawing all these conclusions about me and mapping out my personality when you don't know anything about me. For the record, last week when you dissected who I was, you were wrong about so many things. I didn't have a mother and father growing up or even a sibling, a living sibling anyway. My mother was in labor with my twin brother and me. My father was driving her to the hospital when they were killed by a drunk driver. I'm the only one who survived. I was raised by my Grandma Betty."

He looks slightly taken aback by my confession and almost sympathetic. But then he turns frosty again. "Thanks for clearing that up."

"You're an insensitive prick."

Setting his guitar on the ground, he leans across the much-too-small table and invades my personal space. He gathers my hair in one of his hands, and using it as a handle of sorts, gently guides me closer to him.

Where does he get off acting like this? And, yet, I don't do one thing to stop him.

His eyes bore into mine, "You're a beautiful mess."

His lips curve upward. His smile is dangerously disarming. My heart becomes a nervous grasshopper, fluttering and jumping around inside my chest. He moves his mouth toward mine, and right before his lips touch mine, he releases me and eases back into his chair.

My wits are scattered all over the place, and it takes me longer than I would like to recover them.

I despise him.

I'm drawn to him.

I can't make up my mind.

"You haven't left yet because you don't know what you want. You did at one time. You thought you wanted the white picket fence, the minivan, the two-point-three kids, but when it came right down to it, you realized that you weren't ready. You've only just graduated college and are only, what twenty-one" — narrowing his eyes, he studies my face — "maybe twenty-two. The guy, what's his name, oh yes, *Justice.* He proposed, you accepted, and then you left for Colorado."

"Part of the equation is missing. I found out my friend, Mikayla, kissed Justice, which factored into my decision-making."

He absorbs this new information. "I don't really care about what happened, who proposed, who kissed whom, and by the way, that's a lame excuse for leaving. What I'm really curious about is if the grass is any greener out here in Colorado?"

Yet again, he's strip-searched me with his words, leaving me exposed. But now that I'm privy to the source of all his bitterness and rancor, I know this has nothing to do with me. "You don't care about what I want or did or whether I think the grass is greener. You're not picking apart my relationship with Justice, you're picking apart your own. Obviously, this is all about you and Tonya and how she left you high and dry."

I wait for his opposition, predicting that he'll reject this insight and somehow turn my words inside out and attack me. But he sits still and says nothing, his silence tacit acknowledgment that I'm correct. *I'm right! Take that, Nikeo.* Only, I can't bring myself to gloat. I'm not that cruel.

"I'm sorry. I didn't mean to hit a nerve, but —"

He interrupts. "Here's what I think."

Someone opens the sliding door allowing the bass beat to escape. It pulverizes the air around us, making the moment feel breakable and dangerous.

"I don't want to know what you think."

"I'm going to tell you anyway."

"I'm going inside."

I stand, and Nikeo does as well. He's at my side before I can escape. He pushes my hair over my shoulder and curls his hand around the side of my neck. The pressure of his hand feels perilously intimate and slightly painful.

"It's because of me that you haven't gone back yet."

His eyes seek and find mine. He holds me in place with his gaze.

I swat his hand away. "Given that you're an egomaniac, you would think that."

"I don't think it, I know it."

Disgusted with his incessant verbal games, I turn away.

"Going to join Lizzie and smoke some pot?" he asks me.

I look over my shoulder. "I want to get high as a kite."

His throaty laughter conveys doubt. "I would like to see that."

Impatiently pushing my way through throngs of people, I make my way to the kitchen counter and grab the one and only phone in the house from the kitchen counter. I desperately need to get a cell phone.

"Change your mind?" Lizzie stumbles toward me wearing a goofy smile. She holds a joint in front of my face. "Try it," she urges.

"I never change my mind," I snap.

"Cane, that's like, so cool. Just say no, right?" She laughs.

I make my way down the hall and into my bedroom.

Nikeo isn't right. He can't be right. I'm not staying here because of him. This has nothing to do with him.

I'm going to prove it. I punch in Justice's cell number and anxiously wait.

He answers on the first ring. "You're breaking the rules. Three months, remember?"

It's so achingly good to hear his voice. "Please, can we stop this now?"

"You're the one who left," he reminds me.

"You're the one who made up the rules," I fire back with insistence.

I wait, and in the silence between us, I sense Justice's resolve crumbling. Even though we're thousands of miles from each other, I can feel his love for me. *Forever, for always, no matter what.* It's a relief to know that even though everything else has changed, this hasn't. A burning clump of tears clouds my vision and scalds the inside of my nose.

"Sugar Cane, do you want to come home?"

His voice, a gentle invitation, feels so much like a caress that I actually lean into the phone. "Only if you want me to." Even before I'd opened my mouth, I knew it was the wrong thing to say. When it comes to shooting myself in the foot, I have excellent aim. As expected, a harder, more concrete silence fills the phone line, clogging my ear canals and muting my thoughts.

"That's not good enough. It's not about what I want. It's about what you want. And you have to be sure about what you want. Figure it out before it's too late for us."

Before it's too late? I'm about to ask him what he means when the line goes dead.

CHAPTER NINE

July 1998

"I'm so glad to see you!" Jocelyn says as she launches herself into my arms in front of the baggage carousel.

"I'm glad to see you, too!" I exclaim. "How are you?"

My simple inquiry yields an unexpected reaction. She bursts into tears.

"What's wrong?" I ask her.

Mumbling unintelligibly, she buries her face in my shirt and wails.

I hold tightly to her, soothing her as best I can. People around us start staring and whispering. One guy in his late twenties gives us a dirty look and rolls his eyes. Giving him my most evil, *drop dead* look, I flip him off. He sneers, and if I weren't holding on to Jocelyn, I would give him a piece of my mind and a hearty portion of my fist as a meal.

The carousel starts beeping, and the belt rotates, bringing luggage. Jocelyn's navy and white striped suitcases that I bequeathed to her when I left for college pass by, but I'm not going to let her go until she's ready.

When she reluctantly releases me and pulls back, her face looks like a punctured, oozing tomato. The poor girl has been battling acne for a year now, and she's in the midst of a horrific breakout. Jelly Roll has refused to take her to the dermatologist, saying that medication takes away one problem and creates a dozen more. I think Jelly Roll has more devious motives, like denying her daughter proper treatment to keep the boys away. Jocelyn's a natural beauty and would be stunning if not for the problematic acne.

"I look horrible, don't I," she moans and flattens her hand against her cheeks.

"You look like you've been crying, which you have. Go sit down. I'll get your things. We can talk when we get to the car."

Twenty minutes later when I'm merging into traffic on the highway, she apologizes. "I'm sorry about that."

"It's okay."

"No, it's not. I hate being a blubbering idiot. Mom always says I'm a crybaby. Not that I care what she says anymore. I hate her."

"Are you upset at her? Is that why you were crying?"

Jocelyn glances at me. "I don't want to talk about her at all. And I want to stay here as long as I can. I hate being home. I hate *everyone* and *everything* at home, especially my *mom*."

Her statement, loaded with spiteful subtext, blackens the mood in the car. "You can stay as long as you like, you know that."

"What if Caprice doesn't want me here?"

"I talked to her, and she's fine with it. She might even give you some clients of your own. You could make some great money this summer."

"Okay. That would be great. Because I'm not leaving. Dad said I could stay as long as I needed. I told him he should have come with me to get away from Jelly Roll."

When she says *Jelly Roll,* I know that this isn't a run-of-the-mill quarrel that has her so upset. She knows about the unkind nickname that I had given her mother when I was younger and understands why I had done so, but never once has she used this moniker herself.

"Do you want to talk about what happened between you and your mom?"

She shifts in her seat and crosses her arms petulantly. "No, I don't want to talk about it at all. Ever."

I try another conversational direction, hoping for some information. "What's Justice been up to?"

"Working a lot. Going out to the bars a lot with Mikayla and Jeremy and acting like a big, cranky jerk. I don't know why you can't just make up with him." She glances my way and nervously pinches a loose thread on her shorts. "The whole thing is stupid."

Her observation stings. "You're probably right," I admit.

"What Mikayla did was crappy, but I know that my cousin wouldn't do anything to hurt you."

"I know."

"Then why did you have to leave and mess everything up?"

"There's not a simple answer. You'll understand when you're older."

In response, she scowls and sighs heavily. The lowest blow you can give to a teenage girl is telling her that she'll understand when she's older. I vividly remember how much I resented statements like this.

Sullen, she rests her forehead against the passenger window and stares at the scenery. "It's so pretty it looks fake, like a painting or something." She cranes her neck to get a better view of the mountain-tops. "Can we climb to the top of one of those?"

"Absolutely."

"Can we run and lift weights and stuff?"

"Yes, every day. There are some great paths and hiking trails, and we can go biking with Nikeo. You would love it."

"Nikeo?"

"He's Caprice's cousin. He works for the company, and he lives at the house," I explain.

"Are you friends with him?" she asks.

"Friends?" I laugh uncomfortably. "Kind of."

Friends? Enemies? I'm not sure what label I would assign to our relationship. Given our contemptuous interactions, the term *adversary* may be more appropriate. Regardless of what we are or aren't, I know that I should be avoiding him. And, yet, that flashing neon sign in my brain that tells me to stay away has several faulty bulbs.

Last Saturday, after Lizzie's epic Friday night bash, Nikeo pounded on my bedroom door just after dawn and told me to get up and get dressed.

Never a morning person and definitely not one when someone else demanded that I rise, I rolled over and groaned. "Leave me alone."

"I'm taking you road biking," he said through the door.

"I'm going running, not biking."

"Be outside in twenty minutes."

"Are you deaf, stupid, or both?"

"I put Lizzie's bike shorts, jersey, and helmet outside your door. Wear those," he ordered.

"Do you have a disability? Seriously!" I launched myself out of bed and opened the door to tell him where he could stick it. Before I could get a word in edgewise, he shoved the shorts and helmet into my chest with such force, I had no choice but to brace myself and take them or risk falling on my butt.

"Grab a water bottle. You're going to need it."

Scowling, I slammed the door, but nevertheless, I met him outside. He showed no mercy on the ride; we pedaled fast and furious for thirty miles. Not having the energy to talk, we didn't argue once. When we finished, we wheeled our bikes into the garage, and I was horrified to discover that I had loved every minute of the ride and of the time we had spent together, which is why I couldn't let it happen again.

"Go buy a pair of bike shoes today so you can clip in, and then we'll really ride."

"I'm not buying a pair of bike shoes. I don't even like biking." This was a lie. The endorphins that zinged around in my head were proof that I was already addicted.

Later that day, I strolled down the brick-paved streets of quaint downtown Briar and entered the local bike shop. Twenty minutes later, I was the proud owner of bike shoes, a jersey, and shorts.

"But, I don't have a bike," Jocelyn whines beside me.

"We can rent one from the bike shop downtown, or maybe you can ride Caprice's."

"I'll never be able to keep up with you. Is Nikeo fast?" she asks.

"Faster than me, but don't worry. You and I will go out alone together. I won't leave you behind."

She flips down the vanity mirror. "I hate my face right now. Look at all these zits. It's hopeless," she moans.

"Do you know what we're going to do?" I smile conspiratorially at her. "We're going to call your dad, have him mail us his medical insurance card, and I'm going to make you an appointment at a dermatologist and get you some real medication. By the time you leave here, your face will be back to peaches and cream."

Her vibrant blue eyes, reddened and subdued from her cry, brighten. "You mean it? You're really going to do that?"

"What your mother doesn't know won't hurt her."

When we pull into the driveway, Jocelyn takes a shaky breath. "Think they're going to like me?"

"They'll love you."

Caprice and Lizzie, who are standing in the kitchen starting dinner, warmly greet Jocelyn.

Nikeo, who sits at the bar flipping through a biking magazine, looks up, smiles, and tells Jocelyn he's glad she's here.

Who is this man and what has he done with the real Nikeo? Only yesterday he'd said this house wasn't a daycare for runaways.

Caprice peppers Jocelyn with compliments about her gorgeous blue eyes, and Lizzie asks her all sorts of questions about how long she plans on staying and what she wants to do this summer. Thankfully, she doesn't ask her if she has any pot.

I go out to the car and drag Jocelyn's suitcases in while Nikeo observes from his perch on the bar stool. Like the gentleman he definitely isn't, he doesn't offer to help once. I glare at him, and he responds with a cocky smile.

When I'm finished hauling everything in, I tell Jocelyn that she should call her dad.

"I don't want to call home. Can you?"

"Of course, but are you sure you don't even want to say hi?"

"More than sure," she says looking surly.

She stays in the kitchen, and I take the phone into my room and call the Schaeffer household.

Unfortunately, Jelly Roll answers.

"Hi, it's Cane, we just —"

Jelly Roll interrupts, serving me a series of questions. "She's there? Safe and sound? Was her flight on time? Is she upset? Is she okay?"

"Yes, safe and sound. We're back at the house. Is Samson around by chance?"

"I need to talk to her."

"She doesn't want to talk to you."

"Yes, she does! Give her the phone."

"This isn't up for negotiation," I tell her flatly.

A long silence, then, "*What did she tell you?*"

Her shrill inquiry resonates as unabashed panic, and it's so unlike Jelly Roll to be hysterical that it gives me pause. What happened back home that has both her and Jocelyn so worked up?

"She didn't tell me anything," I respond.

I hear a relieved hiss of air. "Oh."

"Is Samson there?"

"No, he's not. If Jocelyn doesn't want to talk to me, then I'll have to talk to you. Listen closely. I want her to eat three square meals a day and plenty of snacks in between. You've poisoned her with all this talk of eating healthy and exercising and she's obsessed with her body image; thanks to you, she's probably going to develop an eating disorder. I want her in bed every night, no later than eleven, and let her sleep as long as she wants. Don't go waking her up at the crack of dawn to go running. Make sure she calls home every day to check in. I also want —"

She continues, and I tune out. After spending the morning with Nikeo tweaking the company's new website and arguing with him about advertising strategies and then making a drive through rush-hour traffic to get Jocelyn from the airport, I'm exhausted. I flop back on my bed.

"Are you listening to me?"

"Absolutely." Not.

"I'm not at all happy about her being there. She's running away from her problems just like you did. You made more of a mess. Got everything you wanted and what do you do but hightail it out of Savage. There's no making you happy."

"I'm sorry you see things that way." The bedroom door opens and Jocelyn enters and points at the phone, mouthing the question, *who is it?*

Pulling the phone slightly away from my ear, my lips shrink into a tight ball. I raise my brow and give her a pointed look. *Take one guess,* my expression says.

Squishing her eyes shut, she exits the room. She doesn't want to talk to her mother any more than I do.

"I do see things that way, because that's the reality of the situation," states Jelly Roll.

If I pursue this topic and try to defend myself, there will be a fatal collision, and so I change conversational lanes. "Could you send an insurance card for Jocelyn, because —"

"Did something happen? Is she hurt?"

"She's fine. I want it here for emergency purposes," I say quickly, thinking on my feet. "If she gets sick and needs to see a doctor, I want to be prepared."

She takes a moment to process this, and I know her well enough to know that she's annoyed with herself for not thinking of this. Jelly Roll prides herself on covering all the bases.

"I'll overnight it," she mutters peevishly.

"Good-bye."

"No wait! Please." She pauses and sighs. "Please tell her to call me. I need to talk to her. It's very important. Please, Cane. Do this for me."

Her supplication unnerves me, because Jelly Roll never asks politely or begs for anything, she demands. "I'll see what I can do."

"Thank you," she responds, her gratitude authentic.

In the ten years that I've known her, not once has she thanked me for anything.

CHAPTER TEN

Jocelyn, who has spent the first two weeks of her stay sleeping in, lounging around the Briar community pool, reading, and exercising with me twice daily, and refusing to call her mother even though I've asked her to, has decided she's ready to be a working woman. Although she wanted her own clients, Caprice told her that she would have to train with me for a while. Yesterday, she helped Nikeo and me design small advertisements that would be used in the local paper, and when we were finished, we made her our lackey and sent her to the store to buy office supplies.

However, today will be more interesting for her. We're on our way to Arlene and Skeeter's house, and I've just informed her that they are nudists.

"These people are going to be naked?" Jocelyn punctuates the question with a disbelieving laugh. "You're kidding, right?"

"Guess you'll have to see for yourself." I pull up in front of Arlene and Skeeter's home. The front door opens, and through the glass storm door, Arlene waves with both arms. Her breasts jostle with the motion of her limbs.

Jocelyn's eyes travel up the front walk-way, and she spies Arlene in all her glory. "She's naked!" Her hands fly to her mouth.

"Told you. And let me warn you, he's going to be naked, too."

Her eyes widen in abject revulsion. "But, I've never seen a naked man. Ever." She sucks on her bottom lip and shakes her head. "I can't go in! I just can't."

How shortsighted — I hadn't even considered this factor. Her first glimpse of the male form shouldn't be a gravity-riddled scrotum and defeated-looking penis. She might never recover; I certainly wouldn't have at her age.

Panicked, she grips my arm. Her face flames red, making her acne appear angrier. "I can't go in! I can't! I want to help you. But, I don't —"

I quickly come up with a plan B. "Here's what you're going to do. While I clean, you take the car to the dermatologist's office and see if they can squeeze you in. The directions are here." I hand her a piece of paper with written directions. I hope she's better at navigating than I am.

"But my appointment isn't until this afternoon."

"Yes, but when I called to schedule yesterday, they had a nine o'clock opening and a three. Maybe the nine is still available."

"Oh, my God! She's coming outside, she's coming outside!" Jocelyn points at Arlene, who's walking confidently down her front walk.

"Don't point," I say, lowering her hand with mine.

Too stunned to make another comment, she nods dumbly. "Just go to the doctor's office. See if they can squeeze you in, and be back here by eleven to pick me up. If they can't get you in, just find something to do in town."

"Yoo-hoo! Yoo-hoo!" says Arlene, as she smiles and raps on the driver's side window.

I return her smile and open the door.

"I thought you were going to sit out here all day! Is this a friend?" She ducks into the car and smiles at Jocelyn. "Hi, I'm Arlene! Are you going to be helping Cane today?"

Jocelyn, wide-eyed and terrified, has gone mute.

"She just gave me a ride, isn't that right, Jocelyn?" I ask loudly.

Jocelyn snaps out of her *I can't believe what I'm seeing* trance and smiles meekly in Arlene's general direction, avoiding eye contact. "Yep. I'm just giving her a ride."

"What a nice friend you are!" Arlene smiles and then looks at me. "I thought I would help carry things in."

"Oh, that's nice. Thank you."

Arlene helps me unload the cleaning supplies out of the trunk, and at one point as she's leaning forward to grab the canvas bag of rags, her breast flops forward and hits me square in the arm. It makes a weird slapping sound.

"Oops! Sorry about that."

"Oh, that's okay."

"These girls have a mind of their own, and boy, do they like to misbehave!" Laughing, she gives her boobs a squeeze.

Never in a million years did I think I would be working at a job where I would have to worry about naked breasts taking a swing at me.

I tell Jocelyn to drive carefully. She slides into the driver's seat and takes off so fast, she leaves a trail of rubber.

Arlene hoots. "She's sure in a hurry to get out of here, isn't she!"

Skeeter meets us at the door and takes the vacuum from my hands. "Let me help!"

"Thanks," I say, smiling at his face. I keep my eyes trained on his, because I don't have the stomach to see what's going on down there.

As I'm cleaning the master bathroom, Arlene comes in and hounds me about going to a *Bare and There* meeting.

"Have you read the literature that I gave you?"

"Some of it," I say, fudging the truth. I'd read the title on the first page, *Naked Nature: Pure Pleasure.* And, then, I'd dropped it into the recycle bin.

"You need to go to a meeting. I'm telling you, it will change your life! Being naked — it erases all your inhibitions and makes you more aware of who you are as a person."

I bet she would love it if I showed up holding a feather duster and nothing else, and Skeeter would love it more. I should ditch the *Maid Hot* bikini and go straight for birthday suit attire; that's a whole other business direction that Caprice could pursue. I politely decline. "I can't. It's just not for me."

"If you change your mind, they're having a more informal social gathering at the Briar Days Festival."

Caprice had told me about the upcoming Briar Days. Besides the standard carnival, craft and art fair, greasy food, and rowdy beer tent, the festival featured three nights of spectacular music by well-known bands.

"Sure." I look up at her from my hands-and-knees position in front of the toilet where I'm scouring Skeeter's many trials and errors. "I'll think about it."

This appeases her and then she's off, leaving me two hours of uninterrupted time to think.

Predictably, I stew about Justice and Mikayla. Ever since Jocelyn told me that he's been frequenting bars with my former best friend, who not only kissed him, but also declared her love for him, my ire has been on a steady boil.

What is Justice thinking? Why does he have any interest in hanging out with her when he's always made it clear that he doesn't have any tolerance for her behavior and questionable morals?

When Justice and I had been dating for just over a month, we went on a whitewater rafting trip in Wisconsin on the Wolf River. Mikayla and her boyfriend at the time, a guy who called himself Snake, a fitting name since he had so many tattoos on his body that he appeared reptilian, had met us there. While we hiked through the woods in appropriate outdoorsy clothing and swatted bloodthirsty mosquitoes, Mikayla cavorted around in a string bikini and had Snake rub sunscreen oil on her perfect body every thirty minutes. Then, at night, she climbed into the tent with reptile man and put on a porn show for the whole forest to hear.

Still a virgin, it made me uncomfortable and slightly insecure having to listen to Mikayla's vocal performance in the tent next to ours.

I asked Justice if he would prefer I be more like her.

"Absolutely not," he said as he stroked the hair away from my forehead. "She's too obnoxious and only satisfied when she's getting attention. How she behaves? It's not always real," he whispered. "You're real. The most real person I've ever met. That's why I love you so much."

I knew then his devotion was unshakable. But, now, I'm feeling some unwelcome tremors. Are they precursors to a massive quake? Maybe what used to repel him about Mikayla now attracts him. And, if he is in fact hanging out in bars with her and indulging in one too many beers, he's probably been wearing beer goggles. The prescription on those things should be illegal. They make everyone look tempting.

Speaking of temptation, I've got issues of my own. I've been forced to spend quality time with Nikeo four days out of the week now that we're collaborating on marketing and growing the company. Caprice has taken an interest in observing my interactions with her cousin.

When I'd gotten back from a solo run late last night, she and I sat alone on the patio long after everyone else had gone to bed.

"Tell me what's going on with you and Nikeo," she demanded, narrowing her eyes.

"Nothing."

"Bullshit. You've been spending a lot of time together. Biking. Talking. Fighting. Mostly fighting. It's like watching two feral cats circle each other."

I dodged her penetrating stare. "I'm working with him. That's all."

"I don't buy that and neither do you. You like him."

Glowering, I sank lower in my chair. "Like him? He's insufferable."

"Have you talked to Justice at all?"

I briefly told her about the phone call that I'd had with him a few weeks back.

"You're not wearing the engagement ring anymore," she remarked, pointing at my naked hand.

I'd taken it off a few days before. "It doesn't feel right wearing it when everything is such a mess."

She cracked a wicked smile. "I don't think that's it. I've never seen you like this. Nikeo has gotten under your skin and don't try to deny it."

I couldn't deny it last night, and I can't deny it now. He's wheedled his way in like a sliver, and I can't get him out.

Who am I to question Justice's fidelity when I'm struggling with my own?

Skeeter bounds into the living room where I'm finishing up the last of the vacuuming. Appendages are flying every which way. If he gets too close, I'm going to have to duck and cover. Breasts hitting me I can handle. A penis? Not so much.

"Your ride is here!" he announces over the loud whir of the vacuum.

"Thanks! I'm almost finished."

Grin and bear it, I think, or in this case *bare it.* He turns around and bends over, picking up his sunglasses that have fallen off his head, giving me an up-close-and-personal view of his nether regions.

With check in hand and cleaning gear packed and stowed away, I walk outside and open the car door.

Jocelyn proudly holds up two prescription tubes. "I got medication! The doctor says that if I use this morning and night, in two or three weeks, my face will be clear!"

"That's fantastic!"

"Yeah, but since I'm not eighteen, they had to call my dad to get permission for the prescriptions."

I should have let Samson know that I was planning on taking her to the dermatologist. "He wasn't upset?"

"He didn't care, but I told him he better not tell Mom. I don't want her knowing anything," she says spitefully.

Jocelyn helps me load the trunk. After we're buckled up, she tells me all about the doctor and how cute he was.

"Everyone out here is awesome. I want to live here. Maybe I could stay with you and start school here in the fall. That is, if you're staying."

"Don't you miss home?" I ask.

"Not one bit." She jerks down the visor and inspects her acne-mottled skin. "Do you think my face will clear up?"

"No doubt in my mind. You just have to be patient."

"Yeah, that's what the doctor said, but I don't want to be patient. I want it to work now."

"Actually" — I glance over, inspecting her face — "since you've been out here, it's already gotten better."

She smiles proudly. "Probably because there's less stress."

The next stop for the cleaning train: Harriet's house. Once Jocelyn and I have carried everything into the house, I introduce her to Harriet.

"What a sweetie pie! You remind me of my great-granddaughter!" Reaching out with her arthritic hands, she lovingly cups Jocelyn's chin. "Are you going to help Cane clean this summer?"

Jocelyn bobs her head. "For a bit, and then I'm going to get clients of my own," she says self-importantly.

"Such a good thing for a young woman to have financial independence. It's not necessary to rely on a man." Harriet hobbles over to the sofa, which is quite low to the ground, and eases herself down. She winces, and I go over and help her. She smiles her thanks to me.

Jocelyn nods confidently. "I'm never going to rely on a man. I'm going to take care of myself."

"That's the right attitude, young lady," Harriet says approvingly. "My husband was always on me to quit my job as a secretary at a doctor's office, but I refused! When I had our children, I left, but as soon as they were in school, I went back to work. I'll tell you, quite a few tongues were wagging around town. But a woman needs identity outside of her home life. She needs a sense of self, and when she has one, she's always a better wife and mother."

Harriet's wise words resonate. Perhaps I had made the right decision. Granted, I hadn't executed my departure in the most mature of ways, and the timing completely sucked, but deep down I know that this is where I need to be. Jocelyn and I set to work cleaning each room from top to bottom, and it turns out the kid is a natural housekeeper, which makes sense because she grew up in Jelly Roll's house. Jelly Roll has always been a cleaning fanatic. A separate sponge and rag for every surface; she and Misty Moreland would hit it off spectacularly.

At dinner that evening, Lizzie takes out her vegetable tray, again, while the rest us stand in line and fill our plates with basmati rice, grilled meat and vegetables, and a large fruit salad, the meal compliments of Nikeo.

Knowing it must have taken a lot of time to prepare, I thank him for making dinner.

"Don't get used to it, sweetheart, because I don't plan on playing chef on a regular basis. I only made this because we're celebrating. Today I landed the biggest account in Briar," he announces pompously.

"The Aspenwood Condominiums. Two hundred rental units run by Ravenwood Management, and Ravenwood wants *Maid Right in Time* to be their cleaning company."

"What!" Disgusted with him, I push him in the chest with my fingertips. "You're not taking the credit for this, because I'm the one who met with them initially. I got the ball rolling."

"Don't flatter yourself." He raises his eyes to mine. "I closed the deal."

"Only because I'm the one who got our foot in the door and talked to them on the phone for over an hour and —"

Lizzie interjects. "Could you two for once just shut it! You're giving everyone in this house a headache with all your damn fighting!"

I ignore her plea. "Nikeo, come on, admit it!"

"Admit what?" he asks innocently.

Furrowing her brow, Lizzie sighs dramatically. "*Would you two just have sex already and get it over with!* I can't *take* any more of your foreplay garbage. It's driving us all *crazy*."

Jocelyn, who's undoubtedly startled by this outburst for more than one reason, swallows wrong and starts coughing. Nikeo pats her hard on the back.

"You okay?" he asks.

With tears streaming down her face, she quickly bobs her head. "Um, yeah."

Caprice pulls a bottle of wine out of the fancy wine refrigerator that's situated under the countertop, uncorks it, and pours each of us a glass.

"You're giving me some?" Jocelyn asks with a stunned look on her face.

Caprice laughs. "Why wouldn't I?"

"Because I'm only seventeen."

"If you're old enough to work for a living, you're old enough to drink," Caprice rationalizes.

Jocelyn shifts her eyes to me, asking permission. Unable to disagree with Caprice's logic I shrug my consent. A little wine never hurt anyone. She takes a nervous sip and then tries to suppress a smile.

"We landed a big account. It doesn't matter how it happened. Cane and Nikeo are both getting a big bonus," Caprice announces. "Now, let's sit down, eat, drink, and celebrate."

Not wanting to give the slightest credibility to Lizzie's statement, because there isn't any I tell myself, I prudently select the seat farthest away from Nikeo, and Jocelyn, who's completely in love with him, sits as close to him as possible.

My typical truck-driver appetite kicks in, and I dig into my food while watching Lizzie eat only the grilled vegetables. What is her deal? "Do you ever eat anything but vegetables?" I ask her.

"It's a rule I have. I used to be a total heifer as a kid and even as a teenager. You should see pictures. Talk about a disgusting pig."

Jocelyn flinches. Even though she's lost a lot of weight, she's still self-conscious about her body. I don't think Jocelyn recognizes her transformation. When she looks in the mirror, I'm certain she still sees herself as an overweight child.

"Seriously," Nikeo snickers. "There was so much friction between her thighs she could have started a fire."

Caprice defends Lizzie. "She looked fine!"

"No, I didn't. Nikeo's right," she admits. "Then I made up some rules. I had to exercise for at least forty minutes every day. I cut out all junk food — except for one day a week, and on my free day, I had to eat the junk before noon. The last rule, after five at night, only vegetables. It's worked. Look at me now. I'm amazing."

"And humble," Nikeo remarks.

Disregarding his condescension, Lizzie dips a grilled zucchini in her sauvignon blanc and then pops it into her mouth. Is that her version of dip?

Jocelyn, ever the impressionable teenager, brings up Lizzie's rules later that evening as we're running on a bike path that winds around the base of Eldora Mountain.

"I could only eat vegetables after five. If I did that, I bet I could lose the last fifteen pounds."

I'm not going to allow Jocelyn to follow Lizzie's fanatical rules. "Not a good idea. It's not a realistic, long-term option. It's not healthy."

"What do you know? You've never had to worry about losing weight," she grumbles. "I might try the rules," she states defiantly.

Knowing I can't win this argument, I grant her the liberty she craves. "It's your choice."

The bike path narrows as we cross a footbridge over a bubbling creek and then head into an area thick with trees. The pungent odor of pine and resin hangs like fog. In the distance, water of the whitest hue I've ever seen tumbles down a copper-colored serrated cliff and lands into a serene pool tucked under an overhang of rocks. Like Jocelyn, I could see myself living here.

"What Lizzie said about you and Nikeo — do you want to sleep with him?" Jocelyn asks, breathing heavier now that I've ramped up the pace.

"Absolutely not." My immediate and adamant response contradicts my lewd and impure thoughts. Since Lizzie's offhanded comment at dinner, I haven't been thinking of anything other than having sex with Nikeo. What would it be like to have his strong hands pinned to my body and his tongue and mine warring with each other? What would it be like, I think, glancing at the waterfall, to stand naked beneath the water with our bodies connected, pushing toward a blinding pleasure? Until now, I never understood how hate and desire played off each other, heightening emotion and sensation. Even though we haven't even kissed, I instinctively know that if we do, all bets are off. I fear that I'll go against everything I believe in simply for the pleasure of being with him.

What does that say about me?

I try to kick the fantasies of Nikeo and me to the curb where they belong, and Jocelyn unknowingly helps me out by bringing Justice front and center.

"Remember last Christmas Eve when Justice took you sledding, and he told you he was going to marry you soon?" she asks.

I'd nearly forgotten that Jocelyn knew about that very private memory. Like me, she's a sucker for brain candy romance novels, happy endings, and anything that resembles a fairy tale. Over Christmas break, she'd been brooding about a certain boy at school who didn't even know she existed. When she'd said that she would never fall in love and that there was no such thing as a Prince Charming, I assured her that there was. I told her she just had to be patient and then told her about my Christmas Eve with Justice.

Long after Frank and Grandma Betty's annual Christmas Eve extravaganza that boasted enough food to feed an army, hours of live music thanks to Frank's mean trumpet-playing skills, and fireworks and sparklers to cap off the night, Justice had driven me to the forest preserve.

"What are we doing here?" I asked, shivering.

His eyes swept over the landscape. "Having fun in the snow," he said.

He pulled a sled from the bed of his truck. We hiked up the hill where the lone maple tree stood. Struck by lightning on the very same night my parents and infant twin had died and I had been pulled from my mother's womb and lived, the tree was half alive, growing and pulling its dead half along with it. I'd always felt a kinship with the tree and with the place.

Under a clear sky dotted with thousands of stars, Justice and I sledded on the fresh foot of snow until our lungs burned from the cold air. When we finished, he took the sled up the hill, and we lay inside it together under the tree. Despite our many layers of clothes, we made love, his eyes never once leaving mine. He pressed his finger to my reddened and numb nose, kissed my lips, and promised me that very soon he would marry me and make me his for all of time.

Although I'd omitted the part about making love, I'd shared everything else with Joceyln.

"I remember," I say introspectively.

Jocelyn fastens her blue eyes on me. "Don't screw it up. I mean it. He's your Prince Charming. He's your soul mate. You told me so."

Her words and the memory of that night chasten me. Thoughts are just as lethal as actions, and it feels like I've been caught in the act.

Abruptly, Jocelyn changes the subject. "Um, so I was thinking. Lizzie's really cool. Would you mind if I worked with her instead of you?"

It's become obvious that Jocelyn worships Lizzie. She trails her around the house, peppering her with questions and admiring everything from her hair to her outfits to the way she flirtatiously interacts with the men who frequently stop by to see her. While I'm down to earth, Lizzie twirls on the clouds. She has more glitter and star power than I ever will.

However, Lizzie's proclivity for pot, partying, and going panty-less, a habit she brags about constantly insisting on how great it feels, gives me pause. "I don't think so."

"Why?"

"Because I don't think you should be hanging around her that much."

"Please."

"My answer is no." I sound like a strict parent. Here I am laying down the law for Jocelyn, and I can't figure out my own life.

"You didn't say anything when Caprice gave me wine tonight," she argues.

"It was two sips of wine, and that's completely different."

Intuiting my concerns about Lizzie's influence, Jocelyn makes me a promise. "I'm not going to party or smoke pot. I promise."

So says the seventeen-year-old. Famous last words. If something happens to Jocelyn on my watch, Jelly Roll will demand my public hanging, and she'll be the one to tie the noose and kick away the stool.

CHAPTER ELEVEN

"I sincerely apologize. We're installing a business line today with voice mail so this won't happen again," I inform Mrs. Kazinski.

Yet again, Lizzie neglected to deliver an important message, this time from an eighty-three-year-old woman in desperate need of our maid service.

Caprice has made it clear that whomever arrives home first is responsible for listening to the answering machine, recording messages in a log book, and then either calling the clients back immediately if possible or passing the information along to Caprice. Given that Nikeo and I have been insanely busy scouting new clients, meeting with several local property managers about our cleaning service, and designing fliers and news ads that feature Lizzie and Caprice strutting their stuff in the *Maid Hot* bikini, Lizzie is usually the first one through the door and habitually neglects her secretarial duties.

"I assure you, Mrs. Kazinski, this won't happen again, and as an apology, we would like to offer you a complimentary cleaning."

An offer of a free cleaning always seals the deal. I've won her over. I schedule the appointment for tomorrow morning at eight.

When I switch off the phone, Nikeo grabs the complicated schedule of all our employees and shakes his head. "We've got no one free tomorrow morning. We could send Jocelyn, but Caprice won't go for that."

"Then you go and clean," I tell him.

He scoffs. "I. Don't. Clean. It's in my contract. Take it up with Caprice."

He heads over to the refrigerator and pulls out a Pepsi. He consumes three to four cans a day. When he was drinking one outside last week,

I told him if he kept it up his teeth were going to fall out and he'd be diabetic by the time he was thirty. His response was to pull a cigarette out of his pocket and light it. After he took a long drag and blew the smoke in my face, he said maybe he would get lucky and die of lung cancer first.

"You're going to have to get over your fear of cleaning and suck it up. I will take it up with Caprice."

"Be my guest, but I can go get that contract and show you the fine print." He opens the Pepsi, gulps half of the can, and belches loudly.

I roll my eyes. "I'm supposed to be impressed by that?"

The doorbell rings, and Nikeo lets in the phone service technician to hook up the new system. Because *Maid Hot* and *Maid Right in Time* are growing like crazy, Caprice has turned a spare lower-level bedroom into an organized and efficient office where there are now filing cabinets, desks, two computers, and, as of today, a state-of-the-art phone system. The only thing missing is a full-time secretary. Caprice has been conducting interviews all week and has narrowed it down to two applicants. Hopefully by Friday, I will no longer have to put out Lizzie's fires.

I lead the technician down the stairs to the office and then return to the kitchen. Nikeo and I sit down side-by-side and go over the new client contract we've drawn up for the larger businesses, highlighting areas that still need revision and arguing about certain clauses.

I point to the cancellation policy addendum that spans three paragraphs. "We don't need all that mumbo jumbo in there. It's unnecessary padding."

"But we have to cover our asses," he insists. "People are dishonest jerks, and if we don't hold them accountable for payment we're going to get bent over and —"

"But we've already stipulated that they need to pay within twenty-four hours, and this phrase" — I point to the one in question — "is basically a repeat. Too much small print! It might be a red flag for some people. We have to keep it under one page."

"Seeing as how I finished a year and a half of law school I have more insight —"

"Law school?" I ask. I wait for the punch line.

Insulted at my incredulity, he glares at me.

Caprice had told me he'd dropped out of school but never specified what kind of school. I'd assumed undergraduate, not law school.

He frowns. "I don't strike you as the lawyer type."

His barbed-wire tattoo doesn't really fit the mold, but the more I think about it, it makes sense. Stealthy and argumentative, I can see him as a lawyer. "You don't strike me as the type who wants to uphold the law and fight for justice." I hesitate after the last phrase, realizing the interesting wording. *Fight for justice?* Is that what I will have to do when I return home?

I continue. "You strike me as the type of lawyer who's in it for the joy of drawing blood."

"I do love restraining my adversaries and going in for the kill." He raises his eyes to mine, and his lips curve upward into that provocative smile of his.

It's not merely the words he says, but how he says them. Before I know what's happening, my body responds in every off-limit area. I quickly cross my legs and clench my inner thighs together. He's not getting into my head — or my body for that matter.

Noticing my discomfort, his provocative smile widens. "What's wrong?"

"Nothing."

Glancing at my tightly crossed legs, he inches closer to me.

"What's with you and the ring?"

After Lizzie's statement last week and Jocelyn's reaction to it, along with my own debauched state of mind concerning Nikeo, I decided to put the ring back on again and under no circumstances would I remove it. Ever. I feign ignorance. "I don't know what you're talking about."

"You've been playing a game of musical chairs with that diamond ring. One day it's on, next it's off."

"Why are you keeping track?"

"It interests me."

"Why is that?"

"You know why that is," he insists, his voice dropping an octave. "But what you should know is that a ring is just a ring. It's not a good luck charm. It's not a chastity belt. It won't stop you from doing things you want to do."

"I don't want to do anything, and certainly not with you," I declare in the snottiest voice I can muster.

My statement provokes him. He abruptly turns his chair so he's facing me, reaches under the table, and grabs onto the sides of my chair. With ease, he pivots it sideways.

He puts his hands on my stacked knees and forces me to uncross my legs. I intend to wage an all-out resistance, but my tightly clenched muscles instantly turn to mush at his touch.

My legs are spread before him. He runs his hands over the tops of my thighs toward my hips. My breath catches in my throat, and when he grips my hip bones in his hands, my body turns to fire.

"What are you doing?" I ask stupidly, my voice nothing more than a hoarse whisper. We both know what he's doing and why he's doing it.

His hands still on my hips, he yanks me closer to the edge of the chair, forcing my legs to open wider and forcing me closer to him. He takes one of his hands and moves it up to my mouth. He rests his middle finger on my lips and then drags it slowly back and forth until my lips part. The fire that's started in my body has become a raging inferno, and it's liquefying every last bit of me. My resolve to stay away from him and remain loyal and committed to Justice is nothing more than a puddle beneath my feet.

Still resting his fingertip on my lip, he whispers, "This is the last time I'm going to touch you. *The last time.* You're going to come to me eventually. You're the one who is going to have to cross the line and make the move."

"This isn't a game." My voice, all breathy and nervous, withers at the end of my statement.

"No, it's definitely not."

"You're going to be waiting forever."

"I don't think it will take quite that long," he murmurs, and with that, his finger finds its way just inside my mouth.

What is he doing? But, the bigger question is, *what the hell am I doing?*

I'm wearing an engagement ring. I'm in love with Justice.

Yet, here I am sitting before Nikeo, absolutely helpless to his brazen sexual advances that trigger pleasure alarms located throughout my body. I should rebuff his advances immediately and bite the tip of his finger, but, all I can think of is the taste of his salty skin and how he would react should I close my lips around his finger and suck ever so slightly.

"That'll do it! The lines and voice mail are up and running."

I nearly jump out of my seat. Smiling roguishly, Nikeo removes his finger.

Embarrassed at being caught in such an intimate moment, inappropriate on so many levels I couldn't count if I wanted to, I turn the shade of an overripe apple.

The service guy flips his business card on the table between Nikeo and me. "Call if you have any questions. I'll be sending a bill," he announces and lets himself out the front door.

"I'm going for a run," I announce decisively.

Nikeo regards me with a complacent smile. "What? Afraid you might do something you actually want to do?"

Pushing the client contracts at him, I scuttle out of my seat. "Since you're the pseudo-lawyer, why don't you stay here and figure this out."

The back door opens and then slams shut. Jocelyn and Lizzie are chatting excitedly.

Nikeo snickers. "Good thing Jocelyn didn't catch us in the act. She's watching you like a hawk, isn't she?"

"Nothing *happened,*" I hiss.

"Keep telling yourself that." He gathers all the papers we've been working on, stacks them together, and shoves them into a folder.

"Do you think she'll let me?" Jocelyn inquires hopefully.

"Why wouldn't she? *It's like no big deal,*" stresses Lizzie. "Just a few friends hanging out."

Lizzie and Jocelyn enter the great room, and I back away from Nikeo like he has an infectious disease.

When Jocelyn spots us, she smiles at me. "Oh my gosh, Cane! There's this pool party tonight down the street that one of Lizzie's friends is having. You don't care if I go, do you?"

"I don't know if that's such a good idea," I immediately say in a parenting kind of voice that sounds so much like something Grandma Betty would have said to me when I was in high school, I almost take it back.

Lizzie rolls her eyes and fiddles with her diamond necklace.

Jocelyn's smile quickly turns upside down. "Why not?"

I circumvent her question. "Why don't we hang out tonight, watch a movie, and order a pizza?" Jocelyn has become Lizzie's disciple in every way. She wears gobs of sparkly accessories and has taken to wearing hot pink clothes in an effort to emulate the hot pink bikini. Unfortunately, she also subscribes to Lizzie's dietary rules and weighs herself morning, noon, and night to record her progress. I've tried everything to dissuade Jocelyn from doing this, but nothing has worked.

"I'm not eating pizza!" she hollers. "I've lost another five pounds, and I would gain it all back."

"Okay, well, we could go biking," I suggest. Nikeo had taken Jocelyn and me out for road rides three times in the past week, and Jocelyn and I had also gone out several times alone. She loved it as much as I did.

"Nikeo took the rental bike back yesterday," she reminds me.

"I can go back to the store and rent it for another week," Nikeo offers gallantly.

His willingness to help feels contrived, but despite this, I go along with his idea. "That sounds great! Why don't you go pick up the bike, Nikeo, and then you, Jocelyn, and I go for a long road ride," I suggest enthusiastically.

Jocelyn isn't playing along. "No way! I want to go to the party!" she whines. "Please, please, please!" She folds her hands together in supplication and gives Lizzie a *please help me* look.

"It will be fine," Lizzie assures me. "I'll keep my eyes on her."

"No drugs or drinking," I insist.

Nikeo snickers. "Right."

Lizzie, who's standing close to Nikeo, thwacks him on the back of the head. "Hey, it's not like that! It's a *girl's only* swimming party. Just some of my friends hanging out. It's like, no big deal."

Jocelyn looks pleadingly at me. With her skin clearing up thanks to the medication, she looks years older and more confident. Despite my reservations, and I have many, I grant her the freedom she desires. "Fine, you can go, but don't do anything stupid."

She and Lizzie squeal with delight and practically skip down the hall to Lizzie's bedroom, already planning their outfits for the evening.

"Don't do anything stupid," parrots Nikeo. "Famous last words."

I scowl. "It'll be fine."

"Keep telling yourself that."

I drain my anxiety with a long run up a mountain. Still not completely acclimated to the elevation, I gasp and wheeze for the first half hour. When my breathing finally regulates, my thoughts wander aimlessly, ending up in the past on the night that Justice and I had strolled through the Boerner Botanical Gardens in Milwaukee on a clear June evening.

Though I had only finished one year of college and wasn't quite nineteen, I knew that I wanted to marry him and told him this as we walked hand in hand.

"You're sure about that?" he asked.

"I've been sure since I met you, since the night you showed up at Frank and Grandma Betty's wedding when I was in high school."

"Don't get ahead of yourself," he warned. "You might not want to marry me in a few years."

"I'm always ahead of myself, and you know that I never change my mind," I declared confidently. "Don't you want to marry me?"

Justice pulled me into the circle of his arms and kissed me until I was breathless. "Name the time and the place, and I'll be there."

The trail ends. I've summited the mountain and have nowhere to go but down. Pivoting, I look at how far I've come and wish that I didn't have to return to where I started.

*****

At eight that night, I'm in bed reading the last twenty pages of *Love's Last Call,* a rather explicit romance that features a steamy love triangle. The heroine is torn between a bad boy bartender and her nerdy but nice boyfriend banker. I can relate to her plight.

Caprice knocks once, enters my room, and tosses the phone at me.

"Grandma Betty," she says.

I wince. Grandma Betty isn't going to be happy with me. She's called several times this week, and even though for once Lizzie dutifully relayed the messages, I haven't bothered to call back.

"Hi, Grandma Betty, I'm —"

Before I can eke out an apology, she's on me like white on rice. "Sugar Cane! We've been trying to reach you for days. I can't believe you haven't called me back," she gripes.

"I'm sorry. I got the messages, but I've been busy with work." I've also been busy trying to keep my hands and mouth off of Nikeo, but I don't share this with her. I go for a fast and furious subject change. "How's Florida?"

"Absolutely gorgeous. Frank and I have painted and decorated every room. I've done some gardening, but I'm not used to the tropical plants just yet, and the soil is so sandy that I think we're going to have to bring in some topsoil. I joined a knitting club and met some great gals and am planning all sorts of crocheting and knitting projects right now. We finally found a church, nothing like Grace Lutheran back home, but it will do."

"I'm glad."

"You know that I'm not calling to talk about Florida," she says meaningfully. "How are you? What have you been up to?"

I'm wearing my engagement ring, but I almost sucked another man's finger, though I suppose I should be thankful it wasn't something else. I respond generically, "I'm good. Been working a lot and spending a lot of time with Jocelyn."

"Oh, that's nice. So, I called Justice today," she says.

The classic buttinski, Grandma Betty can't help but intervene; nonetheless, her announcement catches me off guard. I leap out of bed, the sudden change in position making me faint. My pulse takes off like a rocket ship, and my stomach drops to my knees. "Why?"

"I called him because all of this is nonsense. I called him because I'm worried about you."

"Why? I'm perfectly fine."

She sighs severely. "I don't think you are. You weren't thinking clearly when you made the decision to leave. You're going to regret this, Cane."

"How do you know that?" I demand, even though I'm already regretting so much of what happened. "I had to get away to think this through. He gave me my mom's ring! What if the same thing happens to me that happened to Mom and Dad? I feel like I'm following too closely in their footsteps. I'm not sure I want to marry so young and live in the same town as my parents and end up pregnant after only a year of being married. What if something happens to me or to Justice? What if one of us dies in some awful way, in a car wreck like they did? I feel like I'm repeating history, like I'm destined to end up dead before my life even starts, just like them!"

"Oh, Cane," she cries, distraught. "Is that what this is about? Is that the real reason you left?"

I've shocked both her and myself with this revelation. I'm continually amazed at how this tragedy that happened so long ago has affected the trajectory of my life. Trembling, I sit on the edge of my mattress.

"Call him and talk to him," she urges. "Tell him what you just told me."

"It's gotten … complicated." I can't and won't tell her of the love triangle in which I'm trapped, or should I dub it a *lust triangle.* What I feel for Nikeo certainly can't be defined as love, can it?

"He's as desperate for news of you as you are of him. Why don't you go home where you belong?"

"I can't. I need more time."

"But what if time runs out?"

I hear Frank in the background asking to talk to me. "Put him on," I say to Grandma Betty.

She passes the phone to him.

"Sugar Cane, how's Colorado?" he asks.

"Beautiful. Jocelyn and I are having a good time."

"That's good. Any thoughts on when you'll be coming to visit us?"

"I'm not sure yet."

"We miss you." In a quieter voice, he adds, "Betty's having a hard time with you being so far away."

"I'm having a hard time with it, too. I miss both of you," I admit.

A long silence follows. Frank meddles only when absolutely necessary, and just when I think he may throw in his two cents about the situation, he asks, "Seen any good storms out there in those Rocky Mountains?"

Frank, a storm aficionado, has cultivated an unusual hobby out of photographing and videotaping thunderstorms, tornadoes, and blizzards. He puts himself in harm's way all the time to capture the perfect footage. He should have been a meteorologist.

"I've seen some spectacular lightning and rain here," I tell him.

"Well then, put that new video camera to use!"

Grandma Betty objects in the background. "Under no circumstances is she going to videotape a storm! Absolutely not."

Frank laughs. "I'm sure you heard that, didn't you? Okay, okay, no storm chasing, but make sure you take some pictures and video footage of the beautiful scenery."

As soon as I'm off the phone, I rummage through my luggage and remove the video camera. I haven't held it in my hands since the night I left. Turning off all the lights, I sit down in the dark, turn on the power, and press play. For the next forty-five minutes, I watch my personal drama unfold. The surprise proposal. The well wishes from friends and family. Drunken, rambling toasts. Uncoordinated dancing. My stunned reaction to the dream house. Mikayla's horror at discovering a secret long kept from her. My absurd reaction to Mikayla's slurred revelation about kissing Justice-I hadn't realized how intoxicated she'd been. Justice's level-headed entreaties.

When it's finished, I push the video camera aside and pick up the silver compass that sits on my night-stand. I'm in a dark room in Colorado miles away from the life that I had always wanted to live.

I'm lost. I don't know if I will fight for the life I wanted with Justice or walk away from it.

CHAPTER TWELVE

At four thirty in the morning I wake in a cold sweat with my hands curled around the silver compass trying to recover from the disconcerting, *very real* dream I'd just had. It's as close as I've come to a vision about Mikayla in a very long time, and what I saw, I couldn't believe.

Flipping on my side, I discover the trundle bed where Jocelyn has been sleeping is empty. My sleepy brain slowly connects the dots. She went to a party with Lizzie. It's four thirty in the morning. Her bed hasn't been slept in. Which means ... *she never came home.*

My adrenaline levels spike, and instantly, I'm wide awake, heart pounding, palms sweating. Is she still at the party? Is she drunk, high, or worse? What if she's dead at the bottom of the pool? What if there were guys at this girl's-only party and one of them took advantage of a young girl!

My mind starts assembling more terrifying hypotheticals. In full-blown panic, I bound out of bed, sprint down the hall, and throw open the door to Lizzie's room. Snuggled deep in a sleeping bag on the floor next to Lizzie's bed, Jocelyn slumbers peacefully.

The adrenaline slowly leaches out of my system. Shaking, I quietly close the door and take a deep breath. Knowing that I'll never be able to go back asleep, not after the dream and certainly not after thinking that something happened to Jocelyn, I decide to go for a run.

When I return home an hour later and am stretching in the garage, Nikeo comes out wearing his biking gear.

He gives me a cursory glance. "Go get your bike shorts and shoes on. We're going for a ride." He lifts his bike off of the ceiling hook and settles it on the ground.

He's right in my field of vision, and I can't help but notice his hard thighs and the way his fitted bike jersey displays defined biceps. "I'm not going anywhere with you."

"Just get dressed and get on the damn bike."

"Get a hearing aid, because I'm tired of repeating myself. The answer is no. By the way, Jocelyn didn't get into any trouble last night. She came home from the party, without incident," I inform him.

He situates himself on the bike seat and clips one of his shoes into the pedal. "So what, do you want me to congratulate you on this, or do you want me to say that I was wrong?"

I snarl at him. "I can't stand you."

"Maybe not, but I can promise you this." He wheels his bike over to me. "You also can't get enough of me. By the way, talked to Caprice last night. You're going to have to clean Mrs. Kazinski's house this morning. I don't clean. Like I said, it's in my contract."

With that pompous declaration, he clips in and rides off into the dewy, cool morning. A coiled snake of hatred sits inside my stomach and is ready to strike him down with venom, but he's too far away for an attack. Disgusted, I stomp into the house.

I take one for the *Maid Right in Time* team and reluctantly load my car with cleaning supplies. Jocelyn is supposed to go with me and help, but she begs off at the last minute to accompany Lizzie.

Wanting to impress Mrs. Kazinski with our professionalism and punctuality, I arrive promptly for the morning appointment. When I survey the yard, I cringe. This might not go as smoothly as I'd hoped.

Littered with rusted-out cars, plastic milk crates, and assorted garbage, including what appears to be a used adult diaper, I haven't arrived at a residence as much as I've arrived at a dumping ground. The house itself, a brick ranch with rotting wood trim, bows out at the bottom and seems to be sinking into the ground. If the exterior is a reflection of the interior, I'm in trouble.

The garage door opens, squeaking loudly and disturbing the fifteen or so cats that have been lurking in the weeds. Caterwauling, they run past me.

"Over here!" Mrs. Kazinski waves me down. "Come in through

the garage. Ain't no way you gonna get in through the front door. My grandson, he's got all his stuff piled high in the living room."

"Okay, be there in a second." I take a deep breath to prepare myself for what I'm about to face, and I instantly regret doing so. Saturated with the pungent odor of cat urine, diesel fumes, and grime, the air is noxious. It's a carcinogenic playground around here.

I lug all the supplies through the garage as instructed. Mrs. Kazinski, who resembles an ailing toad, gives me a toothless smile when I introduce myself.

"This is going to be free, right? No charge."

"That was the arrangement."

She nods. "Good. Start in the bathroom. You'll have to skip the bedrooms. Too much crap jammed in there. Kitchen and living room also need it bad. Not sure the last time I vacuumed. Arthritic knees and hips make it hard to move. How long will it take you?"

"That depends," I respond, noncommittally, knowing instinctively that I should turn around and make a run for it. I follow behind her, traversing the precarious pathway through the garage, stepping over miscellaneous boxes, pairs of shoes, tools, and countless black bags of mystery items. Garbage? Dead cats? Bodies?

I step inside the house and cry out in horror.

Mrs. Kazinski gives me a strange look. "What's wrong?"

What's wrong? Isn't it obvious? I'm in a microcosm of hell! There are things stacked on every surface, shoved into every corner, and spilling out of every cabinet. Rotting food. Magazines. Newspapers. Outdated electronics. Clothing. Wrapping paper. Silverware. A litter box smack in the middle of the kitchen floor that's overflowing with feces and saturated with urine.

My eyes stray to the yellowed ceiling. Why are there Halloween decorations strung across the ceiling … you've *got* to be *kidding* me! That's a *real* spider-web, crawling with *real spiders!*

"Hey!" Mrs. Kazinski shouts.

She then licks her lips and jerks her neck in such quick succession it's uncanny. Perhaps she really is a toad.

"I need to know how long because I've got to get busy canning in the kitchen! I making jam to sell at the roadside stand!" she states emphatically.

That's her stand on the corner? Those cute little jars of jam come from this place? My breakfast considers making a fast reappearance. I back away from Toad Lady. "I'm sorry, but I have to leave."

"You just got here! You have to stay and clean. Now you stay and do what you told me you would do. You said a *free cleaning!*"

"Maybe you should try another maid service. Better yet, try a bulldozer," I remark candidly.

I push open the garage door and head toward my car.

"You come back here!"

I've already popped the trunk and am putting everything back, when Mrs. Kazinski hops over. "I don't understand why you aren't doing what you said you were going to do!"

Is she honestly that clueless? Does she not know that her house should be condemned, that it's unsuitable for humans to be living there, that she probably has mold or something worse growing in her lungs from breathing in the air?

I'm never one to gloss things over, so I hit her over the head with the truth. "Honestly? The reason I'm not staying is because your house is beyond help. It should be bulldozed to the ground. You shouldn't be living in there, let alone making food in there and selling it. I don't have a hazmat suit with me, so, no, I'm not staying."

"How dare you speak to me like that! You're nothing but a smart-mouth brat! If you want to stay in business, then you'll have to act more professional."

Ignoring her insults, I buckle my seat belt and start the car. Stationed at the passenger window, she thrusts her tongue out again and again as if she's trying to catch a fly on her tongue. If she doesn't move, I can't leave. Her feet are in the path of my front tire.

"Please move. I'm going to end up crushing your toes," I tell her.

Before I know what she's doing, she sticks her wrinkled, bumpy arm in through the open window and flicks me hard right between the eyes with all the power her arthritic fingers can muster.

Ouch!

I rub the stinging spot and try to get the eye watering under control. Once I recover from the shock, I frown angrily. "What was that for?"

"If you have to ask, then you're a lost cause! Somebody should have taken the switch to you when you were a girl."

I back out the driveway, spitting gravel in every direction and nearly taking out two cats. Toad Lady raises her fist to me, and I resist the urge to raise my middle finger.

When I arrive home, I'm surprised to find Caprice in the kitchen.

"What are you doing back already?" she asks, glancing at the clock. "You couldn't have cleaned that fast. You've barely been gone an hour."

"See this red spot?" I point to my forehead. "Client abuse. I should have called the cops. Mrs. Kazinski was certifiable." I tell Caprice what had happened and about the appalling condition of her house.

She laughs. "Glad I dodged that bullet."

"I didn't. Shot right between the eyes. I would rather clean for Misty Moreland every day for a month than return to that place."

I open the fridge and grab a Gatorade.

Unscrewing the top, I take a long drink and glance at the clock. I've no desire to work right now. "Want to go running?" I ask.

Caprice gives me a funny look and then out of nowhere says, "You slept with Nikeo, didn't you? You two totally hooked up."

"Absolutely not!" I reply instantly. A scorching blush starts in the tip of my toes, zooms up my legs, ignites my torso, and engulfs my neck and head in flames.

She gives me a *yeah right* smile.

Sighing in frustration, I hold the Gatorade up to my flushed forehead. "It's the truth. I haven't," I say pitifully.

"Seriously?"

"Seriously, no, I haven't, but I can't stop thinking about him," I admit. "You know Justice. You know he's perfect for me-he's good for me. And then, there's your cousin. He's so bad for me, and yet . . ."

"You can't help yourself." She chuckles. "It's obvious he's having that effect. Jocelyn's worried. She came to talk to me the other night."

This news stuns me. "What did she say?"

Caprice, perpetually uncomfortable in her bikini, wriggles her torso and then unhooks the back. Her perfect boobs pop out. Twirling it on the tip of her finger, she launches it across the room. "That thing was driving me nuts!"

It lands on the neck of Nikeo's guitar. She laughs. "He's going to love finding that there."

"Your nudity isn't inspiring. I get enough of it at Arlene's house."

Caprice sticks out her chest. "You love it."

I roll my eyes. "You are aware that you're running a business out of this house? Soon enough we'll have a secretary who probably won't want to see you naked. You can't just start stripping down."

"Why the hell not? I can do what I want, and if anyone has a problem, they can take it up with the boss, who happens to be me," she says in her Italian *don't mess with me* voice. "Come on, let's go running and continue this conversation outside." She swaggers out of the kitchen down the hall.

Once Caprice is appropriately dressed in running attire and we're outside on the path, we continue where we left off.

"Jocelyn wanted me to tell Nikeo to stay away from you. She can see what's happening. She would have to be blind not to. Obviously, I didn't say anything to him. It's none of my business what goes on between you two. Now, if he hurts you in any way at all, then it's my business, and I'll pummel him."

"I have no doubt about that."

We take a conversation hiatus as we ascend a large hill. Caprice's competitive nature takes over; she sets a grueling pace. Not to be outdone, I up the ante, running faster, and by the time we summit, we're both in anaerobic hell.

I push my body to the breaking point. As my heart rate maxes out and my muscles scream for reprieve, everything inside rises to the surface at once, including the worrisome nightmare I had before waking this morning.

When my breathing slows, I tell Caprice about it. "I had a dream this morning. Justice was with Mikayla at a church. They were standing at an altar together. I think they were going to get married or something.

What do you make of that? Jocelyn said that they'd been spending a lot of time together. I don't want to take a step further in my head, but it seemed so real."

"It was only a dream."

Her assurance doesn't calm me. I can't shake the feeling that something is off. My sixth sense, a roaring lion, can't be quieted. No matter how hard I try to clamp my hand over its mouth, I keep getting mauled. "Only, it didn't feel like one. It felt more like one of those premonitions I have when something's wrong with Mikayla."

Caprice cocks an eyebrow. "There are many things wrong with Mikayla, and the only reason you had that dream is because you don't trust her with Justice. For good reason I might add."

We stop to rest and look out over the green, rocky valley. This place doesn't feel like home to me. I'm not sure it ever will. But, it feels like a chance at having a life I never imagined.

CHAPTER THIRTEEN

I'm up on a ladder, attacking dust bunnies that have made their home on the top of Arlene's ceiling fan. Ever since I arrived this morning, she's been following me around the house making small talk. I suspect she's lonely; Skeeter and his infamous peter are out of town on a fishing trip. I only hope he wears clothing. Hooking worms in a boat with a naked man — one wouldn't want a mistake to be made.

Arlene glances up at me. "You okay up there? I don't want you to lose your balance and fall. I hate heights. Get me two inches off the ground, and I'm a basket case."

"I'm good," I assure her.

She straddles a kitchen stool to watch me work. Not for the first time, I think that maybe bleaching the seats should be part of the regular cleaning routine around here.

"How exciting that Caprice is throwing that party tonight. I just received the invitation in the mail a few days ago. I so wish I wasn't hosting book club this evening. Are you going?" she asks.

Thanks to my ingenious marketing skills, though I have to give credit to Nikeo as well, business has tripled since my arrival. Yesterday, right in front of me of course, Caprice stripped out of her bikini for the last time. She's officially finished with cleaning. To celebrate the momentous occasion and thriving empire she's building, she's hosting an elaborate party at The Elephant Ear for the now eighteen staff members and more than two hundred clients.

I climb down from the ladder. "I plan on going. You could always cancel your book club. We would love to have you." *As long as all your bits and pieces are covered,* I want to add.

"Oh!" She snaps her fingers. "I almost forgot." She slides off the stool and runs from the room.

When she's out of sight, I stick out my tongue in disgust. When she or Skeeter moves that quickly, it's far from flattering.

"Found it!" she announces from the other room and hurries back to the kitchen.

She hands me the new Nicholas Sparks book she was telling me about today. "My book club members would lynch me if they knew I read stuff like this! Most of them are former teachers and librarians, and they only appreciate the highly literary. Me, on the other hand, I like a good love story now and then. Something that doesn't make you think too much. I remember you saying you like to read romances, and this is such a good one, you have to read it."

"Thank you for the offer. I'm sure I would like it, but I can't take it." I set it on the counter.

"Now don't be silly. Sure you can!"

"It's just that I'm not sure how much longer I'm going to be in town. I might be leaving," I confess. "Very soon," I add for good measure.

Though I haven't told anyone, not even Grandma Betty when she called last night to once again remind me that I needed to stop being so obstinate and go home and make things right with Justice, I've been plotting my exit strategy.

My relationship with Nikeo has become so intense, I can't see straight. One minute I'm enraged with him for some smart-ass remark he made or something that he did that I'm positive I'll end up on death row for first degree intentional homicide, and the next minute, I want to pull a Caprice and strip off my clothes and throw myself at him. We're like two boxers taunting and circling each other in the ring. We fight constantly, about everything from politics to religion. In all areas of my life, I party with the conservatives, and Nikeo tangos with the liberals. I believe in the Lord and Savior Jesus Christ, and although he doesn't label himself an atheist, he believes that Darwin might have been onto something. Even in our silences there's opposition. An argument is always brewing.

The other evening during a bike ride, we had an animated debate concerning the institution of marriage. He defended his view that it was outdated, unnecessary, and always ends up being a sexless union where neither party was happy. Whereas I vehemently proclaimed that marriage, the ultimate form of commitment and love that was sanctioned by God himself, was a timeless and wonderful tradition. The tradition wasn't screwed up, I argued, people were. They didn't take it seriously enough or take enough time to make sure they were marrying the right person.

Right after this announcement, my tire flatted. Nikeo got off his bike and came over to me. I thought he was going to help fix the flat, but instead, he took hold of my helmet and got right in my face and told me the only reason I believed in marriage was because I wanted security. He waited for my rebuttal, and I'm sure I had one somewhere but I simply couldn't think of what to say. He was two inches from my face. I wanted to kiss him, but I didn't give him the satisfaction. Instead, I demanded that he fix my tire immediately.

Nikeo, who never takes kindly to orders and never seems keen on helping anyway, repaid me by getting back on his bike and leaving me. I was forced to walk the bike two miles home.

"Leaving! But so soon! Don't you like it here?" Arlene asks.

I think of Nikeo in my face the other night and how strong my desire was and how close I was to saying *oh what the hell* and doing something I couldn't take back. "I like it here too much, which is why I need to go back home."

Confused by my response, she furrows her brow and smiles kindly. "It seems silly to leave if you like it here. Selfishly, Skeeter and I would hate to lose you! We've gone through quite a few house cleaners, and it's all because of our lifestyle. They were downright rude and critical. Some wouldn't even come inside the house! I was just about to give up on finding a maid service when Caprice came into our lives, and then a few months later she sent you! Just like her, you're so accepting and such a blessing in our lives!" She places her hand on mine and smiles kindly.

Me, a blessing? She's giving me way too much credit. "Thank you."

"Make sure you think things through. I've learned a few lessons in my time and hasty decisions aren't always the best ones."

She's preaching to the choir, though as for learning that lesson once and for all, I'm not there yet.

*****

Caprice's party may go down in the *Guinness Book of World Records* as one of the rowdiest. A large number of cleaning clients and employees are milling around The Elephant Ear, and they're primed and ready to party.

Over the past ninety minutes, I'd observed shots disappearing off trays at an astonishing rate, people channeling Patrick Swayze and dirty dancing their hearts out, and blatant under-the-table groping between Lizzie and some random, handsome man. The groping had been headed in a *something that would only happen at a Playboy Mansion party* direction, and so I'd walked over and pulled Lizzie's hand off of his crotch. In turn, he discreetly removed his hand from under her skirt, where I'm sure he'd been taking advantage of her *no panties* policy.

My premature intervention hadn't gone over so well. The man closed his eyes in frustration, and Lizzie gave me a dirty look.

"What's your problem?" Lizzie asked.

"Jocelyn's watching," I reminded her. I glanced down at the end of the table where Jocelyn sat chomping on her standard dinner fare, fresh vegetables thanks to Lizzie's influence, and laughing at something Caprice had said. "Not to mention that Caprice would kill you if she knew what you were doing or what you were about to do."

After whispering something into the man's ear, which made him smile and lick his lips, Lizzie rose from the table and pulled me off to the side for a private chat. "Cane, I swear it's no wonder why Jocelyn wants to hang around with me. She told me the other day that sometimes you are so focused on doing the right thing that you miss out on all the fun."

Jocelyn had said that about me? My face must have registered surprise, because then Lizzie said, "What? You don't see it? You act like a self-righteous church lady or something."

"Better than being a drunken, carrot-munching pot addict who sleeps around," I fired back.

"You see?" She pushed her finger against my chest. "Point proven. It's so nice to know that's all you think I am."

She stalked off, and I stood there feeling like a judgmental idiot. If they made muzzles for tongues, I would be the first to buy one.

Now that dinner is over, more guests are making their way to the dance floor. Unarmed Scandal, the same band that had played when Nikeo and I came here last month, is doing a sound check. Jocelyn and Nikeo are sitting at a table near the front of the stage. Lizzie and her groping friend are at the outside bar taking advantage of the free beer; I see him eyeing her skirt. I'm sure he's contemplating his next treasure hunt.

Rolling my eyes, I take a long slurp of my ice water on the rocks with a splash of lemon. I'm living on the edge with this drink. Church lady isn't too far off base.

Caprice, looking disgruntled and on the verge of pummeling someone, sits down next to me. "This night's playing out like a *Girls Gone Wild* video. It will be a miracle if we don't get kicked out, and I hope I don't have to kick someone's ass before the night is out."

"Who are you kidding? You would love to kick someone's ass. It's been way too long since you've gotten in a bar fight and thrown someone across the room."

Junior year in college, Caprice, Justice, and I had gone to a bar to hear a friend's band play. At the end of the evening, Caprice had placed a twenty-dollar bill on the bar along with our bill, and when she turned away, a girl wearing a miniskirt and half shirt that revealed a flabby tattooed abdomen pilfered the money and shoved it down the front of her shirt. I called the girl on it. She denied it. Why bother with words, I thought.

I reached down the top of her shirt and plucked it from her bra where I'd seen her put it. Caprice was infuriated, and so was the girl. Tempers flared. Name calling ensued.

Knowing that a *scratch your eyes out* girl fight was imminent, Justice tried to restore the peace. He handed the money directly to the bartender to pay our bill and then guided Caprice and I toward the door, urging us to take the high road. Caprice had stayed on the high road and even minded the speed limit until the girl called her a, "cheap whore" at the top of her lungs.

Caprice whipped around, ran over to the girl, lifted her clear off the floor, and threw her three feet. She landed in some guy's lap. Sensing conflict, the unruly crowd started chanting, and Caprice, who was all too willing to put on a show, was about to go in for more when Justice picked her up bear hug–style and lugged her out of the bar.

"True. A good bar fight always makes for an interesting night, and" — she smiles mischievously — "this time there's no one to stop me. Did you see what happened over there?" she asks.

"What? More under-the-table hand jobs going on?"

This throws her for a second. "Don't tell me you're serious."

I glance over at Lizzie, who now has her tongue in the guy's ear. "Not completely," I mumble.

Caprice follows my line of vision and spots her cousin getting cozy at the bar, but she doesn't ask for the details. She knows perfectly well what Lizzie does in her spare time.

"Anyway," she continues, "turns out we didn't need to have Arlene show up to get some nudity. The two new *Maid Hot* girls, Lara and Sandy, came straight from work and decided to wear their bikinis."

"I know. I saw them. By the way, Lara's is way too small. Her nipples have been playing a game of peek-a-boo all night. Every time I look over at her one of them is staring at me like some pointy third eye."

"No kidding. She decided it would be a good idea to take off her top. To make matters worse, Sandy followed her lead. They were shaking their tits and had a circle of men around them waving dollar bills in their faces. Good thing I found them and not the restaurant management. It's not exactly the kind of impression I wanted to make tonight."

"Hate to point out the obvious, but *Maid Hot?* Sex sells, and even though it's a cleaning business, you're kind of selling the sex, too. Bikinis. Hot girls. Throwing a party at a bar and grill —"

"I get your point," she says, cutting me off. "Still, professionalism is almost a must. I fired them and told them to leave, which leaves me two employees short. Which means, my cleaning days aren't quite over yet."

Unarmed Scandal finishes up a song, and then the lead singer says that one of his good friends is going to play the next few songs with them.

"This is going to be good. He's going to kill it," says Caprice, rubbing her hands together in anticipating.

"Who?"

"You didn't know?" She drains my ice water, and I can tell she's disappointed with my beverage choice and was expecting something stronger. "Nikeo is friends with Adam, the lead singer. He's playing a set with them tonight. He's been practicing for days. I thought he would have told you."

Now that she mentions it, I have noticed that he's been playing his guitar for hours every night and not once have I heard a Clapton song. "I had no clue, but that's no surprise since we're currently not speaking."

She crunches an ice cube and rolls her eyes. "Why?"

"He made me walk my bike home the other night after refusing to help me fix a flat tire."

Her stare says *you're full of shit.* "You and I both know that has nothing to do with it."

"Remember, Justice? The nice guy? I'm engaged to him. And, Nikeo, he's not a nice guy."

"He's not that bad. He has a good heart. Besides, being nice has nothing to do with attraction. Look at all the guys I've dated. Absolute jerks, but hey, the chemistry was out of this world."

Nikeo takes the stage and picks up a guitar from a stand near the microphone. Caprice looks over at me. "You might want to think about taking Justice's words to heart. He gave you three months of freedom and permission to date other people."

Apparently, in addition to his good looks and killer guitar skills, Nikeo's a natural on stage. Relaxed and playful, he plays with a Pink Floyd line as he introduces himself. "Go easy on me. I'm just a lost soul swimming in a fish-bowl, running over the same old ground," he says. Then, he starts playing a riff with the band backing him up, and all of sudden they transition into the actual song with Nikeo singing lead.

He's doing it so well I wonder if he's ever considered a career in the music industry. A musician. A singer. An almost lawyer. A successful businessman. Is there anything he can't do?

The women in the crowd, including Jocelyn, swoon. If I'm not mistaken, I'm feeling a little faint myself. With my eyes still honed in on Nikeo, I blindly reach for my glass of ice water, thinking that maybe I should dump it on my head to cool myself down.

While he's strumming and singing and winning over all the women, who I'm sure if given the chance would go home with him tonight, he looks right at me with hooded eyes and just enough of a dirty smile to suggest licentiousness. It's a searing look that brands me right between the legs.

Caprice punches me in the shoulder hard and softly says, "He gave you permission, remember?"

I literally have to tear my eyes away from Nikeo. In my head I can almost hear a ripping sound. While I'm trying to figure out what she just said, she lifts a cocktail napkin to my lips and pats.

"For the drool."

Snorting, I push her away. "I wasn't drooling."

"If you say so."

I'm about to disagree when Harriet shuffles over, holding onto her walker and grinning.

I jump up. "You came!" In a display of enthusiastic affection, I wrap my arms around her.

"I wouldn't miss a great party. Oh boy, that young man up on stage, he sure can sing." She gets into the groove of the music, bobbing her head and smiling. "A handsome devil, he is."

"Here, sit, sit." I pull out a chair for her.

"Nice to see you, Harriet," Caprice greets her warmly with a hug. "I miss seeing you every week."

Harriet eases herself onto the chair. "I miss seeing you, too, dear, but this one here," she says, nodding at me, "she's an absolute doll and a sweetheart through and through. Honestly, I've never met anyone as sweet as this child. There's not one bad bone in her body."

That's an oversell. Clearly, she hasn't been around me long enough. I laugh uncomfortably.

Amused by Harriet's glowing praise of my character, Caprice flashes a *I can't believe you have her snowed* smile my way. My best friend and roommate, she's seen the light and dark in me and knows that my true nature is often laced with toxic cynicism.

"I'm glad it worked out. If you'll excuse me, I'm going to go greet some of the other clients who just arrived," Caprice says as she glances toward a group of businessmen who are standing at the bar.

Harriet gives her blessing. "By all means! Go mingle."

Caprice kisses her cheek. "My first and best client."

Harriet pats her hand. "You're such a dear."

When Caprice leaves, Harriet sways in her seat moving to the beat of the music. Nikeo and the band have started a new song, "Omaha" by Counting Crows. He sounds amazing. He looks over at me again, and not wanting to feel the delicious sting of his eyes, I look away.

Smiling wistfully, Harriet looks from Nikeo to me. "I have a thing for musicians, too."

Am I that transparent? I flatten my hands over my flushed cheeks and smile at Harriet. "That's Nikeo, he's just a … friend."

Harriet smiles, and I know I'm not fooling her, or anyone else for that matter.

"Joe played in a navy jazz band. That's how I met him. My girlfriends and I went to a dance hall, and he was up there on the stage in his naval uniform singing his heart out. You've seen that picture of him hanging in the hall, haven't you, the one where he's on stage?"

More than anything, Harriet loves to talk about the past and about the life she spent years building. Most of all, she loves to talk about her beloved husband, Joe. I've learned much about him. I know that after a hard rain, he loved to dance in the puddles with his two daughters. Every Saturday morning, he made pancakes and eggs for his family. Sometimes at night if Harriet had trouble sleeping, he sang to her. I've learned so much about this man that I sense both his presence and absence in the house. Every time I dust that picture that hangs in the hall, the one where he's standing on stage in a black suit with his hands curled around a microphone, his mouth open, belting out a tune that I can almost hear when I close my eyes, a wave of sadness washes over me. "I adore that picture of him. I wish I could have met him," I tell her.

"I was a goner the second I heard him. I knew that he was the one. My, how he could sing! I would like to meet the woman who can resist a man that sings well."

I chance another look at Nikeo, and I can't help but compare him to Justice. Tone-deaf and cursed with two left thumbs, Justice can't carry a tune or play an instrument, despite the four years of piano lessons his mother forced him to take. "I wonder why women go so crazy for musicians."

"My Joe? He wasn't a big talker. Wasn't big on telling me his feelings. Men say what they need to say and that's about it. They don't see the point in talking like us girls, so they close themselves off. Now, when they sing or when they play a guitar like that one up there" — she pauses and regards Nikeo with affection — "they let you in on all their secrets. They show you their soul and let you see all sorts of hidden things."

With catlike grace, Nikeo creeps closer to the microphone. He cradles his guitar like a lover and closes his eyes as he serenades the crowd with the last verse, singing about getting to the heart of the matter and about how the heart matters more. He's not just singing the words. He's feeling them. He's telling his story through the song and uncovering truths about himself and about me.

Then, he looks directly at me. Something powerful passes between us. I'm thankful he isn't close enough to touch, because right now, right this second, I can't even feel the ring on my finger. In this moment, I want to be part of his story, and I would do anything to write myself into his life.

Apparently, everyone around me feels the same way. The crowd chants his name and demands another song from him. He gives them a cockeyed smile. "I'm feeling generous, maybe just one more."

"Don't leave," Harriet says adamantly. Her beautiful, wizened face relaxes around the edges. She wraps her hand around mine. "It would be a mistake." She looks at Nikeo and then back to me. "You have to figure this out."

While cleaning at her house today, I'd told her that I was thinking about going home to the love of my life. And, tonight, I've betrayed my fickle allegiance and humiliated myself. I can deny it all I want, but it's obvious that right now there are two men in my life. The love triangle has been delineated. "I'm not sure I can figure it out," I lament. "I've been trying."

Adam, the lead singer of Unarmed Scandal, asks the crowd to show their love for Nikeo, and they enthusiastically oblige. Nikeo stays on stage for an encore.

"Have a little faith in yourself, dear." Taking off her shawl, she tosses it over her walker. "Now! This is a party, right? Where can we find a bartender! I need a dirty martini, and what are you having?" she asks as she eyes up my empty glass with the dehydrated, flattened lemon wedge. "I'll get you a drink."

I'm not going to let the eighty-five-year-old with a bum hip drink me under the table. "I'll have the same. I'll go and get them," I offer.

Two martinis and an hour and half later, Harriet says that she's all partied out. I'm ashamed to admit that I am as well, perhaps more than she is. After I call the cab service for her and safely deposit her in the back-seat, I return to find Caprice and inform her that I'm leaving as well.

As I'm looking through the crowd and trying not to wobble on my feet from those martinis, it occurs to me that I haven't seen Jocelyn since she was admiring Nikeo on stage. I do a thorough search of the area, but I don't spot her anywhere.

I go from over the legal limit to panic-induced sobriety, and I knife my way through the crowd again. Nothing. Where the hell could she be? She wouldn't have walked back to the house.

I find Caprice chatting it up with some potential clients whom she's invited, and I discreetly interrupt and ask if she's seen Jocelyn.

"Last I saw, she was listening to Nikeo."

"That was over two hours ago." I flash her a *help me* plea with my eyes, but she responds with an impatient, tight-lipped smile.

"She's got to be around here somewhere. Ask Lizzie."

Her suggestion is perfectly logical, and I'm sure if I weren't drunk I would have thought of it. If I find Lizzie, I find Jocelyn. Problem solved. Weaving and bobbing my way through the over-zealous, over-served crowd, I search for Lizzie. I'm not having any luck, and I play detective and interrogate some of the *Maid Hot* employees, but no one is particularly interested in helping me find her.

Finally, I locate Lizzie behind the stage smoking pot with Unarmed Scandal's drummer, bass player, and Lara and Sandy, the two wannabe strippers that Caprice fired earlier this evening.

"Where's Jocelyn?"

She reacts like it's the funniest thing she's ever heard. "Jocelyn? Who's Jocelyn?"

Drunk and peeved, I get in Lizzie's face. "I don't have time for this crap. She's missing."

"How is that my problem?"

"She's your friend."

Lizzie reaches for the joint that's being passed to her by the drummer. "More like an annoying kid sister. It's the first night in weeks that I've had space."

"You have no idea where she could be?"

After taking an indulgent hit off the joint, her eyes glaze over. "Apologize for what you said earlier."

"I'm not going to apologize."

"Then I'm not telling you where she is," she replies in a singsong voice.

"You think this is funny?"

Lizzie crosses her legs and assumes a Zen-like expression. "Chill out. She's fine, okay?"

I remove the joint from between Lizzie's narrow fingers and toss it on the ground. The drummer, who seems to have an aversion to showering, reaches for it, but I move quicker. Planting the sole of my shoe on the lit joint, I drag my foot over it, leaving only a crumbling patch of ash and paper.

"You little *bitch.* That was my *last one!* What the *hell* is your problem?"

I give him an icy stare. "Do you want a list of them? Because I can make one, although it might take me all night. Give me your address, and I'll be sure to drop it by first thing tomorrow morning."

Clearly not comprehending, he shakes his head in a perfect Scooby-Doo imitation and stares blankly at me. "Wait … what?"

I turn my attention back to Lizzie. "Tell me where she is."

She crosses her arms and gives me a jaunty smile. "Apology?"

If it means finding Jocelyn and preventing her face from showing up on the back of milk cartons across the country, I'm willing to flush my pride down the toilet. I deliver an apology that's as close to heartfelt as it's going to get right now. "I'm sorry for what I said earlier."

"I don't know *exactly* where she is, some party. One of my friends said she was having a party, but I can't remember who. Maybe Tyanne? Maybe Becky? Jocelyn wanted to go, so she went."

"Where do they live?"

"They both live in town."

"She's *seventeen,* Lizzie. I need specifics. Addresses. She could be in trouble!"

"I'm not sure where they live. I've never been to either of their houses."

"Last names?"

"No idea."

Drummer boy gives me a nasty look. "Are you a detective or something?"

"Undercover police officer," I respond glibly.

Stoned out of his mind, drummer boy takes this literally and beats it.

"Great!" Lizzie snaps. "Why did you have to scare him away? I like him!"

I snap my fingers. "Let's focus here. How did she get to this party? When did she leave?"

"I think, maybe with my buddy, Kevin? You know, that guy who was sitting with me at the table. They left a long time ago."

With the scum bucket who was playing finger pirate? I'm seeing red, and if my blood pressure continues to rise, I might be coloring the world red, too, because there's a good chance I'll explode. "I can't believe you allowed this to happen! If anything happens to her, it's on you."

"Don't try to pin this on me. She's your responsibility, not mine!"

The statement is a bullet straight to my gut, and I feel the impact and then the sharp recoil of guilt that could bring me to my knees if I let it. She's right, but I'm not going to rescind my statement. Frantic, I run back to find Caprice, but she's getting chummy with Nancy Nielson, a high-powered Boulder Realtor Nikeo and I have been courting over the past two weeks. Caprice sent her a personal invite but hadn't expected her to show. If I interrupt and jeopardize a business deal, Caprice will wrestle me to the ground when we get home.

What am I going to do? And then I spot him, smoking a cigarette, sipping on a gin and tonic, and entertaining a group of women who are probably dying for the opportunity to be groupies.

I walk over and tap him on the shoulder. "I need to talk to you."

Annoyed at the interruption, he dangles his cigarette over the ash-tray and drags his eyes up to mine. "Kind of busy if you haven't noticed."

I narrow my eyes. "Trust me, if I had a choice I wouldn't be bothering you, but I need help."

"That's a hell of a way to start a conversation."

"I need to find Jocelyn. She's gone missing, and the only thing Lizzie can seem to recall at the moment is something about her going to a party and getting a ride from Kevin, a guy who happens to be much older and a complete sleaze-ball. I need to track her down now before something awful happens."

"Go bother Caprice. She'll help you."

"Can't, she's with Nancy Nielson. You're my only option."

He grinds his cigarette in the ashtray and then gives his tumbler a good shake before draining the rest of the drink.

"Are you going to play another set, Nikeo?" asks a leggy blonde.

"Not tonight, sugar," he says to her.

All the girls at the table voice their disappointment and beg him to reconsider.

Knowing that I'm the reason for breaking up the party, Leggy Blonde gives me a nasty look and then turns to Nikeo. "Why not?"

He meets my eyes. "Something came up."

He's actually going to help? I'd expected more of a fight. We walk out to the parking lot together. I give him all the information that I have.

When I finish he says, "I'm not helping until you ask nicely."

I give my pride another swirly in the toilet and flush. "Please, will you help me find her?"

He unlocks his car. "Looks like I already am."

Expecting a wild goose chase, I ask, "Where are we going to start? We don't even know their last names."

He takes a hard left out the parking lot. "I know both of those girls. They're trouble, and their parties are infamous for cocaine, other drugs, and lots of sex. Way to go with letting her hitch a ride with that guy, Kevin. He's a class A asshole. I wouldn't put anything past him."

"I didn't *let* her do anything! I didn't even know where she was for most of the night!" I cringe as the words are out of my mouth. I've just broadcasted my inadequacy as a guardian.

With one eyebrow raised and an evil smile lying in wait, he's obviously about to say something so I beat him to the punch. "No comments. I swear if you say one word, I'll punch you in the face."

The guilt over losing Jocelyn continues eating a hole in my stomach. While I was busy downing dirty martinis with Harriet and telling her all about my boy troubles, Jocelyn was being led astray by these two girls and then climbed into Kevin's car. I'm responsible for anything and everything that happens, and I imagine all the worst-case scenarios. Rape. Drug overdose. Alcohol poisoning. Abduction. Murder. If anything has happened to her, I'll never forgive myself. "Do you think Jocelyn is okay?"

"We'll find out soon enough, won't we?" he remarks.

What a jerk. Had I asked Justice this question, he would have assured me that she was fine.

He speeds down the road, virtually ignoring the traffic signs. I refrain from criticizing his reckless driving.

"Are we almost there?" I ask impatiently.

"Ten minutes."

Nikeo fishes under the seat and removes a CD case. He opens it and inserts the disc into the player in the console. Pearl Jam's "Better Man" blares through the speakers.

Eddie Vedder's lyrics about finding a better man are getting on my nerves and making me edgy. I work my fingers through my hair, pinching small sections and then braiding them. I repeat the process until I'm well on my way to having a head full of cornrows. Then, as fast as I put them in, I take them out.

Out of nowhere, Nikeo says, "You're wearing a skirt." He runs his eyes the length of my bare legs. "I like you in a skirt."

The appreciative sensuality in his voice triggers a full-blooming blush. That spot between my legs that he branded earlier this evening when he was up on stage singing is once again heating up. "That's the first compliment you've ever given me."

"You never give me a chance to compliment you." He rests his arm on the window frame and braces his fingers near the top. "You're always too busy arguing with me."

"I could say the same."

He gives me a piercing look, and I don't know what it means.

"And here we go again," he says matter-of-factly.

Tired of the constant antagonism, I turn the tables. "You can sing."

Will this compliment affect him in the same way that his affected me? I want a level playing field, because I already feel like he has the advantage, and I have a major handicap.

He rejects the praise. "Everyone can sing."

If I don't make this strong, he'll chew it up and spit it out. I take a risk and dare to use the strongest word I know. "I love the way you sing." Then, before I think things through, I add, "I loved the way you sang to me."

I've surprised him. His jaw muscles tighten. He nervously taps his thumb against the crest of the steering wheel. He turns those panther eyes on me. "Don't say things you can't take back."

"I don't take anything back," I state.

He looks at me, his expression unreadable.

"If you wanted a career in music, you could have one."

"I know."

I wait for him to elaborate, perhaps to share his dreams with me, but, instead he glances at me, his eyes boring into mine. "I want other things as well," he adds meaningfully.

When he turns his attention back to driving, I mentally stop, drop, and roll as I try to put out the fire of my desire.

We turn onto a street crowded with cars. "Becky's house," he announces.

Nikeo haphazardly parks the car on the front lawn, blocking three cars. I jump out and make a beeline for the house.

"Wait up!" he yells.

"Like I have time for that!" Obviously, he doesn't understand the urgency of this situation. Like the big bad wolf, I crash through the front door.

"Anyone seen a seventeen-year-old girl? Long brown hair, blue eyes?" I shout.

The guests, too busy with their debauchery, don't respond. If I don't find Jocelyn safe, sound, and unharmed, her mother will order up my head on a silver platter.

Nikeo catches up to me. "I'll find Becky and ask her if she's seen Jocelyn," he says.

While he searches for Becky, I roam through the downstairs and end up in the kitchen. Kevin leans up against the counter holding a shot glass in one hand and a bottle of vodka in the other.

When he sees me, a look of disgust sweeps over his face. "What are you doing here?"

"Where's Jocelyn?"

"Who?"

"The girl you brought here."

He refills his shot glass and drains it. Smacking his lips, he gives me a cold stare. "Lizzie's not here, is she?" He looks over my shoulder.

"Did you give a brown-haired, blue-eyed, seventeen-year-old girl a ride here or not? She was wearing a flowered navy sundress. Flip-flops. Had about twenty sparkly bracelets on her arm."

"Yeah, I brought her here. Only seventeen, huh? She seemed much, much older."

The way he says this makes my stomach curl up into a hard ball. "*Where is she?*"

"Upstairs in one of the bedrooms where I left her."

My fist, cocked and loaded, is ready to make contact with Kevin's nose, but I have to get to Jocelyn first. Nikeo walks into the kitchen, takes one look at my face, and before I know what's happening, he's knocked the bottle of vodka and shot glass from Kevin's hands.

"What the hell!" yells Kevin, who throws his arms up in the air.

"She's upstairs, Nikeo! We'll deal with him later."

Nikeo and I race up the stairs and find Jocelyn passed out on the floor in one of the bedrooms.

I run to her and shake her, and when she barely responds I'm ready to call an ambulance and rush her to the hospital.

"Go call 9-1-1!" I tell Nikeo.

"Let's sit her up." He gets behind her and puts his arms under hers and drags her into a sitting position, and then together Nikeo and I manage to get her on the bed.

Although her eyes are still closed, she's sitting upright with Nikeo holding onto her shoulders. I kneel in front of her. "Honey, can you hear me?"

Dazed, she opens her eyes. Her head bobs and weaves.

"How much did you have to drink?" asks Nikeo.

She giggles sleepily. "Hey, you guys are cheer? Thwat's so cool."

Slurring and confusing words is never a good sign. "Jocelyn, we need to know how much you had to drink."

Reaching out, she touches my face, her hands working over my cheeks and lips like a blind person. "You so pwetty."

Nikeo hoists her upright into a standing position. Though she's wobbly, she at least manages to stay on her feet.

"Come on, Jocelyn, let's get you home," he says.

"No! We have to take her to the hospital," I insist.

"She's coherent. She'll survive."

Jocelyn moves her eyes over to me. "I don't want to go to the wospital. Cane, why is the woom rinning?"

"It isn't. You've just had too much to drink."

"I'm dwunk? My lips are numb." She teeters.

Nikeo and I get on either side of her and guide her arms around our shoulders.

"Hey, where Kevin go?"

"Did Kevin do anything to you?"

Resting her head on my shoulder, she sighs. "He grave me vodka. Two gwasses. Then kissed me and twouched me," she announces quietly with a smattering of confusion.

Nikeo and I share a look, and for once we are on the same page, the same line, and even the same word. There will be no debate or quarrel about this, because there's no question what both of us want to do to Kevin.

I swallow the bile that's risen up and try to put a lid on the steamy anger that's making the inside of my ears burn and ring. "Where did he touch you, Jocelyn?"

"He kwissed me," she says, looking all starry-eyed.

"That's it?" I ask as we near the end of the hallway with the stairs in front of us.

Wrapping her hand around my neck, she leans in close to my ear. "Then he put his hand up my shirt and up my squirt, up inswide me," she admits in a much-too-loud whisper, the alcohol diminishing her volume control abilities.

Nikeo glances at me again, and I can tell that if it comes to it, he's just as willing as I am to end up in jail tonight. I only hope that the police put Kevin in the cell with us.

When we've finally made it down the stairs and are heading to the foyer, I ask, "Did he do anything else?"

"He twied. I said stop."

At her confession, the inside of my intestines twist. Kevin may have preyed on her and taken advantage, but ultimately, I'm the one to blame.

Near the bottom of the staircase, she loses her footing and careens sideways. Nikeo catches her.

Her eyes fill with tears. "I don't feel good."

"We're going to get you home," I promise her.

She whimpers, and Nikeo and I get her safely to the bottom of the stairs and lead her out the front door.

"When we get her settled, I'm going back in," declares Nikeo.

I know exactly what he's going to do, because I'm going to do the same thing. "I'm going with you," I tell him.

CHAPTER FOURTEEN

I hold Jocelyn's hair back while the vodka makes a cameo appearance into the toilet. Her sickness isn't doing my stomach any favors. Keeping my eyes trained on the ceiling, I try not to gag. Hopefully this is the last of it. She's been retching for an hour now.

When she's finished, she sinks to the ground and starts bawling. "I'm never going to feel better," she moans.

"I promise you will." I rub her back and tell her that it's going to be okay. I'm not sure what else I can do. I don't have any more tricks up my sleeve. I've held a washcloth to her forehead, made her sip water, and given her a strong dose of Advil, taking a few pills myself to ease the pain in my cheek and hand.

"I'm going to die!" she announces, and then like a snail, she coils into a ball and wraps her arms around her knees.

"You feel like it, but you won't."

"You don't know wha thi feel like," she slurs, leaving most of her words incomplete.

I know all too well, because *I've been there, done that* more than once. Only, the first time I was certain I would die from drinking, I'd been older than Jocelyn.

Halloween night, sophomore year of college, Caprice and I dressed as sexy wicked witches and attended a costume party at her boyfriend, Chad's, fraternity house. Caprice had been so busy casting a spell on Chad that I was left to entertain myself. Ever the good student and all around do-gooder, I prided myself on my sobriety and wore it like a badge of honor. I'd made it through a year of college without touching a drop of alcohol, a fact that Mikayla found hilarious and also a bit pathetic. Whenever we talked on the phone, she was always telling me to cut loose and live a little.

"You're supposed to party in college, that's just what you do there," she always said.

That night, dressed in fishnet stockings and wearing a jaunty pointed hat with a Cindy Crawford–style mole penciled on my face, I was feeling a bit like a rule breaker and decided that Mikayla had a point. I dipped a ladle into the sweet vat of grape Kool-Aid wop, and after a few sips, the party seemed much more interesting. The sugary taste disguised the potency, and I didn't think I was doing myself any harm at first. But, after four Solo cups, I understood that it was called wop for a reason. It felt like I had been bludgeoned on the head. All my senses had gone rubbery and flat. I tried to find Caprice so that she could walk me home, but she had vanished, probably to Chad's room, and I wasn't about to go knocking on that door.

Somehow I made my way back to our apartment. The world was spinning so fast that I was sure I was going to fall off the edge and plummet to my death. Crawling into the bathroom, I vomited so violently that the blood vessels in my eyes burst. I woke up to the feel of Justice's cool hand against my hot forehead.

"You're here?" I asked in miserable wonderment.

"Yes. You called, remember? I came as fast as I could."

I had no recollection of calling him, but I was so grateful for his presence that I started to cry. He held my hair back while I threw up time and time again. He placed a cool washcloth to my forehead and made me drink sips of water. He tended to me in exactly the same way I had tended to Jocelyn.

Every part of my life and memory is tethered to him, and despite the messy attraction with Nikeo that I can't quite figure out, I want Justice so badly that much of my insides feel empty.

"I want my mom," Jocelyn whines.

I stroke her damp forehead. Although I'm mothering the best I can, I know that there's no substitute for the real thing. "I can go get the phone. You can call her," I offer, fully knowing that if Jelly Roll discovers what's happened, that her innocent daughter has not only gotten sloshed but violated by some pervert, she'll have that silver platter ready and waiting and may possibly do the beheading herself — with a dull knife of course.

"I don't want to talk to her, not after what she did to our family. I hate her. I'm never going home again."

Although she's spoken daily to Samson, to my knowledge she hasn't had one conversation with her mother. Whatever Jelly Roll did, Jocelyn is holding a major grudge.

"I want to go to bed," she declares.

I help her off the floor; she's still shaky on her feet. I wind my arms around her to steady her, and together we shuffle down the hallway. Once we're in the bedroom, I make her sit on the edge of the bed.

I lift the flowered navy dress over her head and pull her aqua nightgown on. Nearly everything she owns is a shade of blue and white, and it's because of my influence. When I babysat her long ago, I told her that I preferred blue and white because it was classic, though in reality I wore these cool tones because I thought other colors clashed with my vibrant auburn hair. Although I've relaxed my wardrobe color rule over the years and have ventured away from my sailor-like color scheme, Jocelyn has remained loyal to it. I wonder if soon she'll start dressing in hot pink swimming suits and bejeweling herself. Although she emulates Lizzie's diet and exercise rules and even some of her mannerisms, with the exception of some accessories, she hadn't yet changed her wardrobe. Selfishly, I want her to be like me. I've watched her grow up. I've witnessed her childhood, her awkward pre-teen years, and full-blown adolescence. I've mentored her, been her friend, and functioned as her older sister. She belongs to me, not Lizzie.

"Will you stay with me until I fall asleep?" she asks.

I sit next to her and hold her hand. "I'm not going anywhere."

She looks up at me, her eyes blinking, and most likely her vision still out of focus. "Why would my mom do that?"

Not knowing what her mother has done or how to answer Jocelyn's question, I hold my palm against her cheek.

She props herself up on her elbows. The glow of the table lamp lights her face in such a way that she no longer looks confident or mature but so youthful and injured that I would do anything to make her feel better.

I'm about to apologize for what's happened tonight when she asks, "But you won't do what she did, will you, Cane?"

The troubled earnestness in her voice gives me pause. Whatever her mother has done, she's afraid of me doing the same. I have no idea what Jelly Roll did to provoke her daughter's anger and disapproval, but I hate the fact that Jocelyn has drawn a tentative line between her mother and me. I'm nothing like Jelly Roll.

Despite not knowing what I *won't* do, my answer is vehement. "Absolutely not."

When Jocelyn finally falls into an agitated slumber, I wander into the kitchen to get the phone and head out into the chilly night to make a call.

It's late here, but even later back home. Staring out into the night, I consider whether I should call him. Behind the rush of water over stone from the nearby creek, the papery rattle of the aspen leaves, and the lonesome sound of Nikeo's guitar, there's a thread of stillness that has the flavor of loneliness. Ignoring the late hour, I nervously dial his cell phone and wait.

After eight rings, I'm about to hang up when I hear a voice I'm not expecting.

"What do you know?" Mikayla trills. "I was wondering when we'd get to talk again. We kind of ended things on a bitter note."

Mikayla's answering his phone at this hour? She's tripped a jealousy wire; I feel a series of small explosions inside my chest. "Why are you answering his phone?"

"You're a college grad. I'm sure you can draw a conclusion."

"Are you seriously going after him?"

"Cane," she sighs wearily. "I don't want to talk to you yet. About anything. I'm not ready. *Okay?*"

"Fine, then give the phone to Justice." I barely disguise the desperation in my voice.

She's silent, and in the background there's evidence of a party. The telltale cackle of men who've had too much beer. Bass staccato of dance music. A high-pitched whine of a blender pulverizing ice. And then breaking through it all and rising to the surface, the calming sound of Justice's voice.

"Who are you talking to?" he asks her with blasé curiosity in a tone that sounds all too cozy.

I'm about to make another demand when the line goes dead.

"Spec-tac-u-lar!" I yell. I dial his number again, determined to give whoever answers a verbal lashing. But I don't get that far, because it goes right to voicemail. Defeated, I toss the phone onto the table and sit down.

I'm familiar with Mikayla's powers when it comes to men. In that, she has all the power, and they have none. One of the ways in which Mikayla and I are alike is that when we want to do something, or in her case *someone,* we'll stop at nothing even if it means destroying everything and everyone in our path. When Justice said that he wanted us to see other people, was he already entertaining the notion that he might trade up for Mikayla? It would be trading up, and not just because she's six inches taller, more successful, and certainly more beautiful. What may tip the scales is her wild desire to have a good time. She's the life of the party, and as Justice knows, I'm not.

Nikeo opens the sliding door and joins me on the patio. "She asleep?"

"Finally." I stare off into the distance. Rings of moonlit fog circle the mountain peaks like halos.

He rolls his shoulders forward and then backward. He sits. "How's your cheek?"

I tentatively run my fingertips along the ridge of my cheekbone and wince. "Feels splintered."

"I wanted to kill him," he states calmly, with an undercurrent of menace in his voice.

"You would have if I hadn't pulled you off."

His expression darkens. "I'm not good at self-control. It's either all or nothing."

Once Nikeo and I had gotten Jocelyn safely to the car and buckled her into the backseat, I'd sprinted back into the house, ignoring Nikeo when he told me to wait up. I found Kevin sitting on a lawn chair in the backyard swapping getting-laid stories with another guy. Like two seasoned fisherman, they boasted about their bait and catches and the trophies they had accumulated over the past few years. Disgusted, I circled around and stood in front of him.

He frowned and rolled his eyes when he spotted me. "Didn't you find her? I told you where she was."

"*Stand up,*" I commanded.

"Why?"

"Because I want to see you fall down when I kick your ass," I explained tensely.

"I'll be a gentleman and stand, but I'm not falling for you under any circumstances," he said, grinning at his clever statement. Placing his beer on the ground, he rose out of his seat and raised his hands. "Happy now?"

Balling my fist, I spring-loaded my arm and gave him a right hook to the jaw. His conceited expression crumpled under the pain. He staggered sideways.

"Now I'm happy," I announced. Ready for round two, I prepared to give him a left hook when he blasted me with the back of his hand across my face.

Mismatched in size, I fell to the ground. He followed up the assault by calling me a stupid bitch.

Nikeo happened to step outside at that moment. Surmising what had happened, he attacked Kevin mercilessly. Although Kevin was beefier and taller, Nikeo was faster and angrier, which gave him the clear advantage.

Kevin's friend tried to intervene without success.

I sprang to my feet. Stunned, I watched the violence escalate. Blood flew. Muscles bulged. Jaws tensed. It was animalistic and uncivilized, and yet … fascinating. Because Justice was always a lover and never a fighter and prided himself on turning the other cheek, I'd never witnessed anything like this.

Fascination, however, quickly turned to horror as I realized that Nikeo believed that the wages of sin were death.

"Nikeo, stop!" I shouted and roughly yanked on one of his arms. When he looked at me, his green eyes were fierce and uncomprehending.

I look at Nikeo now, sitting in the dark, shaded by the shadows and wonder if the fierceness has left his eyes. "How are your hands?"

Gingerly flexing his fingers, he inspects his knuckles. "I iced them. You should ice your cheek."

"Thank you for what you did tonight."

"I didn't do anything."

I rise out of my chair and walk over to him. "Pull your chair out."

He scoots his chair backward away from the table.

I gently pick up his hand in mine and raise it to my mouth. Our eyes lock. I place a tender kiss on each of his knuckles. I pick up his other hand and repeat this process.

When I finish, he takes my wrist and pulls me onto his lap and wraps his arms around me. I don't question whether it's right or wrong, whether it will lead to something more or whether I want it to. Instead, I relax against his chest and tuck my head under his jaw.

It's the first time since leaving home that I've felt like I made the right decision and that I'm supposed to be here.

And it scares me like hell.

CHAPTER FIFTEEN

"Over there!" Nikeo pedals toward the bike shop, his thin road tires splicing through the standing water on the pavement.

Jocelyn and I, shivering and soaked to the bone, are anxious to get under the bike shop's large awning and out of the deluge.

"We never should have gone out!" moans Jocelyn. "Lizzie said it was going to rain."

We'd been three miles from downtown when the storm attacked. Jocelyn, frightened of inclement weather, started hyperventilating and still clipped into her bike, fell over, scraping her leg. Sobbing, she refused to go any farther. Nikeo and I insisted that she had to, but she was more interested in pitching a fit than in listening. Disgusted with her behavior, Nikeo got off his bike, physically picked her up off the ground, and smacked the top of her helmet with his palm.

Stunned by the jarring slap, Jocelyn immediately quieted.

"You can stay out here on the trail and get struck by lightning. Or you can suck it up and get back on your bike and follow me to town and live to see the next day."

His tough love tactic, although not well received by Jocelyn, who stuck her tongue out at him, nevertheless worked. She got back on her bike as instructed.

"You didn't have to hit her," I yelled at him disapprovingly as she rode ahead.

"I didn't hit her. I whacked her helmet." He jumped back on his bike and looked at me over his shoulder. "It worked, didn't it?"

Nikeo makes it to the awning first. Jocelyn and I, not far behind him, unclip from our pedals, hop out of our saddles, and run our bikes over to the shelter. Our shoes click against the steaming pavement. Finally out of the storm, we rest our bikes against the building and wipe the water from our faces.

"I want to go home," announces Jocelyn, who refuses to make eye contact with Nikeo.

He shakes his head. "We aren't biking home until this rain clears up."

"I'm freezing," she complains. "I'm going to go inside the store and warm up."

Jocelyn tries the handle, but it's locked.

Nikeo points to the sign. "Briar Days. They close at six because of the festival," he explains.

Jocelyn, still peeved, glares at him. "I figured that out. Are we going tonight?" she asks, directing the question at me. "Because I really, really want to! I'm tired of staying home."

Ever since her drinking-and-disappearing act last week, I'd been keeping a tight leash on her. Although I never officially doled out a punishment, I've been playing the role of overbearing parent. This past week, I'd insisted on a ten-thirty bedtime, forbid her from hanging out with Lizzie, and kept her by my side at all times.

Considering what happened, I can't take any more chances by giving her freedom.

"Drunken locals. Sketchy-looking carnies. The rancid smell of fried food." Nikeo takes off his helmet and runs his hand through his dark hair, shaking out the water. "The music is the only good thing about it."

Clasping her hands together, Jocelyn looks at me pleadingly. "Can we go?"

"I'm not sure."

"Please!" she whines. "I promise I won't get into trouble."

I'm not worried about her behavior; I'm worried about my own. Nikeo will be doing an acoustic solo performance right before Unarmed Scandal takes the stage. Given what happened between us last week and the fact that Justice hasn't returned my phone calls, I'm primed for transgression of the worst sort.

As if reading my mind, Nikeo meets my eyes. "You told me you were coming tonight. You're not going back on your word, are you? Because, that wouldn't be like you, would it?"

He has a point.

Two people huddled together under a large umbrella approach. "Yoo-hoo! Yoo-hoo!" tweets the woman, who's waving like crazy.

"Cane, it's so wonderful to run into you!" she remarks excitedly as she approaches.

I vaguely recognize her.

"You kids were biking in this weather! It's madness out here!" says the man next to her.

I audibly gasp and then try to smooth over my rude reaction with a polite smile. Her beautiful, shoulder-length silver hair. His jovial voice. It's Arlene and Skeeter wearing jeans, white linen shirts, and sandals. Miraculously, they're wearing clothes. In their matching outfits, they look the part of a conventional retired couple. Jocelyn swings her eyes to me and grins. She's figured it out, too.

"Nice to see you! Are you here for the festival?"

"Yes, but let's hope this rain eases up," says Skeeter, as he sticks his hand out from under the umbrella and catches some rain in his palm. "Arlene and I were hoping to go to the carnival and hop on some rides."

"Oh, yes! I love the tilt-a-whirl. It's my absolute favorite," says Arlene.

"Mine, too!" declares Jocelyn. "Maybe Cane and I will get to go on it later."

"We could all ride it together," Arlene suggests.

Taking an unfortunate mental leap, I picture Arlene and Skeeter riding the tilt-a-whirl naked. *Keep your hands at your side — hazardous flying body parts,* I think. Not willing to commit to spending time with my nudist clients for fear they might be wearing less should the rain clear up, I offer a noncommittal, "Maybe."

Skeeter gives me a jolly smile. "Well, no matter! I'm glad we ran into you so that we could say good-bye again."

Effusive with her affection, Arlene ducks out from under the umbrella and throws her arms around me. "We're going to miss you!"

I'm thankful that this time she's wearing clothes, because when she'd done that earlier this week, I had her breasts mushed against my stomach. At least her husband hadn't tried to embrace me, because breasts I could handle, but a wrinkled penis pressed up against my stomach … not so much.

When she pulls away, Nikeo fires a *what the hell* look at me. Obviously, I hadn't mentioned it to him yet, nor to Jocelyn, who has blown up her cheeks like a puffer fish. Only Caprice and Grandma Betty knew my intentions, and of course Samson, who has already purchased Jocelyn's airline ticket. Leave it to Skeeter and Arlene to open the bag and let the cat out, though I shouldn't be surprised. They love to expose things.

Arlene rests her hand on my shoulder. "Honey, I know you're leaving town next week, but if you get the chance, swing by the *Bare and There* social gathering at the beer tent at nine thirty. There are such wonderful young people in that group. You would have a blast with them."

Nikeo, wearing a wicked grin, steps forward. "Sorry, I don't know if you remember me, but I'm Nikeo. I came to your house once with Caprice."

Arlene grins and takes Nikeo's hand. "Oh yes! I remember now! Nice to see you again, young man."

"Cane has told me all about *Bare and There.* She would love to go," asserts Nikeo. "I'll take her myself."

I widen my eyes at him, and he gives me a *gotcha* smile.

"Oh wonderful," Skeeter says in a booming voice. "Nice running into you three. We best be off and let you get home and get some dry clothes on."

"Or we could leave them off," proposes Nikeo.

Skeeter points at Nikeo. "Now you're talking."

Arlene laughs and waves. "We'll look for you later this evening!"

As soon as they're out of earshot, Jocelyn blows the hot air out of her mouth, deflating her puffy cheeks. "You didn't tell me we were leaving! We can't leave! We just can't."

"We can't stay out here forever. Both of us need to get home."

"I'm not going."

"I already talked to your dad. You fly out next Wednesday, and as soon as I drop you at the airport, I'm driving back."

Jocelyn narrows her eyes. "This is so unfair. Why are we leaving?"

Nikeo lowers his eyes to mine. I know that, like me, he's remembering last Friday night. My lips on his hands. Our bodies molded together perfectly in that chair with the mountains in the distance.

I pull my eyes away from him. "Because we have to," I respond.

"Unbelievable," Nikeo growls under his breath. He climbs back on his bike and pedals toward home.

Jocelyn and I watch him leave. When he's out of sight, she carelessly jerks her bike around so that it's facing the street.

"*Because we have to* isn't an answer," she grumbles. "It sounds like something Jelly Roll would say."

"You shouldn't call your mother, Jelly Roll. It's disrespectful."

"I don't care. And like you should tell me not to call her that. You say it all the time. You're such a hypocrite."

Knowing that what I say from here on out can and will be used against me, I wisely hold my tongue.

The rain has given up, and the ominous clouds skate back out over the mountains. The violet, opaque light of evening bathes the streets. In the distance, lights from carnival rides flash, and clown-like instrumental music floats from the speakers near the games where cheaply made stuffed animals are strung from twine, waiting to be taken home as a prize.

"You know what? I don't want to go tonight." Jocelyn straddles the middle bar of her bike and clips one foot into the pedal. "I don't care what you do, but I'm staying in my room."

*****

Caprice meets up with me outside the beer tent and takes the beer I've bought for her from my hand. "Sorry I'm late," she says.

"That's okay. Nikeo and I got held up inside. Or, more accurately, felt up," I comment drolly.

"Felt up? Hey, how much do I owe you?" she asks, shifting the two lawn chairs to one arm and reaching into her pocket.

"It's on me."

Circling back to my comment about being felt up, she asks, "Was it good for you?"

I offer a wry smile and curt shake of my head. "Apparently, *Bare and There* isn't only about nudity. There are also some very active and persistent swingers."

She chokes out a laugh. "Come on, you're not serious."

"Cross my heart and hope to die." I turn my head and glance at the beer tent to make sure the swingers haven't decided to swing my way. "Believe me, I did want to die of embarrassment. Nikeo and I were propositioned by Barry and Jane, a couple in their thirties. It was like some wacky speed dating thing. They came up to us, told us that we were attractive, and wouldn't it be fun if we swapped partners."

"That's kind of rude. They didn't even take you out for a romantic dinner first."

"No dinner, no buttering up. They cut right to the chase and tried to take us to bed. When I flat-out refused and told them they were crazy, they offered to give us their medical history, an official doctor's report that ensured they were free of all venereal diseases. Like a clean bill of health would make me change my mind."

Howling with laughter, Caprice hands me her beer and pries open the lawn chairs for us. "It would have been more interesting if you would have played along with it just to see what they would've done."

"Nikeo did. He said that he would like to see their medical report, and the woman actually offered to go back to their house and get it! Then he started asking about how many other partners they had, if they ever had parties, if drugs were involved, what their favorite sex toy was. He was on a roll, and they were taking the interview seriously! They thought we were considering it. I couldn't believe it."

We sit, and Caprice slaps her palm against the armrest. "I can't believe I missed out on that. I would have loved to have been there if only to see your face."

"Which was contorted in disgust."

She laughs knowingly. "Oh, I bet. Here comes Cane galloping in on her moral high horse."

"Don't start." Caprice, much like Nikeo, is an all-star for the liberal lefties. It's been the source of many contentious debates during the four years we've known each other.

"You aren't exactly known for your open mind," she comments.

"Not when it comes to garbage like that. It's revolting."

"Don't be judgmental," she reprimands. "They aren't hurting anybody. If they're both into it, then I say *go for it*."

"I'm not being judgmental, I'm being factual. Swapping partners is disgusting."

"So says the conventional Lutheran girl who still feels guilty for having sex with her longtime boyfriend because she hasn't officially tied the knot."

I click my tongue in a sound of denial. "No way. I don't feel guilty."

She gives me a *yeah right* roll of her eyes.

I don't say anything further, because, I wouldn't be able to hold my ground. There's a modicum of truth in her statement. After all, aren't I breaking the Christian code by having sex outside of marriage? Thanks to my religious upbringing, I was taught both in church and at home that premarital sex wasn't about love but lust, and that it was a sin of the flesh to be avoided at all cost. When that kind of seed has been in the ground for years and watered at regular intervals by the church and authority figures, it's hard to pull up the roots.

I know firsthand that premarital sex can be about love, but I can't discredit lust that is sometimes so powerful it wrestles love to the ground. Coincidentally, I'm thinking this as I raise my eyes to the stage and study Nikeo. He's wearing loose-fitting Levi's that hang low on his trim waist and a button-down black shirt that's begging to be unbuttoned. In this instance, love is down for the count, and lust raises its hands in victory.

"What I don't understand is how you let him talk you into going to the beer tent when you knew about the meeting?" Caprice asks.

"Too much drama. It slipped my mind." I had forgotten about

the meeting, because I'd still been stewing about what had happened between Jocelyn and me. Once we'd gotten back to the house, we'd spent an hour battling like mother and daughter.

She told me that she wasn't going home and that if I tried to make her get on that plane, she would run away. She even went so far as to bring Kevin's name into the argument. She threatened to call him. That's when I lost my temper. I gave her more than a piece of my mind, I gave her the whole thing. I lectured until I was blue in the face and red in the eyes. She retaliated with a lecture of her own, telling me how stupid I was for leaving Justice behind and that I didn't deserve him or the dream house he was building or the future he was offering me. She told me I wasn't good enough for him, an opinion her mother shared and had not so subtly delivered over the years.

"Apparently Nikeo *didn't* forget," I continue. "He took me to the beer tent under the pretense that he wanted to sample some brews from a new brewery, and guess who was there? Skeeter and Arlene, who were of course thrilled that I showed for the meeting. They introduced me to their good friends, Barry and Jane, swingers extraordinaire."

"You think Skeeter and Arlene buy into that lifestyle?" asks Caprice, genuinely curious.

Crossing my arms and tensing my shoulders, I bounce my foot up and down and around in a circle. "I don't know, and I don't want to know. Seeing them naked is almost more than I can take."

Nikeo, confident and at ease, takes the stage and positions himself behind the microphone. When he looks directly at me with those panther eyes of his, I immediately still. My foot stops moving. My shoulders relax. The tight loop of tension that's ever present in my stomach unfurls in a way that leaves me awash with desire. Nikeo and I are more than fifty feet apart, and yet, I feel like we're touching.

He strums a complex series of chords, offering a tease of what's to come. My heart mimics the pleasing sound of the notes, and I'm left breathless with the change in rhythm. I press my hand over my chest to try and settle the beat.

Caprice, who's watching me closely, catches my response to Nikeo. She flicks my hand. "You can send Jocelyn home, but as for you taking off? It isn't such a good idea."

"But Justice and Mikayla are probably —"

"Yeah, yeah." She exhales sharply, expelling a puff of air. "I've heard this all before, but it's not about Justice and Mikayla and what may or may not be going on between them. It's not about Justice ignoring your phone calls and not returning your messages. It's about you. You aren't ready to go home, and if you do, you'll be making a huge mistake. I know that, but more importantly, you do, too."

She gives me one of her shrewd, no-nonsense stares, and I glance away.

Nikeo leans close to the microphone. "How are you doing tonight?" he asks, in that velvety voice of his. His lips curl only slightly at the edges so that he looks pleased to be there but not overly eager. Shifting his body to the side with understated swagger, he adjusts his guitar.

The local crowd knows who he is. They pump their fists and chant his name. He finds my eyes again, inclines his head slightly, and says, "How about … 'Good Riddance.'"

As he sings the Green Day song, it isn't as much of a performance as it is his good-bye to me. It has a bitter edge that leaves me with a sour feeling in my stomach. His eyes repeatedly seek me out, and I do my best to dodge his line of sight.

Near the end of the song, Caprice nudges me in the ribs and nods her head in Nikeo's direction. "If you go back home, it's not going to work with Justice. Not when you're still thinking about Nikeo."

The Green Day lyrics are too personal tonight. I'm standing at the fork in a road, and Grandma Betty is grabbing me by the wrist and telling me to go home, while Caprice is holding onto the other one and telling me to stay.

After his set, Nikeo vanishes behind the stage and doesn't reemerge. Caprice and I stay put to enjoy the concert. We listen to Unarmed Scandal, shimmy to the music, and raise our blood alcohol level to a not-so-legal limit.

When Unarmed Scandal makes their exit, I start plotting mine. I'm all partied out and don't want to risk running into Nikeo on a night where becoming one his groupies doesn't sound like such a bad idea. I fold up my chair and crumple up my empty beer cup. "I'm going home."

Bossy as ever, Caprice says, "No, you aren't. You can't miss the fireworks. They're going to start soon."

I offer a paltry but valid excuse. "I want to talk to Jocelyn and smooth things over."

Caprice waves her hand, dismissing my idea. "She's seventeen. She'll get over it. She's probably already over it and snoring away."

"I'm leaving."

Like the bully she aspires to be, she grabs the chair out of my hand, opens it back up, and gives me a try-to-leave-and-I'll-take-you-out-look.

Along with everything else, my foot is feeling a little weak; I don't have it in me to put it down. Giving in, I plop back into the chair. "Fine."

"I'm going for a refill," she announces as she stands. "When I get back, you will be here."

"Sure."

Narrowing her eyes, she appraises me, trying to decide if I'm telling the truth.

"I promise."

Satisfied, she nods and plucks the crumpled cup from my hand. "Want anything?"

"I've already had too much."

"Live on the edge. I'm getting you another."

"I can't handle any more."

"Ha. You can handle more than you think. Besides, we're celebrating the fact that you're going to stay here the rest of the summer."

She waits for me to say something, but I remain mute.

"That's settled then," she says and saunters off toward the beer tent.

I've already made my decision, and no one can change my mind about it. As to whether or not the decision is good or bad, the jury is still deliberating the verdict.

A high school band takes the stage and starts playing something that sounds like a cross between grunge rock and jazz. It's a confusing, jarring kind of music that makes me long for earmuffs.

"Look, it's Cane!" a woman yells.

Her barely familiar voice fills me with dread.

Before I can make a mad dash for the beer tent and drown my sorrows in a pint of ale, Jane, swinger extraordinaire, rushes up to me and takes hold of my arm.

She bends down and sticks her narrow, fuzzy face in my personal space, so close that not only can I see she hasn't waxed her mustache in quite some time, I can also smell her rank breath. She's eaten a corn dog. Definitely a stick of cotton candy. And, possibly, washed her meal down with fresh lemonade.

"I'm so glad we found you, because we wanted to run something by you," she says.

"Whereas I want to run away from you," I respond bluntly, the alcohol having diminished what little impulse control I have.

She pulls away from me. Thank God. Free at last. She's offended and will storm off, and I can go on with my evening. Then, she throws a wrench into my plans by tilting her head back and cackling as if it's the funniest thing she's ever heard.

"Did you hear that, Barry? Did you hear what she said?"

With all the swinging that Jane does, possibly from a rope (I can't help but think of Tarzan and Jane), she's probably had quite a few mishaps along the way. As in: head injuries. This lady is cracked.

Obviously, Barry didn't hear what I'd said to his wife, because he was a good ten feet behind her when she shoved herself and her mustache into my personal space.

She's laughing so hard that tears are running down her face, causing her mascara to smear. Reaching up, she runs a finger across her spider-leg-like eyelashes trying to control the damage.

Barry, now on the scene and eyeing me like I'm made out of sugar, says, "So we meet again." His slightly jack-o'-lantern smile grows larger, and he runs a hand over his atrocious comb-over and licks his lips.

Is he attempting to look … suave? Sexy? Mysterious? Standing, I tense my muscles. Where is Caprice when I need her? She should be back by now! "Well, Barry, I can't say I'm happy about that."

Jane sways her hip to the right and bumps her husband. "Isn't she a card, Barry. An absolute riot."

"Only sometimes I'm not. I don't have a sense of humor," I deadpan.

"Almost had me there," Barry says with a laugh and fashions his hand into a makeshift gun, points it at me, and does that irritating double click out of the side of his mouth.

This must be his signature go-to gesture. I saw it at least four times during our brief encounter in the beer tent.

"We got off on the wrong foot." Jane, who resembles and behaves like a fly, sneaks up close and cups her hand around her mouth as if sharing a confidence. "Sometimes we're a little forward."

There's no easy way to get rid of these two, so I decide to make a game out of it. "No! I don't believe it. How could anyone say that?"

"I know! I know! But it's true!" she exclaims with outrage. She buzzes ever closer, and I resist swatting her away.

"Here's what we're thinking." She rubs her hands together as she shares her scheme. "Maybe you and Barry could get to know each other a little better. Go off and have a drink. Watch the fireworks together! You have my permission and my blessing."

"I would love to take you over to the beer tent." Barry wiggles his bushy brows. "I want to learn what Cane Kallevik is all about." He rests a hand on my shoulder and squeezes once and then again, smiling greedily and feverishly licking his lips, as if he's trying to determine how I'll taste. Shivering, I swat his hand away.

"Disgusting. And let me make this crystal-clear, I will not be doing anything with you ever, not this evening, not in the future, because —"

"Because she's with me. Exclusively." Nikeo grins a guard-dog kind of grin, pulling back his lips and baring his teeth. He slides his arm around my shoulder.

Grateful for his sudden, out-of-thin-air appearance, I beam at him and play along with his game. "It's true. I'm with him and only him." I hold up my left hand, showcasing my engagement ring.

Jane, looking like she's been smacked with a fly swatter, bounces back and lands in Barry's arms. "I remember what it's like to be newly engaged. You don't have any desire to go looking for something new."

I flinch. Newly engaged with my betrothed thousands of miles away, and I've already found something new.

Nikeo's lips twist into a cynical smile. "She has no desire at all."

"But then, after a few years boredom sets in, you have to go looking for something to keep things fresh and alive. You'll see what I mean," she says.

"If you ever change your mind, look us up. We're in the phone book under Adams." Barry points his finger at me again and clicks his tongue.

With arms linked, Barry and Jane walk away, their eyes scanning the crowd, looking for potential lovers.

"I saved you," Nikeo says, his voice rough from singing his heart out on stage.

"Don't give yourself too much credit. I was doing fine on my own." That lust thing is really getting on my nerves. I slip out from under his arm and turn to face him. "Where've you been the whole night?"

"You missed me."

I glance up at the stage. The horrible grunge rock, jazz band has finished their short set. "I miss your music," I clarify.

"Semantics."

My eyes dart around everywhere. "Have you seen Caprice?" Nikeo rescued me from swinging Jane and Barry, and now I need my best friend to rescue me from her cousin.

He moves closer to me, pushes my hair of my forehead, revealing my birthmark that resembles a small cross. Nikeo puts his fingers to it and traces the small shape, and I wince. Justice patented this move; he does this all the time, an affectionate gesture that follows our disagreements, of which there are few, and our lovemaking, of which there is plenty. Now that Nikeo has done this, I'm reminded of the direction in which I'm headed. I don't need Frank's silver compass to tell me that my behavior has gone south.

I'm about to walk away when Nikeo says, "Your eyes are blue tonight. I've never seen them like this before. They're usually gray, gold, or green. Sometimes a combination of the three, but never blue. They're beautiful."

A lone rocket fires and squeals in the background, a precursor to the fireworks.

Given that Nikeo usually makes cutting assessments about me and rarely gives a compliment, I'm taken aback by this observation. "You noticed my eyes?"

"I notice everything. Like how you smile right before you say something nasty and the telltale scrunch of your nose after you say something you regret."

Why is he doing this? Is this one of his games? Or, and this would be more dangerous, is this real? "You're laying it on thick, aren't you?"

"If I don't mean it, I don't say it."

My pulse accelerates. My eyelids grow heavy, and I resist the urge to shut them and lean into him. "What is this between us, anyway? Because I don't do casual." I aim to sound adamant, but my voice comes out like whipped air.

"I don't want this to be casual." He places his mouth near my earlobe. "And neither do you."

Above us, fireworks hurtle into the night and fracture the sky like lightning bolts, leaving behind streaks of brilliant colors.

"You don't want to leave. You're not going to leave," he murmurs into my ear.

He's right.

Even though I told everyone I was packing it up and packing it in, I know that I won't be able to go through with it. I can't picture myself back in Savage, Illinois, surrounded by cornstalks. I can't even picture myself with Justice.

I can't leave until I understand what this is or is not with Nikeo. I have to get to the bottom of my obsession with this man who I'm sure is wrong for me, who will not give in to what I want, and may not even give me what I need.

Before I hop on my moral high horse, pass judgment on myself, and ride off into the night, I lasso Nikeo to me, living up to his prediction that I would be the first to touch him.

I fix my arms around his shoulders and press my body against him so that there's no question what my intentions are. He strokes the sides of my neck with his hands and curls them around the base in a kind of seductive, stranglehold. His thumbs move back and forth across the dip at the base of my throat. But, he's not going to kiss me. He's waiting for me.

In the sky above us a series of cataclysmic detonations are followed by an eerie, anticipatory silence, and that is when I choose to close my eyes and fit my lips over his. He tastes smoky, citrusy, and exactly right.

His hands find my hips, and he jerks me closer to him. The kiss steadily intensifies, and it's already taking us to places far beyond this night. The future that I'd always pictured, the one with Justice, is suddenly erased, and it's thrilling and terrifying.

His lips war with mine, and we are about to take our affection to places it shouldn't go in public when I sense a presence. Slowing the cadence of our kiss, I pull away from him.

Cautiously, I look to the side, and she's standing there.

CHAPTER SIXTEEN

"How could you do this?" she yells over the reverberating racket of the pyrotechnics.

Backing away from Nikeo, I take a step toward her. "Jocelyn, I —"

"Justice would never, never do this to you! How could you, Cane? You're engaged to him! You promised you wouldn't do this! How could you do this?"

I shake my head. Valid question. *How could I do this to Justice when I love him?*

I look briefly at Nikeo, and I immediately know why and how. When I'm around him, I behave unscrupulously and irrationally. He provokes emotions in me that Justice never has. He unsettles me, challenges me, pushes me, and enrages me. He makes me question who I am and what I believe. He brings out things in me I didn't know were there and things I don't like to acknowledge that are.

How am I supposed to relay this to a girl who only cares that I have upset her world and betrayed Justice? "I'm so sorry, Jocelyn."

"My mom said the same thing when I found out she cheated on Dad!"

The news stuns me. That explains why Samson insisted that Jocelyn get away and why Jelly Roll was pleasant to me on the phone when I spoke with her and why she was curious to know if Jocelyn had said anything.

Still, Jelly Roll cheating? It's preposterous. Who in their right mind would cheat with an unhappy, overbearing, critical woman like Jenny Ryanne Schaeffer? I'm not proud of the fact that this is my first thought, and I'm even more destroyed when it occurs to me that perhaps Jelly

Roll and I have more in common than I care to admit.

"*Why?* Why did you *do* this?" she asks.

I cast a helpless look at Nikeo, hoping he'll bail me out by taking responsibility, but then I realize this is only something Justice would do. Justice saves the day, while Nikeo delights in how a day can unravel.

I'm going to have to fight this battle alone. "I don't know what to say. Can we go back to the house and talk about this?"

Near hysterics, Jocelyn gulps and swallows a sob. "Does everyone cheat? Is everyone unhappy? You cheated. My mom cheated. Mikayla's mom cheated. Mikayla went after Justice! What's wrong with all of you?"

My face burns with shame. "I don't know what's wrong."

"You don't deserve him! You don't!"

"You're right," I agree sadly.

"You're not going to marry him. I'm going to make sure of it." Crying, she turns and bolts.

Sick with shame and guilt and every negative emotion there is, I look at Nikeo. "I should go after her."

Ever contrary, he says, "Give her space."

"I don't think I should give her any space! What's she doing here anyway? Lizzie promised that she wouldn't let her out of her sight." Lizzie, who had stayed home with a bad headache, had solemnly sworn to serve as a warden and not let Jocelyn go anywhere. Although I hadn't had a Bible, I'd made her raise her right hand.

No surprise that she hadn't done her duty. Because of her negligence, Jocelyn witnessed my lip-lock with Nikeo. Now she's furious and hurt, and I'm afraid of what she may do. My biggest fear is that she'll run to that snake, Kevin. I suspect she has a soft spot for him, because she's mentioned him a few times over the past week and has told me all the things that he'd said to her, one of them being that she had a gorgeous face. Maybe her mother had been on to something by not treating her acne. Thanks to my harebrained scheme of sending her to the dermatologist, her peaches and cream face is attracting all sorts of attention. Despite making it abundantly clear to Jocelyn that Kevin is a scumbag and took advantage of her and that he should be castrated and locked up for his crime, I know that part of her doesn't believe me or doesn't want to believe me.

"You never should have trusted Lizzie to watch her," remarks Nikeo.

All that molten chemistry that we'd shared minutes ago petrifies. "Thank you for pointing out the obvious," I snipe, my tone dripping with sarcasm.

"It's what I'm best at."

Caprice shows up carrying two beers and looks from Nikeo to me. "Trouble in paradise?" she asks as she hands me a lukewarm beer. "Sorry this is so late in coming, but I sealed the deal with Nancy Nielsen. She's agreed to refer us to several of her wealthiest clients and also set up a meeting with a prestigious property management firm!"

"Business always interrupts pleasure," Nikeo remarks.

"It wasn't business that interrupted anything," I disagree. "It was something else entirely."

"Not something, *someone*," he specifies. "If she wouldn't have interrupted, what then? Would we have possibly taken it horizontal?"

Like a bull ready to charge, I push a stream of air through my nostrils. "That's what you're worried about at the moment? Unbelievable! That's all this is for you then, a roll in the hay?"

"You have me so figured out, don't you? Keep on jumping to your conclusions and see where you land. But sweetheart" — he snatches my left hand and holds it up in front of my face so that I have a clear view of my ring — "this ring isn't doing you or me or Jocelyn a whole lot of good right now. It's confusing the hell out of everyone."

I hate it when he's right. I yank my hand away. "I hate you."

"Why don't you stick with that emotion, because it might make things a hell of lot easier for both of us."

He walks away, and I shout after him. "You're not going to help me find her?"

He pauses midstride and throws a heartless comment over his shoulder. "She's your problem. Not mine. Besides, she's not drunk or lost, she's pissed off."

Caprice takes a drink of her beer. "Apparently a lot happened in the past half hour."

"You think?" I dump my beer on the ground. "I have to find her."

Caprice, who thankfully has a cell phone, calls home, hoping to get in touch with Lizzie.

Caprice shakes her head and tucks her cell into the front pocket of her sweatshirt. "No luck."

"It's a long walk from the house, which means Lizzie probably made a miracle recovery and gave her a ride here."

Agreeing with my theory, Caprice and I split up to comb the fairgrounds, agreeing to reconvene in twenty minutes just outside the beer tent.

Nineteen-and-a-half fruitless minutes later, I'm standing outside the beer tent frantically braiding my hair and avoiding Barry's finger gun. Caprice shows up looking grim.

"I found Lizzie, and shockingly, she's lit up like Christmas tree."

Seeing my furious expression, Caprice grins. "Don't worry. I hit her for you."

"I should have never trusted her!"

"Lizzie said Jocelyn came to her about twenty-five minutes ago wanting to leave, but Lizzie pawned her off on Kevin."

"You're kidding me."

"It gets worse," she says grimly. "They left together. Lizzie thinks they were going to his place to have a beer."

Apparently Kevin hadn't learned his lesson last week. Bowing my head, I place my fingertips on my throbbing temples. No way am I ready to be a parent, much less the parent of an adolescent. As soon as I find that girl, I'm going to kill her and then send her packing tomorrow morning. "This is a nightmare. How are we going to find him?"

Caprice holds up the back of her hand. An address is scribbled on her skin. "Lizzie was coherent enough to give me his address."

"Let's go!" I say, already sprinting toward the parking lot.

Caprice and I drive across town to his apartment and pound on his door like a SWAT team. I wish I packed heat, because I would love to wave a gun in his face. That would be much more effective than a beatdown.

A grisly man in his thirties with lumberjack attire and pungent body odor answers the door. "What the hell do you want?" he roars impatiently. And then, he hesitates. He assesses Caprice's body and then slides his eyes approvingly over me. Delighted at his windfall, he amends his statement. "What can I do for you gorgeous ladies? Come on in." He tries to wave us inside.

"Where's Kevin?" Caprice asks in a no-nonsense detective voice.

"Not home." He grins and stands up taller. "But I am."

She continues the interrogation. "Has he been home at all in the past hour or so? Have you seen him with a teenage girl? Brown hair, blue eyes, about five feet six inches?"

"Afraid not. He's at the fair. You're a sweet little thing, aren't you?" He appraises me. "You and all that gorgeous red hair. I have a thing for red hair."

He reaches out to take hold of a tress. I'm about to smack him, but Caprice beats me to the punch, literally. She karate-chops his arm.

He shakes it out. "What the hell was that for?"

"Make another smart remark or try to touch us, and I'll do it again. Does Kevin have a cell phone?" she asks.

Narrowing his eyes suspiciously, Lumberjack Man looks over our shoulder. "Don't tell me you guys are cops. Man, I'm so sick of this. Kevin needs to get his shit together and go after girls his own age."

Caprice and I share a look, and my stomach falls to my ankles. If Kevin is really a predator, then Jocelyn is in serious danger.

Caprice folds her arms and assumes a tough-guy pose. "Yes, we're cops. Undercover. We need Kevin's cell number."

"He doesn't have one. Good luck finding the bastard." He's about to shut the door, when I stick my sneaker in the doorjamb.

"Hold up a second. What's he done in the past? What's he been accused of?"

He snarls. "If you really were cops, wouldn't you already know?"

I remove my foot just as he slams the door.

"Holy. Shitty. Balls," says Caprice. "Let's go."

We drive back to the house, breaking all the rules of the road. If Jocelyn isn't there, we plan to call the police. As soon as we pull into the driveway, we jump out of the car and run into the house calling her name. When I flip on the light in our shared bedroom and discover that her dresser has been emptied and her blue and white striped luggage is gone, I scream for Caprice.

She comes in the room.

"She's gone! Do you think she went somewhere with Kevin? Where do you think she is? Do you think that guy would do something?" I cry.

Caprice shakes her head. "I'll call the police."

I try to swallow the leaded ball of fear that sits at the back of my throat. "I need to ... I should call her parents. Let me talk to them before we call the police."

I rush down the hall to the kitchen to grab the phone, and Nikeo walks through the front door at the same time. He looks at me.

"I saw Lizzie at the fair," he says. "Jocelyn is with Kevin?" he asks, seeking confirmation.

I snatch the phone from the charger. "Like you said, I'm sure she's fine."

"Come on. I'm sorry. I'll help you find her."

"Too little, too late. I don't have time to deal with you." I'm already walking down the hall as I say this. He runs after me. "Cane, I want to help you find her."

I walk into my bedroom and kick the door shut in his face.

Caprice, palming her cell phone, looks to me for direction.

"Go talk to Nikeo. Maybe see if you can get in touch with anyone else who knows Kevin. I'm going to call Samson."

"I'll be right outside the room if you need anything. We'll figure this out."

Before I lose the nerve, I dial Samson's cell phone, but he doesn't answer. I dial his office. Again, no answer. Heaving a big sigh, I dial their home number.

Lady luck is giving me the middle finger. Jelly Roll answers.

"You've really done it now. Haven't you? *This takes the cake.* I can't believe you've done this to Jocelyn! Can't believe it, although I can't say I'm surprised one bit. You've always been a selfish little thing, intent on getting what you want when you want it and not caring who you hurt."

I process her words as swiftly as my muddled brain allows. If I'm interpreting correctly, Jocelyn has spoken with her parents, which means that she's alive and most likely hasn't been kidnapped or accosted by Kevin. "Can I please speak with Samson?"

"He's on his way to Chicago already. He wants to be there in plenty of time."

"She's flying home," I say, hoping it sounds more like a confirmation than a question. But, Jelly Roll can sniff ignorance a mile away and calls me on it.

"Huh! I should have known. I bet you were trying to get in touch with Samson to tell him that you had no idea where our daughter was. Why else would you be calling this late? You don't have any idea where she is, do you? You can stop searching. She's safe and sound at the airport. Some nice young man named Kevin took her there. We booked her on a late flight."

Kevin didn't kidnap her after all, though I sincerely hope that he hadn't demanded any kind of payment for his chauffeur services. If only Jelly Roll knew what that nice young man had done to her innocent daughter last week.

Filled with relief, I take a deep breath and rest my head against the wall. "This is all my fault."

"Yes, it is. You owe many people an apology, don't you?"

Although I would like to rub Jelly Roll's face in her own transgressions, I have to clean up my mess first. "Can I speak with Justice?" I ask in a small voice. "Please. I need to speak with him."

"He's not home," she answers merrily, taking pleasure in this announcement.

I wait for her to tell me where he is, but she's silent. If I want to know anything, I'll have to give her the upper hand for now.

"Can you please tell me where he is?"

"Where he's been ever since you left. With Mikayla." She punctuates her statement with a terse laugh. "Not that it matters, does it? Because from what Jocelyn told me, you've moved on as well."

CHAPTER SEVENTEEN

August 1998

"Want to go for a bike ride?" Nikeo asks as he rests his guitar on the counter.

"Absolutely not."

Thanks to the fifteen miles I ran earlier this morning to get my mind off Justice and his blatant lack of communication despite fifteen calls in the last seven days, I'm cranky, sore, and my stomach is throwing the ultimate temper tantrum. I could eat two large pizzas. Pulling open the refrigerator, I apathetically scan the shelves. The gourmet choices for the evening: celery, a head of broccoli, five red peppers, a suspicious box of Chinese that's been in there for three weeks, and a stack of processed American cheese.

His usual stealthy self, Nikeo sneaks up behind me, and I bristle at his presence. Turning, I give him a look that could freeze ice. "What do you want?"

"Get over yourself," he says as he, too, takes inventory of the food.

Dissatisfied, he frowns. "We're going to The Elephant Ear," he announces.

I push the fridge shut with my elbow.

"But put something else on," he says, glancing at my holey sweatpants and long-sleeved shirt that looks like it's been rubbed over a cheese grater.

"Have you lost your mind? I'm not going anywhere with you." Seven long days, countless arguments, and mounds of sexual tension later, Nikeo and I still haven't mended any fences. If anything, we've knocked a few more down and spit on each other's property. Although problematic in that it's difficult living with him and working with him, at least I'm no longer putting my relationship with Justice in jeopardy. However, at this point, what difference does it make?

Lizzie breezes into the room and grabs her veggie stash from the fridge and gives me a dirty look. "Don't eat my stuff."

"I wasn't going to."

The phone rings. Nikeo answers. "Just a minute." He hands it to me. "Some guy for you. I'll wait for you. We're going to dinner."

My blood sugar levels aren't conducive to arguing, and if I don't go get something to eat, I might cannibalize myself. "Fine."

He smiles in victory.

I press the phone to my ear, hoping against hope that Justice is finally calling me back. Heart fluttering, mouth drying, I squeak out, "Hello?"

"Hi, Cane. Samson here."

At least *he's* returning my calls. I walk down the hallway and seek privacy in my room.

"How is she?" I ask.

"Still upset. Still doesn't want to talk to you. Or anyone else for that matter."

I've been trying to make contact with Jocelyn ever since she left so that I could properly apologize and repair our relationship, but she isn't ready to make nice or ready to back down.

Last week, fresh off the plane and home for barely twenty-four hours, she'd made a public service announcement and told everyone what had happened between Nikeo and me. She'd even called Grandma Betty in Florida, who immediately called me and read me the riot act, telling me that I was acting like a fool and was going to lose everything I'd ever wanted. I didn't have the heart to tell her that in all likelihood I'd already lost it.

I don't fault Jocelyn for tattling. Wronged by two of the people she holds most dear, her mother and myself, I understand why she put on the boxing gloves and beat me down. I wish she'd chosen her mother as the target, but I know that family comes first.

"I wish I could take back what I did," I tell Samson and then cringe at my word choice. "I'm sure I'm not the only one who's said that to you lately."

A long silence follows. Although I've spoken to him two other times since Jocelyn arrived home, it's the first time I've indicated that I know about Jelly Roll's affair.

When the silence persists, I know I've screwed up big-time. Samson doesn't feel comfortable with personal topics. He's a meat-and-potatoes kind of guy, and not just when it comes to meals. He likes to stick to the facts, and when it gets too personal, when there's a meal of emotions to talk about, he loses his appetite and walks away from the table.

What's wrong with me lately? As Grandma Betty told me on the phone, *stop making poor choices.* "I shouldn't have said anything," I say meekly.

"What happened with you … it's different from what happened between Jenny and me. We're married. You're not."

Although I still haven't nailed down the details of Jelly Roll's affair, as in who she nailed, I'm not about to make Samson any more uncomfortable than he already is by asking for the sordid story. "Maybe," I concede and then ask for advice. "Justice won't return my calls. What should I do?"

He waits a beat and then says, "You already know."

I should go home, that's what he's implying. That's what Grandma Betty and Frank told me to do. Whether it's pride, anger, or the fact that the timing doesn't feel right or the reason doesn't feel right, or plain stupidity, I can't do it.

Using one hand, I clumsily braid a strand of my hair. "That's not going to happen just yet," I tell him.

"I figured."

I need to ask him the question that I'm dying to know, the reason I'd called him in the first place. My future is hinged on his response.

"Mikayla and Justice. They're together, aren't they?"

I sense his hesitation. I visualize him removing his ever-present Cubs baseball hat and bending the bill nervously in his hands. "They're spending an awful lot of time together. Jeremy is with them, too. I don't think they're a couple, but ... I don't know. I'm not sure about anything anymore."

That makes two of us, I think. After I hang up the phone, I replace my homeless-looking apparel for pencil-tight jeans and an Oscar the Grouch sweatshirt and meet Nikeo out front.

At the restaurant, I don't talk. I eat. I inhale a bowl of soup, a large salad with grilled chicken, and then steal half of Nikeo's burger and fries. When I'm finished, all that's left on my plate is a pile of crumbs and a smeary mess of ketchup and ranch dressing that looks like a finger-painting.

Finally sated, I crumple up my napkin and throw it on my plate. "Let's go."

Nikeo pulls out his pack of cigarettes and places it next his Pepsi. "I'm not leaving."

"We came to eat. We ate."

He pulls out a cigarette and cups his hand around the end as he lights it. His green eyes find mind. He takes a puff. "What's with you?"

"Nothing. Can we just leave?"

"You've been acting like an absolute bitch for a week now, and I can't figure it out."

I know that he didn't intend the statement to be inflammatory, but I'm already inflamed and looking for a reason to burn something to the ground. "You did not just call me a bitch."

"Relax." He blows smoke out of the side of his mouth. "I said you have been *acting* like a bitch. There's a difference."

I look at his cigarette with disgust. "Why are you smoking?"

He gives a cursory glance to the cigarette and then looks at me. "You're going to tell me what's been going on with you."

"No way are we going to sit here and discuss my feelings," I say, throwing back the same phrase he used on me in June.

Impatient, he rolls his eyes and then glares at me. "I didn't ask to discuss feelings, did I? Now, *talk*."

"Fine. You want to know what's been going on? In all likelihood, Justice has dumped me for my best friend. I can't confirm or deny this, but I'm guessing that's what has happened since he won't return any of my calls. Then there's Jocelyn, who also isn't speaking to me because she happened to see me kissing you. To make matters worse, she ratted me out to everyone back home. Now my grandmother calls every chance she gets to remind me that I'm making the biggest mistake of my life. She's telling me I should run home, get on my hands and knees, and beg Justice to forgive me. I'm worried that everything has changed and that it will never get back to the way it was."

After this verbal purge, I feel physically ill. Nauseous and agitated, I press my back against the chair and bounce my foot to offset the roiling in my stomach.

He considers this for a long moment. "Why is change such a bad thing? More importantly, why would you want things to go back to the way they were?"

"Because, it's what I know. It's what I love. Because it's right."

He stabs his cigarette into the ashtray. Signaling the waitress over, he orders two gin and tonics.

When she leaves, he looks over to the stage. "Chad Smith, one of my good friends, is going to play tonight. He does an acoustic set. He's amazing. We should stay and listen."

Leaning forward, I rest my elbows on the table. "Aren't you going to say anything about what I said?"

"Do you want me to say something?"

I half-chuckle, half-snort. "You always have something to say."

"I don't tonight." He tosses me his pack of cigarettes. I catch it in my hands.

"Take one," he says.

Narrowing my eyes, I crush the pack of cigarettes in my palm and then drop it. "I don't smoke."

He raises one side of his mouth into something resembling a grin-sneer. "Now that's not true, is it? I've seen you smoke with my own eyes."

As soon as the drinks arrive, Chad Smith, a scrawny bean pole of a cowboy with enormous boots and an even bigger hat, takes the stage and gives a shout-out to the crowd and thanks them for coming. Too bad I'm going.

"Please, can we leave?" I ask, using my sweetest voice.

"The drinks just came."

"I don't want one," I say forcefully.

"I've heard that before."

It just so happens that Chad's voice is much brawnier than his body. He sings about sweet home Alabama, and it triggers a memory.

Last summer, Justice and I had taken a road trip to Florida. We'd driven through Alabama around midnight. Exhausted and barely conscious at that point, this song had come on the radio. Justice cranked up the volume, and we sang along at the top of our lungs. Afterward, we pulled over into a grove of trees intending to catch a few minutes of sleep. Instead, we made frantic, sweet love in the middle of nowhere in the Deep South on the sultriest of nights.

"In this case," — Nikeo glances at my hyperactive foot that's picked up velocity —"it's not about wanting, it's about needing."

It takes me a second to realize Nikeo's referring to needing a drink, because in my mind, I'm still in Alabama on the side of the road with Justice wanting and needing him. Forcing my foot into submission, I tuck it under the chair. "Alcohol doesn't solve anything," I mumble halfheartedly.

Nikeo stirs his drink with his finger. "A few drinks never hurt."

I fix my face in a Puritanical expression. "It doesn't necessarily help."

Visibly annoyed with me, he shakes the bottom of his glass. The ice cubes knock against each other, and the lime almost flies out. "You're exhausting. It's no wonder Justice moved on."

Nikeo likes to throw the truth like a dart, and his aim is incomparable. He always gets a bull's-eye. His words pierce my raw nerves. I know I'm exhausting, because, sometimes I exhaust myself. Before I'm able to slop a bunch of indignation over my hurt, tears sting my eyes. I try for a steely tone, but my voice shakes like a leaf. "I need to leave. Please."

Nikeo reaches across the table, takes my hand, and stands. Fearing I may cry or scream or do a freaky combination of both, I don't fight him when he pulls me out of my seat and leads me to the dance floor.

There's so much noise inside my head that I'm trying not to let fly out my mouth, I can barely hear Chad singing "If Tomorrow Never Comes," by Garth Brooks.

Nikeo wraps his arms around my waist. "Don't think about anything. Dance with me," he commands.

Contact with him makes it impossible to hold on to my anger or anything else for that matter. He forces me to be so present in the moment that I can't forecast the future or remember the past.

I relax into his arms. Pressing my forehead against the top of his chest, I lock my hands behind his neck. "What are we doing?"

"You said that you wanted things to go back to the way they were because it's what you know. Don't do something because it's familiar or because it's easy. Fear-based decisions are the worst kind."

His aim is as accurate as ever. If I make a decision out of fear, I'll end up sabotaging myself and taking everyone else down with me.

His luminous green eyes lock with mine. When he looks at me like this, I feel like he's dredging the bottom layer of my soul and discovering things I didn't even know existed.

"No more one step forward, two steps back. Stop pretending this isn't happening, because it is. Stop pretending you don't want it to happen, because you do. I'm not what you know or what's easy. I may not even be what you love. But, I'm what you want," he says.

And then, he kisses me. It's deliciously unhurried and long, and I lose myself in it. He pulls away before I want him to.

"Now we can leave," he says, releasing me.

He leaves me stranded in the middle of the dance floor, but we both know that I will follow him anywhere he wants to go.

CHAPTER EIGHTEEN

"You're going to have to suck it up. Let's go over the plan again. You hand her the letter, profusely apologize, and then clean her house from top to bottom, twice if you need to, without saying one negative word to her. In fact," says Caprice as she hands me an envelope, "you have to kiss her ass up and down until it's covered in lipstick marks."

"I could kill you right now. You promoted me two weeks ago, remember? *Vice president of marketing.* Pay raise. A share in the company. I don't clean anymore."

"Not entirely true," she reminds me. "You clean for Arlene and Skeeter. And Harriet."

"Only because I like them and care about them. I can't go back to Misty Moreland's house. I might commit homicide. Or worse. We're talking grand jury indictment. Nationwide news coverage. Interviewed by Barbara Walters. Life in prison."

"If you want to keep your job, you're going."

I grind my back teeth together. "There's no other way?"

"Nope. Cane, don't screw this up. I mean it. If you do, I'll fire you. I don't care if you're my best friend. I can't afford to blow this opportunity. This is a huge break, not just for me, but for you, too. And if all goes well, maybe you'll consider staying here permanently."

It's not like I hadn't known this day was coming. Caprice had won over high-powered Realtor Nancy Nielsen back in July at the Briar Days beer tent. Nancy had been ready to refer us to many of her clients and business associates in Denver and Boulder, which could double, perhaps triple our income potential. However, just before Nancy started making her calls, she happened to have lunch with one her oldest and dearest friends, the hospital-bootie-wearing Misty Moreland, who didn't have such nice things to say about our company, especially me. The deal had almost been dead in the water, but lifeguard Caprice had rescued and resuscitated the agreement, promising Nancy and Misty that she would do everything in her power to make things right.

I stick the envelope in my back pocket and sigh. "You know that you're sending me into a war zone, and Misty is going to be hoping and praying that I step on a land mine and blow up."

Caprice kicks me hard in the butt as I'm walking away.

"Jeez!" I yell, rubbing my backside. "What was that for?"

She smiles innocently and shrugs one shoulder.

When I arrive at Misty's and step out of the car, my butt still aches, which I'm positive had been Caprice's goal. She'd wanted to leave me with a reminder to behave myself.

Misty and her wandering eye meet me at the door. "I honestly didn't think you would show up."

I hand her the apology letter that Caprice had drafted and that I had signed the night before. "I'm truly sorry. I behaved unprofessionally and immaturely." In fact, I had acted like a fool, and I was truly sorry for that. No matter how right I may have been.

Deliberating the authenticity of my words, she eyes me suspiciously with one eye. "You didn't bring any supplies?"

"No, I understand that you prefer to use your own."

She plants her hand on her hip and raises her chin. "Come in. Shoes off. Hospital booties on. No mask today, though. I ran out of them. I'm going to have you start upstairs. I already have all the supplies out. The knobs in the house are filthy."

I step inside and obediently remove my shoes and stretch the blue booties over my feet.

I make a show of rubbing my hands together eagerly and season her with a sweet smile. "I'm ready to go."

"After you polish the knobs, you will spray each of them individually with Lysol, but make sure you hold a paper towel under the knob while you are spraying it, because I don't want anything to get on the floor beneath. It would ruin the finish."

I could bang my head against the wall right now, and if I had Misty's helmet hair, it wouldn't hurt in the least. "Absolutely, whatever you say."

She trails me up the stairs "I'm not thrilled that you're here," she says.

I'm not exactly doing a happy dance either.

"But Nancy told me that she has faith in this business. So I'm taking her word for it. Because believe you me, I didn't want to have one more thing to do with the company. Not after the appalling things you said."

When she gives me a sharp look, I know this is my cue to grovel. "I'm sorry for how I acted. Thank you for giving me an opportunity to make it right."

"I suppose everyone deserves a second chance," she says begrudgingly.

After carefully observing my cleaning methods and hovering for over an hour, Misty, though not delighted, is at least mollified by my diligence and repeated apologies, which I deliver at regular intervals.

"I'm going downstairs to work on some things."

About time.

"I'll come and check on you in a bit to make sure you're doing everything properly. After you're finished up here, vacuum out the vacuum canister and then rinse it with bleach and water."

"I will absolutely do that," I vow heartily, trying to keep the sarcasm from oozing out of my mouth or slipping unwittingly into my expression.

When she's gone, I pucker my lips and then relax them. They're stiff from all the butt kissing.

While I vacuum in neat fan patterns, dust dust-free surfaces, and scrub the nooks and crannies of the room and windows with the handy-dandy industrial cleaning cotton swabs that Misty provided, I remind myself that this is for the benefit of the company and the good of my karma. What goes around comes around, and I'm hoping I'll be handsomely rewarded, should I stay.

Nikeo and Caprice have been trying to convince me that I need to move out here permanently, though each for different reasons.

"You need to stay. I want a relationship with you. I'm tired of this cat-and-mouse game. Anyway, what's the point in the chase, when one of us is going to get pinned down in the end," he'd said last week after a ten-minute make-out session on the couch that had left both of us breathless and wanting more.

Given my state of mind and the position of his hand on my thigh, the pinning would have happened then and there had Caprice not arrived home early from her date, flipped on the lights, and caught us groping on the couch like two teenagers. Embarrassed, I'd literally slinked off the couch and hid in my room for the rest of the night.

The morning after this episode, Caprice poured me a cup of coffee and worked her angle. She told me that I'd become indispensable to the growth of the company and that she couldn't stand to lose me.

"I'm not letting you leave without a fight. It's not just because you're my best friend. I mean, obviously, it's been amazing having you here, but you and I make a great business team. You can't go home at the end of the month. Give it a year. Six months. Let's see where all of this goes," she said.

"I don't know. I mean, I want to stay. I love you. I love the company, but I can't commit to anything right now. I'm not in the right frame of mind to decide anything."

Everyone counts on me to be decisive and committed. It's who I am, and so when I said this, I couldn't quite believe it and neither could Caprice, who pressed the back of her hand to my forehead. "Are you sick?"

"It wouldn't surprise me," I replied.

Determined to get her way, Caprice sweetened the deal by giving me the promotion, a substantial pay bump, and a share of the company.

I can't say that I'm not tempted to make the Rocky Mountains my permanent address, because the farm fields of Savage, Illinois, aren't exactly offering a bountiful harvest right now. The Schaeffer family, with the exception of Samson, despises me. Mikayla and I aren't on speaking terms, or any terms at all for that matter. Grandma Betty and Frank are enjoying their golden years watching the golden Florida sunrises. And my future with Justice isn't so much hanging in the balance as much as it's falling, and I don't think I'll be able to catch it before it splatters on the ground.

I'd managed to get in touch with him once, and it had been a miserable conversation because I'd set the wrong tone right from the start.

"Shocking. You finally answered the phone," I sniped. "I've been trying to get in touch with you for weeks now."

"I thought we agreed not to talk. Until the end of August," he reminded me. "It's the beginning of the month."

"Thanks for clarifying the date. I've left so many messages, I've lost count. I told you it was important, and you didn't call back. You've been ignoring me, which I think says it all right there."

Taut, charged silence followed. Then, in a much-too-calm voice, he said, "If it was that important, you would have gotten in your car, driven back home, and put an end to this. But word around here is that you've been busy making new friends, which is why I assume you haven't come home."

When provoked, Justice fought an impressive passive-aggressive fight.

Instead of owning up to my indiscretion, begging him for his forgiveness, and claiming it wasn't what he thought, which would insult both him and me as it was precisely what he thought, I turned the tables on him. "You're seeing Mikayla."

He made a sound of disgust. "You would think that."

"Don't try to deny it."

"Yes, because what would be the point of that," he stated evenly.

He bulldozed me with this admission, and I staggered backward and sat heavily on the edge of my bed as I processed the reality of them being together. "How could you do this to me?"

The petrified stillness that followed only validated his appalling revelation. Fever-like symptoms set in. My body grew hot and then cold. My brow broke out into a sweat. My teeth chattered. I wanted to know everything, all the awful, intimate details of their relationship. "How long has this been going on? Did it happen right after I left? Is this permanent? Are you in love with her?" I fired off these questions, but Justice continued waging his passive, silent war.

"Have you had sex with her?" I blurted out.

Instead of answering, he strategically turned the table. "Have you had sex with Nikeo?" he asked, saying Nikeo's name like it was a dirty word.

Shutting off the vacuum, I carefully remove the canister, empty the contents into a garbage bag, and then carry it to the utility sink in the basement to give it its bath. Maybe I should wipe out my mouth with bleach and water to cure me of my impulsive, careless way with words. I should never have responded to Justice in the way that I had, because it ended our conversation and mortally wounded our relationship.

Misty with her bleach radar finds me in the basement. "Are you finished with that floor already?"

With gloved hands and sponge at the ready, I plunge the canister in the water and bleach. Scrubbing and smiling, I respond pleasantly. "Yes, I'm finished."

"That's impossible." She presses one hand against the top of her chest. Her hair quivers. "What about the knobs? Are they polished? Did you spray them with Lysol? Because school will be starting soon, and those boys bring home so many germs it's a constant battle trying to keep this house free from viruses, bacteria, and other nasty things."

Have you ever considered spraying your sons with a mixture of Lysol and bleach after they come home to make sure they're not carrying any diseases? This is what I want to say, but I'm going to toe the line and keep my tongue on a leash if it kills me. "I did everything that you asked. Please go inspect and see if I overlooked anything."

"I think I will," she says and sprints up the stairs.

For the rest of the day I'm a humble servant, pleasing Misty and making up for my behavior earlier this summer. Six miserable hours later, I'm finished.

"I'll be telling Nancy that I fully approve."

"That's good to hear. I'm glad that I had an opportunity to make things right."

"Although, you did miss a few spots in the bathroom and in the hall closet and some other areas in the kitchen."

"I'm certain that I cleaned everything," I say politely. My hands and knees can vouch for that fact, as they are sore from all the needless scouring. My singed nose hairs and throbbing head are also key witnesses; the bleach has stripped all my membranes raw.

"Not that well. I took my light wand around the house."

"What are you talking about?"

Exasperated, she pulls a wand out of her back pocket. "You know, a light wand!"

Still clueless, I stare at this unusual tool and shake my head.

Shocked by my ignorance, her eyebrows dart upward and her mouth falls open slightly. "It's a slim battery-powered black light that shows me all the areas where bacteria and germs reside," she explains as if it's the most common thing in the world and everyone has one stashed in his back pocket should an invisible dirt crisis arise.

"Next time, please use more bleach on the counters. Be sure to spray the Lysol in the back corners of the closet. Don't forget to use a new rag for every surface."

Rolling my lips inward, I hold them there. I'm trying to prevent my tongue from busting out of its restraints.

Misty isn't tolerating my silence. She taps her foot, and her wayward eye goes one way and then the other. "Does that *sound* reasonable?"

What would be reasonable is sticking that light wand, all your rags, and the Lysol where the sun doesn't shine. If I open my mouth, these will be the first words to come out, and I'll ruin everything for Caprice and myself. I keep myself occupied by removing my hospital booties and tying my shoes.

Huffing impatiently, she again asks, "Does that sound reasonable?"

Unable to safely speak, I smile and nod, smile and nod.

As soon as I get in the car, I take the leash off my tongue, open the windows, and let out a war cry followed by a bubbly stream of curses as I drive away.

When I arrive back at the house, Nikeo meets me by the back door. He isn't his usual domineering self. He looks subdued. His body is slack, but yet tense at the same time.

My heart crawls up into my throat. "What's wrong?"

"Harriet. She's had a heart attack. Her daughter called. She said that Harriet wants to see you," he says quietly.

My heart somersaults from my throat all the way to the bottom of my stomach. My mind can't quite grasp this unexpected tragedy. "But I saw her yesterday. I was at her house. She was fine. We talked about her husband, Joe. I told her that I was going to Misty Moreland's house today, and she told me that I should behave myself." We'd also talked about Justice and Nikeo and how confused I was. I'd admitted what I'd said to Justice, and I'd asked her what I should do.

"We should go now, Cane," he says urgently. "She's not … she's not doing so well."

He tries to soften the blow, but it's all the more powerful because of what he omits. *She's going to die soon.* I sink into the notion slowly, and like quicksand, it pulls me further down and holds me there. My eyes blur with tears, and then they spill down my face. "I can't believe this."

Nikeo opens his hand and shows me the keys. "I'll drive you to the hospital."

*****

I meet Harriet's daughter, Ellen, outside her hospital room.

"You must be Cane."

I nod. She gives me a hug and then holds me at arm's length, this woman who's an exact replica of Harriet, same eyes, same hair, only twenty some years younger.

"You've been such a blessing in my mom's life. She's told me so much about you."

"She's been a blessing in mine. She's become a dear friend."

"You were the first person she asked for when she finally woke up."

"I was with her yesterday. She told me you were coming to visit last night for dinner. She was excited."

Ellen glances at her husband, who is conferring with a doctor. "That's when it happened. Just after dinner when we were playing cards together." Ellen's voice is pinched with sorrow.

"She's going to be okay, right?" I ask, my voice barely more than a whisper.

Grimacing, Ellen blinks back tears. "It's her second major heart attack. She's not well enough to have surgery. The doctor says she's in congestive heart failure now. There's not much they can do."

That quicksand that I'd gotten stuck in earlier now circles my neck. "I didn't know she was that ill."

"You wouldn't have known. No one did. Mom puts on a great front." She inclines her head toward the hospital door. "You should go see her."

I push open the door.

Harriet, who had been resting, stirs and smiles at me. "You came."

I walk over and kiss her forehead. "Of course I did," I say as I sit on the chair next to the bed and take her hand. "I'm so sorry this happened."

"Now there's no reason for that! Everyone's acting like it's the end of the world. It might be the end of me," she chuckles weakly, "but it's not the end of the world."

"Don't say that. Don't joke around."

"People are too afraid of death, and I don't understand it. I've lived a long life. I've loved. I had the love of a lifetime. I was married to him for over forty years. I've had children. I've watched them grow. I've watched them have children. I've watched my husband die. Now, I'm at the end, and that's okay."

"You're going to be all right."

Harriet squeezes my hand, but there's not much strength behind the gesture. Her spirit may be strong, but her body is weak. "I don't think so, but that's okay."

"You're my friend. I don't want to lose you."

"You're my friend, too. My dear, young friend. Did you behave yourself today?"

Her question about the mundane details of my life surprises me. "You remembered that I was going to see Misty today?"

She cracks a smile. "My heart may be on the fritz, but my memory is working fine."

"I was on my best behavior, even when she showed me her germ wand."

Puzzled, Harriet blinks several times. "A germ wand?"

I tell her the story, and her laughter is cut short when she's overcome with a coughing fit. The episode taxes her and frightens me. Closing her eyes, she rests for a moment.

"Some people are crazy, aren't they?" she asks.

I nod, and her smile fades as she grows more serious. Reaching out she takes my hand and brushes her thumb back and forth over mine.

"I wanted to see you today, because I've been thinking about our talk yesterday and about those two men in your life."

"Don't waste any time thinking about me," I chide. "It doesn't matter."

"It matters to you, and," — pausing, she squeezes my hand again —" it matters to me. I've been stingy with advice, haven't I?"

I shrug noncommittally even though this is very true.

She winks. "I know that you've wanted me to say more than I have."

Smiling sheepishly, I admit, "At times, yes." We'd spent many hours talking about my dilemma this summer, and whenever I asked her for her opinion or asked her what I should do, she told me I was wise enough to figure it out myself. She said that if I made mistakes, which I most certainly would, it would only make me wiser in the end.

"I know that you're lost right now and that you're struggling with who you want to be with, where you want to live, what you want to do with the rest of your life. Cane, you're such a marvelous young woman. Don't rush to try and figure everything out. Be patient with yourself and with those you love. You have your whole life ahead of you. The most important thing, the only thing that will lead to happiness, is following your heart. If you try to do things because you think you should do them or because it's what's right or because it's what someone else wants you to do" — she stops to take a breath. Shaking her head, she continues — "in the end you'll pay a price. You won't be happy."

"Lately, my heart has a terrible sense of direction. It's hopelessly lost."

Smiling compassionately, she nods her understanding. "It happens to everyone at some point. But, there will come a point and time when you will no longer be confused. Everything will come into focus for you, and your heart will lead you to where you're supposed to be."

"Thank you, but," — I smile dryly — "it would have been more helpful if you would have said the name Justice or Nikeo, or if you didn't want to be that specific, you could have said Illinois or Colorado."

She laughs softly. Her grip loosens on my hand, and her eyelids droop low.

"You're tired. I should go," I tell her.

"I'm so glad that I got to meet you." She smiles at me, and it's a smile that says good-bye. "I wish I had more time so that I could see how it all turns out for you."

I attempt to swallow the scratchy lump in my throat, but it's embedded like a prickly burr.

When Nikeo and I arrive home, I change into my biking clothes.

Nikeo meets me in the garage. "I'm coming with you," he announces.

"No mercy on this ride." I hop up onto my saddle and clip in. "I'm going fast and hard."

His eyes find mine. "Is there any other way?"

"Not right now there isn't."

Forgoing the warm-up, I take off at a breakneck pace. My leg muscles burn from the unrelenting cadence, and I shed emotions like a layer of skin along a thirty-five-mile stretch of road. I'm so focused on this solitary therapy session of physical punishment that I'd forgotten Nikeo had come along for the ride until we're back in the driveway.

"Go shower," he says, removing his helmet. He wheels his bike into the garage. "Then I'm taking you out to eat."

"I don't want to eat." Scowling, I rip the rubber band from my hair, freeing my ponytail. I shake my head dog-style, and sweat flies. "Don't order me around."

"You need to eat. We're going out."

Predictably, Nikeo gets his way. An hour later we're seated at a round table in a kitschy Italian restaurant that reminds me of Sorrento's, and the memory of Justice getting down on one knee, the engagement celebration, and the catastrophic party in the woods rolls through my mind.

I fidget with my silverware, bounce my foot, and if left alone for five minutes my entire head would be braided into cornrows.

"Eat something." Nikeo butters bread for me and practically shoves it in my mouth.

I push it away from me. "I'm not hungry."

"You cleaned all day. You spent an hour at the hospital. We went for a thirty-plus-mile ride. You need to eat."

I raise my wineglass. "I'm thirsty, though."

"That's your second glass of sangria," he points out.

"Thanks for keeping track."

He stares at the bread on my plate. "Eat."

I sigh. "Fine." I gobble up the bread, and when I swallow, I realize that the burr of sadness that had been embedded in my throat is gone. It's amazing what a little wine can do.

Eating the bread stimulates my latent appetite, and I manage to put away most of the bowtie pasta with vegetables that I order. Feeling bold, unruly, and ready to follow the direction of my heart no matter how right or wrong it may be, I think as I spy my engagement ring, I place my elbows on the table, steeple my hands, and make an announcement.

"We're going to sleep together. Tonight."

I've never taken Nikeo by surprise. It's always the other way around, but I've definitely shocked him with this. He gives a subtle shake of his head and clears his throat. "You're drunk," he says conclusively, dismissing my proposition.

He signals for the check.

"Come on." I offer an enticing, inviting smile. "That would solve everything, wouldn't it? It would tell me and you *everything* we needed to know."

"This is the wine talking, not you."

"Funny thing" — I point to my lips — "this is my mouth moving."

Nikeo hands our server his credit card.

"I'm surprised. Given the way that you boss me around, I would think by now that you would have told me to have sex with you."

His eyes linger on my mouth. "Can't say I haven't thought about it."

"Then why haven't you said it?"

"We aren't having this conversation tonight," he says.

He signs the receipt, unwraps one of the complimentary mints, and pops it in his mouth.

"Yes, I think we are having this conversation."

"You've had a rough day. I'm taking you home."

"I want to go out. We should go to that party." As we were leaving for dinner, Lizzie and Caprice had tried to coerce Nikeo and me into coming to a hot tub party. "It would be fun."

"I'll drop you off there."

"I want you to come with me."

He stands. "That's not going to happen."

"I always get my way." I slip my hand into his.

"Not with me you don't."

I decide to forgo the party only because I can't convince Nikeo to come with me. When we arrive home, I open a bottle of wine, flip on the gas fireplace, and strew large pillows on the floor.

Nikeo brings his guitar out of his room as I'm pouring myself a generous glass.

"Isn't this better than a hot tub?" he asks as he tunes his guitar and then strums a few chords.

I plop down on a pillow and rest my feet on the coffee table. While I lounge and make the wine disappear, Nikeo sets the night to music, playing one song after another with barely a pause, so that when he finally stops I look around the room to see who turned off the stereo.

He comes over and takes the wineglass from my hand. "You've had too much."

I look at the half-empty bottle. "It doesn't matter."

He sits down next to me. He pushes my hair away from my face, exposing the cross-shaped birthmark. He runs his fingers down the side of my face.

My body flares at his touch. Nerve endings light up like fireworks. I lick my lips in anticipation. The wine flows through me. My bloodstream hums with it. My brain swims against the current of it. Closing my eyes, I prepare myself. I'm close to the point of no return. There will be no going back.

I open my eyes and sit up. I ease myself onto Nikeo's lap, straddling him so that we are face-to-face. "I love the way you play music and the way you sing." I kiss him on the mouth. It's a tease, a chaste gesture that sets us both on edge. He wants more and so do I.

He looks affronted by this. "That's all you have to say?"

"Not even close," I respond, my voice gruff with desire.

"What else?" He gives me an *I dare you* look.

It doesn't matter that I'm scared as hell. I always accept a dare. "I love the way you argue with me. I love that you never give in to me. I love how you boss me around. I love how you refuse to make things easier. I love how you challenge me. I love that you don't believe in the same things I do. I love that you talk back to me, that you get angry with me. I love how it feels when I touch you and when you touch me."

"This isn't the wine talking?"

I place my palms against his face and stare into those eyes that have been observing me, judging me, and hunting me from the day that I arrived. "This is me talking."

He kisses me then, until my lips are bruised and my body wants to be. When he pauses for a moment, I hold my hands on the back of his head, breathe in the sauna smell of his skin, and whisper in his ear. "What do you have to say?"

His eyes find mine. "I love you."

His admission surprises both of us. I never expected that he would feel this, let alone admit it, and judging from his expression, I don't think he did either.

Shaking my head, I rest my fingers over his mouth as if to tell him to shush. "You can't possibly."

"I think I do."

"Thinking and knowing aren't the same."

He settles his hand on the back of my neck and pulls me closer until only a sliver of air separates our lips. "Then I know," he says, and I don't hear the words as much as I can feel them form against my mouth.

He kisses me, silencing both of us. With my legs wrapped around his waist, he stands and carries me to his room. He kicks the door shut. I'm past the point of no return. I'm falling without a parachute.

CHAPTER NINETEEN

"How did she look?" Caprice asks.

"Not good. Her daughter said she would call with any updates."

"She's such a sweet lady. I want to do something for her. Send her a big bouquet and maybe some candy or something."

"She loves peanut butter and chocolate. That's her favorite combination."

"Then we'll go downtown to Briar Chocolates and see if we can find something."

I nod. "We should do it today."

Caprice, who runs alongside me, glances my way. "She's not doing great, is she?"

I give a curt shake of my head. "She all but said good-bye yesterday."

We continue to run. Another mile passes. We've managed to make it almost five miles without her bringing up what she witnessed early this morning, but I know by the way that she's slowing the pace and keeps throwing these I'm-dying-to-know glances that it's only a matter of time before she asks me what happened.

Appropriately, as we are making our way across the footbridge that crosses a small creek, she brings it up.

"I saw you last night" — pausing, she sneaks a look at me, her brow shooting skyward — "sneaking out of Nikeo's room and back to your bedroom."

"We'll cross that bridge when we come to it? Is that what this is?"

Confused, she looks over her shoulder at the small bridge we just traversed and then back to me. "Clever. But, I still want to know what happened."

"I don't want to talk about it."

"Come on. Lizzie and I spent the entire morning speculating about you two."

I already know this. Thanks to my open bedroom window, I'd heard their entire back-and-forth conversation. As they sipped their coffee and their spoons clinked against their cereal bowls they discussed my life. *I saw her sneaking out of his room! At one in the morning. Obviously they had sex. Did you hear any noises or anything? Don't be disgusting, and besides, I wasn't exactly listening. I didn't think she would go through with it, because I'm pretty sure she loves Justice. I guess you're right … she's still wearing the ring, isn't she? What's the story with that anyway? Who knows what she's thinking. Whatever happens, I hope she stays.*

"You weren't exactly quiet. I heard every word."

She grimaces. "You're not mad, are you? Lizzie and I were just trying to make sense of it all. I don't want you to get hurt, but I also don't want my cousin to get hurt."

"An awkward situation all around, isn't it?" I ask.

"I don't want to run anymore," I announce. I stop and make my way over to a bench. I sit and look down the path. "Too much wine last night. I feel like I've been dragging my ass the whole way."

Caprice sits next to me and reaches forward, stretching out her hamstrings. "I would like to hear more about that awkward situation."

Leaning forward, I rest my elbows on my knees and cradle my head in my hands. "I'm not discussing it."

"Why?" She nudges my knee. "Was it that bad?"

Sighing, I turn my head in her direction and peek through my fingers. "I'm having a crisis of faith."

"Did you have sex with him or not?"

I sit up and turn to face her. "I'm not talking about this with you."

"I can't accept that! I'm your best friend."

"Right, and as my best friend, you have to respect and accept it."

"Don't kiss and tell? Is it something like that?"

I'm physically and emotionally dehydrated and defeated; I give my friend a give-me-some-space look.

She holds up her hands. "I'll back off."

I push myself off the bench and turn in the direction from which we've come. The distance seems insurmountable. I think back to the night of the engagement party in the woods and how Justice had carried me on his back through the woods. If he were here now, would he carry me or would he walk away?

Energetic from her six cups of coffee, Caprice pops up and tightens her ponytail so that it sits higher on her head. Shaking her arms like a swimmer itching to jump into the water, she smiles eagerly. "Ready to go?"

For the first time in my life, I've run out of energy. My reserve tank is as dry as a bone, and I'm not sure I can afford to fill it back up. "I have to walk back."

Stunned, Caprice stills her arms and studies my face. "I'm worried about you."

I start walking. She catches up with me.

"You're worried about me, and I'm worried about Mikayla," I say, continuing our conversation.

"If you're seriously worried about her, I'm going to have to slap some sense into you."

"I'm worried about what she's doing," I clarify. "I had another dream, like the one I had earlier this summer. She was standing at the altar in her wedding dress. She was getting married, and the groom was none other than Justice."

Caprice guffaws. "*No way.* Be reasonable. It was *just* a dream."

"You don't know how real it was. I heard her saying the vows. With everything that's been happening, it makes total sense. He's finished with me."

"You're not only paranoid but completely out of your mind. I know that guy, and there's no way he would marry her."

"It was a vision," I declare. "I know it's real. I saw her wedding dress, her flowers, how she was wearing her hair. It's making me crazy."

"Because it is crazy. Let me remind you that with your other *Mikayla visions,*" she says making air quotations with her fingers, "it's always been about her being hurt or in danger."

"She is going to be in serious danger if it's true."

When we arrive home an hour later, Nikeo's in the driveway, working on his bike. Standing there in his bare feet wearing nothing but greasy, low-riding jeans with his dark hair tousled, he exudes sexiness. He glances up and gives me a crooked smile.

Caprice looks at him and then me. "I'll be inside."

She leaves me standing in the driveway.

Feeling awkward and embarrassed, I cross my arms and avoid eye contact.

Working a rag over the bike chain, he removes dust and debris. "You're awfully quiet," he says.

"I'm not sure what to say."

"A first for you."

"In this case, I guess it is." I walk over to him. "About last night . . ." I try to say the words I need to say, but I can't do it yet.

Crouching down, he rifles through a pile of wrenches and finds the size he needs. I try not to stare at his dark, strong arms that only hours ago held me captive.

Without making eye contact, he asks, "What about it?"

"You're going to make this difficult on me, aren't you?"

He shrugs. "Nothing about this relationship has been easy, has it? Then again, easy is boring." His statement has a punch of anger.

"Volatility is overrated, too."

"Is it now?" He looks me directly in my eyes with such desire that I lower mine. "Because if last night was any indication then I would dare to say you're lying."

"I don't lie."

He makes the ultimate confrontation. "Do you have any regrets?"

Too many to count, I think. But it wouldn't be fair to answer in this way. "It's too early to tell."

He accepts my answer with a nod, turns away from me, and resumes tinkering with his bike.

Inside the house, Lizzie and Caprice are arguing about something. Caprice is on the warpath, and I can tell from her tone of voice that she may start throwing punches if someone doesn't intervene. Too bad for Lizzie. I don't have the energy to break up a fight, and I seriously doubt

Nikeo will come to Lizzie's rescue.

I study him working and watch the way his capable hands effortlessly wield the wrench. My thoughts return to last night, remembering the way that he undressed me and worked his fingers over my body until I felt as broken and vulnerable as I'd ever been.

"What happens next?" I ask.

He grits his teeth and much too carefully places the wrench on the ground. With barely contained frustration, he looks up at me, "I don't know, but don't take too long to decide."

I hear a crash inside the house, and then Lizzie yells, "Come on! Like, stop overreacting!"

"I'm not overreacting! I can't believe this, Lizzie! How stupid!"

Looks like I'm going to have to referee. I enter the house, and Lizzie and Caprice immediately stop what they're doing and stare oddly at me.

"What gives?" I ask, directing the question at Caprice.

Instead of responding, she looks over at the messy countertop that's covered with a week's worth of mail and miscellaneous papers, receipts, and random articles of clothing. That kind of disorganization drives Caprice crazy, and because she's been badgering all of us to make sure we clean up after ourselves, I'm assuming this is what set off the argument. Lizzie, the biggest offender in the house, probably threw something onto the pile. In fact, there's a bra sitting there that I hadn't noticed earlier.

Caprice swings her eyes back to me. Stepping forward, she hands me a piece of paper. "Lizzie has something to tell you."

Lizzie, obviously peeved, glares at her cousin. "She can read."

"Tell her!" yells Caprice. "Or so help me, I'll punch you in the face."

Lizzie adjusts the row of sparkly bracelets on her arms and heaves a big sigh. "You are such a bully, Caprice, do you know that? It's not that big of a deal."

She tries to leave the room, and Caprice grabs her forearm, causing the bracelets to clink against each other. "Stay put."

Lizzie growls like a trapped cat. "Let go!"

"No," Caprice says and looks at me. "Cane, look at the paper."

I raise the sheet of paper from my side and quickly skim the words.

Mik and J getting married Saturday at six. Should come home. Samson.

My stomach inverts. My hand flies to my mouth. That moment Harriet had told me about, when it would be clear what direction my heart wanted to go in, it's here.

I'm so close to hyperventilating, I'm eyeing up the brown paper lunch bags on the counter.

"Are you all right?" Caprice asks.

"Let me go!" Lizzie twists herself free from Caprice's grip and rubs her red arm. "I can't believe you're treating me like this! You're such a controlling bitch. I should quit. If I leave, I'm taking all my clients with me," she warns. "I could be making so much more money and I know that —"

Apparently, rage is more effective than paper bags. My lungs inflate with so much hot air it feels as if I could take flight.

I interrupt Lizzie's nonsense complaining. "*When did he call? When did you take this message? How come you didn't tell me? Why didn't you give this to me?*"

"I don't know. Monday or maybe last weekend. I can't remember. *Okay?* But at least I wrote the message down."

"You mean you could have taken it *before* this Monday, as in they could *already be married?*"

"No. I think, I mean, I *know* that I took the message this week."

I cast a helpless look at Caprice, and she gives me the reassurance I need. "That has to be the case, because the kitchen was spotless last weekend."

Scrunching up the piece of paper, I whip it at Lizzie. "I can't believe you didn't tell me."

"You know what, Cane? Join this century and get a cell phone. The rest of the world has one. Then you could take your own messages, because I'm sick of writing all of them down and trying to remember to give them to you. I'm not a secretary, you know."

"All of them? Please don't tell me that there are other ones."

Dodging my stare, Lizzie fiddles with her enormous diamond hoop earring.

"Lizzie, tell me."

Sighing, she shuts her eyes. "There might have been," she admits in a childish voice.

Furious, my eyes sweep the counter, and I begin sifting through the chaos looking for other scribbled messages. How many people have tried to call and tell me about this? Had Mikayla called to brag? Had Grandma Betty found out and called to warn me?

"I'm going to rip that earring out of your ear!" bellows Caprice.

Recognizing that her cousin may very well do that, Lizzie retreats, taking giant steps backward. "You two can both suck it. *I'm sorry,* but I don't see how it's *my* responsibility to keep track of who called or when they called or how many times they called and what they said. It isn't part of my job."

With this proclamation, she stalks out of the room.

"It's called common courtesy, Lizzie, but obviously you wouldn't know anything about that!" Caprice yells after her.

Had Justice called me? Had he told me that he was moving on and that he decided to marry Mikayla? Why would he do this? He might love her, but jump into marriage? A sickening thought occurs to me. There's only one reason a gentleman like Justice would marry Mikayla so quickly. I wonder if the wedding invitations had a shotgun as the logo.

Caprice comes over to my side and puts her hands on my shoulder. "Calm down. It's going to be fine. I'll call the airline for you and get you a flight."

I look at the clock and choke back the sobs that are creeping their way up my throat. "It's almost eleven, which means it's almost noon there. Six hours. That's not enough time."

"You'll make it in time."

"The vision was true."

Mystified, she shakes her head.

"When I talked to Justice a couple of weeks ago, he asked me if

I'd slept with Nikeo, and do you know what I said to him?" I look at Caprice. "I said, 'I wouldn't call it sleeping since I was wide awake and enjoying every second of it.' I had to run my big mouth and say something stupid."

Caprice gives me a sympathetic look that I don't deserve. She reaches for the phone book and starts paging through it. I cover my face with my hands, allowing myself one second of weakness and self-pity.

The side door opens and closes. Nikeo, greasy and sweaty, breezes into the kitchen and gives me a smoldering stare.

Caprice halts her airline search and looks at me. *You have to tell him what's going on,* she says without uttering a single word. "I'm going to go down to the office. We have more phone books there," she says.

When she leaves, Nikeo crosses his arms and leans against the refrigerator. "This is it then. Your decision is made."

"You know I'm leaving?"

He raises one shoulder. "I'm not deaf. The windows are open."

Despite my desire to go home and stop Justice from doing this and get him back, I can't pretend I don't have strong feelings for Nikeo. Confusing as they are, they're nonetheless real.

"Don't leave," he commands. "Stay here. With me."

"He's getting married."

"And you're running home to try and stop it? That doesn't make sense to me. It's ridiculous." He makes a sound of disgust. "Don't know what you have until it's gone? Is that it?"

"I love him." Under the circumstances, I recognize how cruel my proclamation is.

"Trust me." His eyes bore into mine. "That was established rather definitively last night, wasn't it?"

I dodge his gaze. Blood fills the capillaries in my face. "I'm sorry, Nikeo. I have to go."

As I turn to walk away, he says, "Make your choice right here and right now."

My eyes find his. The intensity of what I feel for him startles me still, and even though I've already made my decision, my heart aches.

He closes the distance between us, pushes my hair away from

my eyes, and places his hands on my face. There's vulnerability in his expression that I've never seen before. I'm hurting him. All this time I thought he had more power over me, and now I know for certain that it's the other way around.

"I don't give second chances," he says.

"I wouldn't expect you to."

CHAPTER TWENTY

"Maybe it's all a misunderstanding," Caprice says as she takes the airport exit. "Maybe Samson was trying to get a rise out of you or something."

"No way." I unwind the dozen or so braids that I've put in my hair. "He would be the last person trying to get a rise. It's his wife who's always trying to get a rise out of me."

"You're going to try to call them again, though, right?" she asks.

Before we'd left, I'd called the Schaeffer household, Samson's office, Samson's cell, Justice's cell, even Mikayla's cell, and finally Grandma Betty and Frank's home number hoping to get to the bottom of this mess and stop it before Justice pulled the trigger on the shotgun. But no one had answered. "If I have time."

"You probably won't," Caprice says, glancing at the clock on the dash. "Thirty minutes until your flight, and they'll be boarding by the time you get your ticket and make it through security."

She looks at me out of the corner of her eye. "Are you sure you want Justice back? With him marrying Mikayla, and with how you feel about Nikeo — it doesn't make sense to me."

"I wouldn't be here if I wasn't sure. What I have with Nikeo? It wouldn't work."

"But you love him," she asserts. "I know that you do, and from what I can tell, he feels the same about you."

Closing my eyes, I think back to the night before and what happened with Nikeo. "But, I love Justice more."

"I could turn around and go back to the house." She looks at me. "Last chance."

I place the strap of my duffel bag over my shoulder. "I know what I'm doing."

She looks at me skeptically. "What if he goes through with marrying her? What will you do?"

"I haven't thought that far ahead. I can't think that far ahead."

She whips the car into the terminal lane and speeds up to the curb, earning herself a middle finger and a series of honks.

"Thank you so much." I give her a quick hug.

"Go! Call me as soon as you can."

I fly out of the car, and mere minutes later, I'm flying in the air. The flight seems excruciatingly long, and I can't sit still.

I jiggle, bounce, and tap, and earn a scolding stare from the elderly woman who had the unfortunate luck of being seated next to me.

When she's had enough of my constant motion, she makes a tsk sound and glares at me. "Ants in your pants or something?"

In no mood to be called out on my anxiety let alone apologize for it, I respond sassily. "That's what Grandma Betty tells me. I've had ants in my pants from the day I was born. They're quite something. Want to have a look at them?"

She gives me a sharp look of disapproval. "No, I do not, young lady."

Sitting on my hands, I close my eyes and click my heels together three times. There's no place like home.

Two miserable hours and twenty minutes later, we land. Having only a carry-on, I bypass the luggage claim and sprint toward the Avis rental counter where a car would be waiting for me, another detail Caprice had seen to while I'd showered and packed in less than half an hour.

Once I've signed all the dotted lines and the keys are in my hand, I glance at the clock. It's four thirty. I barely have enough time to make it, but I have to at least try to get in touch with Justice. I dash over to the phone booth, whip out my calling card, and dial his cell number. It goes straight to voicemail. Groaning in frustration, I dial the Schaeffer household, hoping by some miracle he's there. It rings seven times, and I'm in the process of hanging up when someone says, "Hello."

I press the phone back to my ear. "It's Cane!" I exclaim, breathy with urgency.

"Well, well, well," Jelly Roll says slowly as if she has all the time in the world. "Samson said you might be calling."

"I need to talk to Justice."

"He's at the church with everyone else," she informs me, her voice tight with impatience. "You weren't invited for a reason."

It occurs to me for the first time that I have no idea where he's getting married. "What church?"

"Grace Lutheran."

His betrayal astounds me. How could he get married in the church where my great-grandmother, Grandma Betty, and my mother were married? Is he deliberately twisting the knife, or is this Mikayla's brilliant idea? "Where's Mikayla?"

"She's there, too. I don't have time for all of this, you know —"

I slam the phone down, because I don't have time either.

Once in the car and on the road, I set the compass next to me along with the map. I'm operating on such a high level of panic, I'm scarily calm. Cruising well over the speed limit and constantly on the lookout for state patrol, I'm making excellent time. Although I won't be there for the start of the ceremony, I pray that I'll at least arrive before Justice says, *I do,* because *I don't* think I could recover from that.

Harriet told me that my heart would regain its sense of direction, and it has. At the beginning of the summer, I'd taken a crazy, out-of-the-way detour, and I'd gotten hopelessly lost and distracted by Nikeo, in more ways than one. But this morning when I discovered that Justice was marrying Mikayla, my disoriented heart knew which path to take. Because, for me, all roads lead back to Justice.

Valentine's Day the first year we were dating, I'd spent an entire Saturday cutting three hundred and sixty-five hearts out of red construction paper and decorating them with glitter. On each of those hearts, I'd written one thing that I loved about Justice so that over the course of the next year, he could read a new one each day.

I love your absurd fascination with alien movies. I love your crooked dimples. I love the way your face lights up when you see me. I love the way your lips curve into a smile even when you're sleeping. I love how you never raise your voice at me even when I deserve it. I love your absolute kindness. I love that you always choose to see the good in people. I love the way you calm me down just by looking at me. I love the way you make my heart race when you look at me from across the room. I love your patience. I love your strong values. I love how you let me beat you when we play basketball. I love how finicky you are about your food not touching on your plate. I love how you giggle like a little boy when I tell you a dirty joke ...

When I'd embarked on the project, I thought it would be difficult to come up with hundreds of things, but in the end, I could have written many more.

What I'd loved more than making the gift, was watching his face when he received it. He'd treasured it so much that the next year I'd done something similar. Only instead of writing what I loved about him on the hearts, I'd offered my services and myself in three hundred and sixty-five different ways. Some of those ways were innocent. A home-cooked meal. A car detailing. A fishing excursion up north. Some of them weren't so innocent, and those were the ones that he cashed in first.

How ironically bitter that I think about this gift now when only hours before I'd told Nikeo what I'd loved about him. I hate myself for betraying Justice in this way. The only thing that assuages my guilt is that while I'd told Nikeo what I loved about him, there are also things I can't stand about him, things I hate about him. Love tainted with hate isn't love at all. I only wish I'd realized this sooner.

The scenery has changed. Cityscape and suburbia has given way to cornfields and random groves of sturdy trees that guard the landscape like gnarly giants. I keep my eyes trained on the road, determined to get there in time, and then I realize that arriving is only half the battle.

What am I going to do when I get there? Because I've been so focused on getting across the country, I hadn't actually thought about the process of stopping Justice from making the biggest mistake of his life. In all the movies I'd ever seen, it's always the man rushing in to stop the ceremony. If I bust through those double church doors and shout at the top of my lungs, why would Justice bother to listen to a word I say?

After all, I'm not a knight in shining armor. I wouldn't even consider myself a fair maiden, because my behavior of late has been anything but fair. I can't sweep Justice onto the back of a steed, or in this case into the front seat of this Geo Prizm, and ride off into the sunset, not that there would even be one because the skies are fraught with pissed-off clouds. The reality is that I'm a scrawny, freckly young woman with a big mouth and even bigger ego whose knee-jerk reactions injure everyone, though in the end, they injure me the most.

I'm interrupted from my verbal self-flagellation when the car starts to misbehave. It vibrates violently beneath me. The engine makes a grinding, squealing kind of noise that sounds ominous, and I white-knuckle the steering wheel and let a string of expletives fly. Just when I think that the engine might explode or at the very least catch on fire, the car regains its composure. I remind myself to breathe.

I'm filling my lungs for a second time when the check engine light on the dash flashes. The car starts to shake, rattle, and gasp, and this time it isn't misbehaving. It's taking its last painful breaths and preparing to die. This isn't supposed to happen in a rental car!

I pound on the console, threatening and cajoling the car. "Don't you dare quit on me! I know you can do it! We're almost there!"

The check engine light defiantly flickers in my face one last time, and then the engine perishes. I rock all one hundred and five pounds of me forward and backward like a madwoman, hoping the momentum will keep the car moving; but this object in motion doesn't care about Newton's Law, because it's not going to stay in motion. Maneuvering the vehicle onto the shoulder, I stomp on the brake and throw it in PARK.

Now what?

I don't have a cell phone. I'm stranded two miles from the church, and the ceremony has already started. The cherry on top of my day? A wicked thunderstorm is brewing. Impressive stacks of robust clouds stretch across the sky like a defensive line. Poised and ready to tackle, they're throwing off bolts of lightning as a warning.

About the only thing I have going for me is that the car has conveniently managed to break down next to a horse farm. Galloping through the doors of Grace Lutheran Church on a white steed would make quite a statement. However, my equestrian experience is limited, and I'm fairly certain the owners would frown on me jumping their fence and thieving one of their mighty stallions.

All I know is that I have to get there in time to take the pastor up on his invitation to *speak now,* because there's no way that I can *forever hold my peace.* Not in this instance. I don't have it in me.

I have no choice. I have to run. Digging in my bag, I trade my flip-flops for my running shoes. I yank them on, jump out of the car, and start sprinting just as the defensive line in the sky takes action.

I dash through the pouring rain, maintaining a grueling pace where breathing is a luxury I don't have time for. My lungs catch fire from the effort, and I can't even feel my body. I see the sign for the church, and because I'd used that sign as a marker when running in high school and training for the marathon with Justice, I know that I have one more mile to go.

Time warps, and although I know that I've been running for only minutes, it seems like hours. Lactic acid chomps away at my muscles. Wind and rain push against me. The thunder shakes the ground beneath my feet. Everything conspires against me, but I'm not going to give up. I can't.

In the distance is the brick edifice of the church, the steeple, and behind it, the cemetery where my parents and brother are buried.

A quarter mile to go. In the parking lot, there are a dozen cars, including Justice's truck and Mikayla's yellow Corvette, which has been decorated with tin cans and balloons. In the back window, in block, bubble letters, the signature style of Jocelyn, is the phrase *Just Married.*

I stop. That fragile thing that lies in the deepest, most hidden part of my heart shatters. Lightning strikes a tree in the cemetery, splitting it clean down the middle, and I reflexively clutch at my chest, feeling like the same thing has happened to me.

For the first time since this morning when I held my head in my hands and allowed myself one moment to wallow in self-pity, I hesitate.

I hold my hands straight out to the side, tip my head back, exposing the cross-shaped birthmark on my forehead, and allow the storm to baptize and drown me.

Give up, turn around, and leave, or bust through the double doors?

I can't stop who I am. I take off in a dead run.

I throw open the first set of doors and step into the narthex. A curving wall and another set of doors block off the vestibule. Through the slender, stained-glass windows that line the curving wall, I see them standing at the altar.

She's not supposed be standing next to him. I am.

That fragile, shattered thing inside my heart blisters, and instead of doubling over from the pain, I stagger forward, push open the doors, and scream, "That's supposed to be me!"

Only, when the groom turns around, *it's not Justice.* It's Jeremy. I'd been so sure ... Mik and J are getting married, only the J hadn't been Justice, it had been Jeremy.

Relieved, I grab onto the end of a pew to steady myself. Justice, who stands next to Jeremy as the best man, looks the opposite of relieved.

Through the incredulous expressions of the guests, which are thankfully limited to the Schaeffer family and Mikayla's father, I see my actions for what they are, self-serving, reckless, and a whole lot of crazy. Ashamed not only for this impetuous act, but for all the hotheaded decisions that brought me to this point, I go crimson with shame.

Mikayla, looking aggrieved by the interruption, shakes her head. "You didn't honestly believe I would have done that to you?"

Jenny Ryanne, incensed that I've interrupted her son's wedding, screeches, "Get out of here this instant!"

"Jenny," Samson intones softly, resting his hand on her upper arm.

"What?" she asks him. "She's ruining this wedding."

"I'll take care of this," says Justice. Wanting to restore peace and order, he starts making his way toward me.

"No." I hold up my hand. "She's right. I've ruined this. I'm so sorry, Jeremy and Mikayla."

I could break down and cry and never stop, but I won't give myself permission. I hold onto what remains of my dignity, which is sopping wet like everything else on me. "I'm so sorry."

"Cane," Mikayla looks me in the eye. "I'm sorry. I wanted to call," she says softly.

Not trusting myself to speak, I'm only able to nod. Dripping wet and shaking from more than cold, I leave the church.

I saw how Justice looked at me with disgust. Knowing that he won't be coming after me and that I've lost everything, there's nothing more to say or do. In the pouring rain, I put one foot in front of the other and begin the slow walk back to the rental car. I'll change into dry clothes, wait the storm out, and plot my next move.

Progress is slow. I'm nursing a blister thanks to my feverish run without socks. Tired of favoring my heel and hobbling, I take off my squishy shoes. Walking barefoot on the shoulder of a highway in the pouring rain is not how I pictured my evening. Had I stolen the horse, at least I would have had some form of transportation.

I'm a football field's length from the church, when I hear him yelling for me.

I stop and turn around, shielding my eyes from the drops. He's standing at the edge of the parking lot holding an umbrella.

"Come back! Don't be ridiculous!" he yells.

Too late for that. I'm beyond ridiculous. I cup my hand to my mouth. "Go back inside!"

"It's over!"

CHAPTER TWENTY-ONE

Those two words bring my heart to a complete stop.

Seeing him standing there in the rain under the umbrella, his tall, muscular frame clad in a tailored tuxedo, his mouth taut with frustration — I can't fathom why I ever left.

I could not love him more.

The fear that made me run is nothing compared to the terror of losing him forever. And, I think I have.

When he starts walking toward me, I hold up my hand. I don't want him making the effort. I'm the one at fault for creating this absurd mess. I start walking, slow and steady at first, but I can't help myself. Barefoot and desperate for him, I start running.

I duck under the dome of his umbrella. I look into his aquamarine eyes, the color of tranquil, shallow ocean waters.

"I've missed you so much," I say, reaching up to touch his cheek.

He catches my wrist and holds it there in midair. "Don't."

His rebuff, though deserved, isn't expected. Justice, who usually forgives and forgets easily, looks furious. My throat is clogged with sadness, and I push words through it. "I'm sorry."

He releases my wrist. "That may be the case, but that doesn't quite cover it, does it?"

I bring back the words that he yelled. "You said it's over between us? Are you sure?" Devastation rocks my expression, and it's only a matter of time before my features crumble. "Is that what you want?" I ask.

"I was talking about the ceremony."

My heart skitters around in my chest. "Oh."

"We have a lot of things to talk about."

"The understatement of the century."

"There will be a small reception at Sorrento's. I have to go. I can talk to Samson to see if you can come."

I look back toward the church. Jocelyn stands behind the double doors watching us. Because of the rain, she's only a blurry outline. I put up a hand and wave, but she quickly turns, refusing to acknowledge me. "Samson would be the only one who wanted me there." I pause, wanting and needing him to say that he wants me there as well, but his silence is withering and answer enough.

Justice fixes his eyes on some nondescript point over my shoulder. I lower my eyes to the ground. Murky water swirls around my bare toes. I'm grateful for my numb feet, because there's so much pain everywhere else I can barely stay upright. "I can't go. I've already ruined enough things. Mikayla and Jeremy are married? Why didn't you call me and tell me? I don't understand how any of this happened or what's going on."

He recycles my phrase. "The understatement of the century."

From his tone and the way that his eyes bore into mine, I know that he's not referring to the wedded couple.

Behind us the church doors swing open, and Jenny, wearing a silver dress that resembles a Christmas tree ornament, yells for Justice to bring the umbrella back. He turns and holds up one finger letting her know that he'll be there in a minute. Dissatisfied, she glares at me and huffily turns, raising her hands and saying something to Samson, who's accustomed to her tirades and merely shakes his head at her.

"Where's your car?" he asks, his eyes scanning the parking lot.

"I have a rental car. It broke down two miles from here. I can walk."

"I'm not letting you walk in this weather," he says firmly, fishing his keys out of his pocket. "Go sit in my truck. I'll be there in a minute."

He turns and walks away, leaving me in the downpour. Samson, who stands near the entrance waiting for Justice, waves at me. I wave back and walk to Justice's truck.

After I start the engine, I crank the heat on high and hold my pruned and frozen fingers up to the vent. Out of the corner of my eye,

I see a tornado of silver coming my way. Seconds later, Jenny stands at the passenger door glaring at me. With her squat and flushed, fleshy neck, she looks like an aggressive rooster.

She bangs on the window with the wooden handle of the umbrella that she's holding.

This should be good. I hit the automatic button to lower the window.

"How dare you show up here like this and ruin everything!"

"From what I understand the ceremony was over."

"You've had your chance with this family, with Jocelyn, with Justice. Your chance has come and gone. You're not welcome anywhere near us."

Normally I'm not great at keeping my temper in check, but my flattened spirit doesn't have much oomph today. "I haven't done anything to you, Jocelyn, or to any of the rest of your family."

"Didn't *do* anything? First off, you had my daughter go on some insane rabbit diet, and she came home starving and emaciated. You wouldn't even take her to work with you. You pawned her off on this girl named Lizzie. Not only that, you forced her to go the doctor to get poisonous medication for her acne! I found the stuff in her bathroom, and she told me that you're responsible."

Looks like Jocelyn has been bending the truth this way and that. "Poisonous medication? Isn't that an oxymoron?"

This comment goes unnoticed as she continues her rant. "You neglected her because you were too busy with your new boyfriend. You don't know how devastated Jocelyn is because of what she saw and what you did. Now you come back here, interrupting my son's wedding all so you can get Justice back. After what you put him through and what you've done, you don't deserve him. You cheated on him, and so in my book, you're through. There are no second chances. I want you out of here tonight. Go back to Colorado."

Her imperious gaze dares me to say something in return, and I don't want to disappoint her.

"You know, you might want to think about revising your book," I say spitefully.

She jerks her chin upward, her fleshy jowls wobbling with the motion. "What's that supposed to mean?"

"There are *no second chances?* You of all people *know* that's not true. Your husband is giving you a second chance after you cheated. And since we're keeping score here, I know that Jocelyn is more upset by what you did than by what I did. I'm not married. You are. So what *you* did to Samson is worse."

She retracts her neck. The extra skin gathers around her triple chin. Her eyes noticeably shrink.

"*What?* You didn't think I would find out the reason Jocelyn came to Colorado? You cheated."

"I did no such thing," she states feebly.

"At least I have the dignity to own up to my sins. I've already apologized for interrupting Jeremy's wedding, but I'll say it again. I. Am. Sorry. I'll spare you further embarrassment." I press the button and roll up the window.

Samson, who has been watching from under the eaves by the church entry, calls for his wife. Before she turns to leave, she gives me one last contemptuous stare. I prudently ignore her.

Twenty minutes later after everyone has left the parking lot and avoided eye contact with me, Justice finally opens the door. He throws a duffel bag onto the seat.

"I have a change of clothes in there." He unzips it and pulls out a pair of jeans and a T-shirt. "Wear these."

"I'm okay."

He gives me a dubious stare. "Your lips are blue. You're freezing."

The soaked clothes are glued to my body like an icy second skin and have lowered my body temperature at least five degrees. Despite the blasting heat, I'm freezing. I do as he says, quickly shedding my clothing. Justice, who only months before would have taken pleasure in watching me undress and taken advantage of the situation, keeps both hands on the steering wheel and his eyes trained out the driver's window. His aloofness makes me want to cry.

I pull on his jeans and shirt; they're so oversized I feel like a toddler. He puts the truck in gear and drives to the rental car.

"I'll get your things," he says.

Before I can protest and tell him that I'll do it, he jumps out of the truck and runs to the rental car to retrieve my purse, luggage, and keys.

When he's finished transferring everything to his truck, he looks at me. "I'm the best man. I have to go to the reception."

"I understand," I say in a small voice.

He regards me briefly, his expression inscrutable. Nodding, he puts the truck into gear and drives away.

The silence between us, uncomfortably stifling, makes me anxious. The windshield blades swish rapidly. Raindrops ping aggressively on the roof of the truck. Justice taps his thumb against the bottom of the steering wheel.

"I want to explain everything," I say suddenly, trying to break the tension and make some conversational headway. I admit that I was wrong to jump to conclusions about him and Mikayla. I inform him that she answered his phone one night at the bar, and because of what she said, I assumed they were together. Jelly Roll insinuated the same thing, I add.

"Then, when I talked to you on the phone, you didn't outright deny it. When I talked to Samson, he didn't know if you and Mikayla were together, and he certainly didn't mention anything about Mikayla and Jeremy. And, Lizzie, Caprice's cousin, she's horrible at relaying messages. Samson had left a message about the wedding, but it had said Mik and J are getting married. I thought it was you."

I give him the rest of the pertinent details concerning my frantic morning and the trip across the country to try and make it to the wedding in time so that I could put a stop to it.

When I'm finished, he doesn't say anything.

"I'll drop you off at the house," he says in a clinical tone. "We'll talk later tonight."

When he turns off the highway miles before the Schaeffer Farm, I say, "I thought we were going to the house."

"We are."

Still confused, I turn in my seat and look over my shoulder at the stretch of gravel road behind us.

He settles his eyes on me for a brief instant before focusing back on the road. "We're going to my house."

That one little pronoun, *my,* tells me everything I don't want to know.

By the time we reach the rutted and muddy driveway, the rain clouds have scooted away, revealing a sloppy orange sunset that looks like melted sherbet, and it has dripped onto the tops of the trees that surround the house that he's building.

He puts the truck in PARK and hands me his cell phone.

What was once a concrete hole in the ground is now a beautiful Craftsman home, an exact replica of the one that I had admired in Chicago.

"It looks amazing."

"I still have a long way to go. It's not finished yet, but it will be in another few months. The front door is open. Call the rental car place, explain what happened. They can arrange to have the car towed."

Sticking only to the logistics, he has emotionally vacated the premise. "We can talk then, right? I really want to work this out. Don't you?" I ask.

He extends his neck and loosens his bow tie. "We'll talk when I get back."

I gather my things and have to hold onto the waist of the pants I'm wearing so they don't slip to my ankles. I awkwardly step out of the truck.

Before I close the door, I look at him. "I love you, Justice."

He turns toward my gaze, and I recognize that open and exposed expression. I'm positive that he's going to say it in return, but then he faces forward and drives slowly away.

Dazed by his rejection, I lose my grip on my bag, purse, and on the waist of Justice's jeans. Everything falls to my feet, including the pants. I stand there half-naked in front of the half-completed dream house.

CHAPTER TWENTY-TWO

"Did you have sex with him?"

I'm startled awake by these words. After crying on the floor for at least two hours and probably causing extensive water damage to the plywood subfloors, I'd fallen into the kind of fitful sleep that follows emotional and physical exhaustion. My face, crusty with dried snot and tears, is swollen and tender. I prop myself up on my elbows.

Justice sits next to me with his arms resting on his knees. His white tuxedo shirt, rolled at the sleeves, hangs open, revealing a white undershirt.

"Did you have sex with him?" he asks again.

When Nikeo had closed the door to his room and come to the bed, I'd been more than willing to give myself to him in every way. And I almost had, but when I'd closed my eyes in the moment before, I saw Justice. My heart had revealed what was most important, and knowing that, I couldn't go forward. I'd immediately stopped Nikeo.

"No, I didn't have sex with him," I answer honestly, but my tone reveals guilt.

"But you did things with him, didn't you?"

I nod, more with my eyes than my head.

"Cane." A tortured look that blossoms into saddened rage takes over his face. He purges his lungs of air and runs his hands through his dark hair. "*I want to kill him for touching you.*"

The menace in his voice is unfamiliar. "I wish I could take it all back. The whole summer," I tell him.

His eyes are glassy with emotion. Always stoic, Justice has never cried in front of me. Knowing I'm responsible for evoking such emotion is unbearable.

He looks at the ring on my left hand. "I wish I could take it back, too," he says. "We both made a lot of mistakes. I should have told you about Mikayla kissing me. I should have reacted more calmly when you told me you were leaving. I shouldn't have let you leave. I shouldn't have made up those stupid rules. I didn't want you seeing anyone else. When Jocelyn came back and told me what had happened with you and that guy, I wanted to book a flight, go get you, and bring you home."

"Why didn't you?"

"I knew that if you didn't find your way back on your own, you wouldn't really be mine."

"I've always been yours. I came back."

"But only because you thought I was marrying Mikayla."

"That's not true. I came back because I love you. I want to marry you. I want to spend the rest of my life loving you."

"*Then why did you leave?*"

"Because I panicked. It was too much, too soon. My graduation. The proposal. The party. The dream house. Talking about our future kids. You gave me my mother's ring. I kept looking at it and thinking, what if we end up like my parents? It felt like I was living their life. I was scared. I needed time to sort it all out, and I needed to get away from here."

Incredulous, Justice searches my face. "Why didn't you tell me all of this before you left?"

"I don't know."

"Cane," he breathes my name, reaches out, and takes my hand.

"But I was always going to come back to you. You have to know that."

He looks into my eyes. "I'm not sure I do."

"Where does that leave us?" I ask finally.

Leaning forward, he kisses me on the lips, and my heart rebounds. It feels right and good and intimate like it always has with Justice. It's going to be okay. But when he pulls away from me, there's a distance in his expression that I've never seen before.

"This time it's not you who needs time and space," he says. "It's me."

To be continued ...

Stay tuned for the third and final installment of *The Ugly Tree*. See www.facebook.com/authortamaralyon or www.tamaralyon.com for updates.

First chapter sneak preview …

CHAPTER ONE

Late September 1998

Not that I have a watch, clock, or anything else to tell me what time it is, but I'm guessing it has to be near midnight, because the programming quality has tanked. While lounging on my sleeping bag and cramming ketchup-riddled microwave popcorn into my mouth, I channel-surf. Since I've managed to misplace the remote to my barely nineteen inch television, circa 1988, and am too lazy to get up every time I want to change the station, I'm using my big toe. Had I taken Grandma Betty's advice and used Velcro to adhere the remote to the side of the television like she's told me to do multiple times, I wouldn't be in this predicament. My toe accidentally grazes the power button. The screen makes an electric snapping noise and goes black.

Spectacular. I'm going to have to get off my butt.

Setting my snack aside, I army-crawl over to the television, push the power button, and change the channel the old-fashioned way. I land on an infomercial where a slick con-artist named Lester Stanford tells me that I can make millions buying real estate even if I have poor credit and no money. Apparently, intelligence is also not a prerequisite! I ease myself backward, resume eating, and listen to Lester, who promises that I can quadruple my wealth in a matter of weeks. If I mail him fifty nine ninety-nine, he'll send me a booklet and CD that will explain the simple process, and I'll be well on my way to being a billionaire.

Sold! Let me get out my checkbook and run to the post office to overnight the money!

Who actually believes this crap?

Extending my big toe, I'm about to axe Lester and his empty promises from my life when I hear a musical chirping. With surprising toe dexterity, I mute the television.

What is that? It sounds like a small bird trapped in a closet. Oh, wait! It's my new cell phone. Only I have no idea where it is. Leaping up, I spill my popcorn all over the top of the television. A few kernels with ketchup stick to the screen, one landing right on Lester's head. From this angle, it looks like he shot his brains out.

Racing around my new apartment and hurdling over stacks of boxes, I discover my phone in my bathtub. I must have left it there when I was hanging my new frog shower curtain.

Bending down, I grab it and answer on the last ring. "Did you survive the trip?" I ask breathlessly.

My best friend, Caprice, emits something of a growl. "Holy. Shitty. Balls. That was the longest drive known to mankind. The longest. Do you know how many miles it is from Colorado to Illinois? Too many."

"You could have spared yourself the misery. My suitcase isn't that big-you could have brought it on a plane." I'd spent the summer out in Briar, Colorado, with Caprice, helping grow her cleaning company, *Maid Hot,* the Hooters of the cleaning industry where the maids are required to wear bikinis. In my haste to leave and start my new marketing job at Schaeffer Dairy Farm back in my hometown of Savage, Illinois, I'd inadvertently left a suitcase filled with the majority of my business clothes. Because I'm excessively thrifty and only buy things when they're on clearance or in a second-hand store, I've been rotating three dress shirts and two skirts for the past two weeks.

"Obviously that would have been easier, but I didn't want the hassle or expense of renting a car once I got here. Never mind that I don't know how long I'm going to be stuck in Chicago dealing with my family. My cousin's upcoming wedding? Absolute nightmare. Turns out there are dozens of events planned. Since I'm the oldest, I'll be expected at all the showers, parties, fittings, all that shit. Besides, if I would have flown, I wouldn't have been able to bring your present."

Caprice has been mysterious about the housewarming gift she's bringing me. "You don't have Nikeo stashed in the trunk, do you?" I ask half-jokingly. It's occurred to me that Nikeo, her handsome and antagonistic cousin, may have come along for the trip because he too might be attending the wedding. Nikeo and I'd had a summer fling that had flung my life into the gutter. Two months later, and I'm still trying to crawl out from where I landed.

"Don't panic, I left him back in Briar. Although, what I brought you does resemble him," she says enigmatically.

"Come on, you have to tell me what it is."

"No hints. It's a surprise. Did you get everything moved in?"

"Justice and Samson are bringing the furniture tomorrow, but all the boxes are here. Lots of unpacking to do."

"I can help when I get there."

"You won't have to. Grandma Betty will be here in the morning, and she won't let us go to bed until everything is cleaned, unpacked, arranged, and put away. She's abides by the *a place for everything and everything in its place rule*."

"My kind of lady. *Maid Hot* could use a woman like her. Think she would wear a bikini?"

"Hot pink isn't her color."

Caprice laughs. "Too bad. I bet she would be popular with the senior set."

Fist planted over my mouth, I stifle a yawn and sit on the edge of the tub. "So when are you getting here?"

"Tuesday night, and I can't stay long. Probably just a night."

"I wish I didn't have to work-"

"I wish you would ditch your job and come back to Colorado with me," she interrupts.

Ever since I left Colorado, she's been hounding me to return. "Not possible. I signed a six-month lease on this place. The job at Schaeffer Diary is going well. Not to mention that Justice is here. I need to be where he is."

"How are things with him? Good?"

Good? Try the antonym of that. Because of what happened with Nikeo, my relationship with the love of my life, Justice Price, isn't on the rocks, it's buried beneath the rubble. Our interactions, once loving and playful, have become frosty and formal. I would prefer to spend every second together, moving forward and planning our future. Instead, we have scheduled dates, every Wednesday and the occasional Friday night. This was his brilliant idea. It feels like we're a couple on the verge of divorce trying to give it another go and acting all fake and upbeat. It's thoroughly depressing and taxing, especially since I'm doing everything in my power to make it work.

In the past four weeks since our pseudo-breakup where he said he needed to slow things down and put our future plans into an indefinite holding pattern, I've sent him flowers, surprised him with the fancy fishing rod that he's been wanting for two years, which by the way was obscenely expensive and not on clearance, wrote him a two-page love poem, and treated him to a candlelight picnic in the woods.

The picnic had been memorable but not exactly successful. Justice had been about to kiss me when one of the pillar candles had somehow tipped over, rolled down an incline, and landed under a pine tree. The brittle, dead branches at the bottom caught fire and burst into flames, an event that seemed more like an omen than an unfortunate accident. Once we made sure there wouldn't be a forest fire and Smokey the Bear wouldn't put us on any Wanted posters, we packed it up and packed it in.

Justice, though politely appreciative of my wooing, hasn't been over the moon about it. I fear it's only a matter of time before he signs his walking papers. Worst of all? I'm positive he has his eyes on someone else, and I'm hoping that's all he has on her at the moment.

Pressing the phone between my ear and shoulder, I free up my hands and ease myself backward into the claw-foot tub. My legs dangle out over the edge. I weave small sections of my hair into scalp-hurting braids. "We're making progress," I respond generically, sparing her the less than stellar details.

Twenty minutes of conversational nonsense follows, and when I switch off the phone, I stay planted in the bathtub, gazing up at the plaster ceiling and running my hands over my half plaited head. I doze off, but wake up because my bony butt has gone completely numb and my neck feels broken. Sore and groggy, I climb out of the tub and shuffle into the living room.

Collapsing onto my sleeping bag and mound of pillows, I stare dumbly at the television that's mucked up with ketchup and popcorn. It's quite a mess, and I can't make out what new infomercial is airing. I should clean it properly before it dries and gets crusty, but I don't have the energy to find the paper towels and cleaning supplies. They could be in any one of the boxes strewn around the room.

My eyes are drawn to the lower half of the screen, where an advertisement for a psychic hotline scrolls.

The purple words emit a smoky haze. The ad reads, "Our certified psychics will tell you everything you need to know about your life. We have the answers you seek. Find out your destiny. Only $1.99 for the first minute. Call 1-888-550-5000 right now!"

I didn't like what Lester was selling, but this concept appeals to me. My life would be much simpler if I knew what was going to happen, and I don't even have to mail a check and wait for a booklet and CD that will explain everything. I can charge $1.99 to my credit card and hear everything I need to know straight from a psychic's mouth. Instant gratification-the one thing Americans can agree on. I bet Lester would be rolling in even more dough if he set up a hotline.

Where is my wallet?

Thirty minutes later, I'm entering full-blown panic mode because it's nowhere to be found, and, then, I remember the last time I had it was when I came home from work, carrying a gallon of Schaeffer Dairy Cow Pie Ice Cream. I yank open the freezer door, and there's my wallet, sitting right on top of the ice cream. Perfectly illogical, just like the rest of my life at the moment.

Now that I have my credit card and am ready to find out my destiny, I've forgotten the stupid phone number. I sit, eyes glued to the television and wait another ten minutes before the advertisement comes on again. Cell phone at the ready, I punch in the numbers, read the operator my credit card number, and impatiently wait to be connected to psychic extraordinaire, Rhonda Riddle. I'm already skeptical. The name sounds more like a stripper than a psychic.

"Hello, this is Rhonda Riddle," says a nasally voice. "Thank you for calling. What's your name?"

"Cane Kallevik."

"Ohhh! That's a pretty name. How old are you, sweetheart?"

"I turned twenty-two on August, fifteenth."

"Such a young thing! A Leo, which means that you are enthusiastic, faithful, and loving."

Enthusiastic and loving? Maybe. Faithful? Up to a point. "I don't know about that."

"The stars tell me that you are all those things," she states emphatically. "What would you like to know about your destiny?"

What didn't I want to know? If she could hand over a detailed outline of the next year of my life that would be ideal, but it boils down to one thing. "I want to know if I'll end up with Justice."

"End up with justice? Something happened to you. Someone hurt you. I'm sensing an assault, a robbery, a horrible crime, a murder."

Go fish, I mumble under my breath. I'm quickly losing faith in Rhonda's ability. "I'm not talking about justice as in legal justice, I'm talking about the man I love, Justice Price."

"Is he a lawyer? Because it would be perfect if he was. *The price of justice?* Justice Price! Get it!"

It would have been more effective had I flushed two bucks down the toilet and spared myself the humiliation of this call. I flick my credit card at the television. It knocks off one of the kernels. I wait to see if she'll say anything else.

"You're deeply upset right now. You love Justice. You want to know what's going to happen with him."

Not exactly intuitive since I've spoon-fed her this information. "Rhonda, can we cut the crap? You and I both know that you aren't psychic."

"I am," she insists, employing a mystical tone of voice.

Give me a break. She doesn't have a psychic bone in her body, but I desperately need someone who's impartial to hear my story and give me feedback. Since I don't feel like cruising any more channels looking for a therapy hotline, though I'm positive I could find one, I'll settle for the non-psychic.

"Here's the deal, Rhonda. Four months ago, I graduated college, came home, and Justice popped the question in front of a hundred friends and family. I said yes. After that, he drove me to my surprise party where he proceeded to show me the dream house he was building for us. Then at this very same party, in a very public and humiliating way, Mikayla, my best friend from childhood, found out the secret I'd been keeping from her for years: years ago, while we were still in high school, Mikayla's mother cheated on her father, not with a man her own age, but with Mikayla's boyfriend. To make matters worse, she got pregnant and had his love child. Mikayla was furious at me for keeping this from her, and then she dropped her own bomb. She told me she was in love with Justice and made out with him!

"It was all too much. Graduating college? Getting married? Building a dream house? Finding out Justice and Mikayla had kissed and that she loved him? I needed time to process everything. I took off for the summer, met this guy named Nikeo, and fell for him. Things got complicated between us, more than complicated actually, but in the end I knew it was Justice I loved and wanted to be with.

"Just when I figured this out, I got this cryptic message that said Mik and J were getting married! I assumed that it meant *Mikayla and Justice* were getting married. I rushed home to stop the wedding and ended up crashing the end of the ceremony. But, it wasn't Mikayla and Justice, it was Mikayla and Justice's cousin, Jeremy. I felt like the biggest jerk. I was hoping that Justice would be ready to move forward with our relationship, but then he told me that he needed time to think things through.

"To make things more problematic, I'm working at Schaeffer Dairy Farm for the owner, Samson Schaeffer, who just so happens to be Justice's uncle, and Justice also works for the company. And, so does Samson's son, Jeremy, who's now Mikayla's husband. One big happy family. Did you follow all of that? It's been a bit awkward and tangled to say the least."

After that verbal purge, I need a gin and tonic, heavy on the gin, light on tonic. Unfortunately, the only liquid I have in this apartment comes from the tap.

Rhonda lets out a low whistle and abandons the mystical tone of voice. "Wow, it's like a storyline from *General Hospital* or *The Young and the Restless.*"

"Not a soap opera, just my life." I snatch a kernel off the top of the television, throw it up in the air, and catch it with my mouth. "So, what's going to happen?"

"Sweetheart, I have absolutely no idea, but I'm dying to find out! I'll give you my home number. I want you to call me back!"

CPSIA information can be obtained at www.ICGtesting.com
Printed in the USA
LVOW101508300613

340852LV00002BA/2/P